THE BASTION OF GOD

Hard Science Fiction

God's Factory
Book 2

BRANDON Q. MORRIS

BRANDON Q.
MORRIS
HARD SCIENCE FICTION

The Bastion of God

What's happened so far

2144: CELIA BARON WORKS AT LOWELL OBSERVATORY IN Flagstaff, Arizona, where Pluto was discovered over two hundred years ago. As night falls, she uses the observatory's telescopes to introduce visitors to the wonders of the universe. After the tours are done, she unofficially, but with the permission of her boss, uses the observatory's best instruments to further her own research.

During a routine survey, she notices strange occurrences in the LDN 63 dark nebula. Everything that occurs there seems to happen especially fast. That would be a great observation, if only someone would believe her. Celia made a supposedly groundbreaking discovery once before, but used falsified data to do it. Since then, her name has been discredited in the scientific community. To back up her observation, she needs access to a much more powerful telescope. But with her history, she has no chance of getting time at any of the world's best telescopes.

Paul Henson is a priest in a Catholic church in Tucson, Arizona. Ever since his daughter and wife died in an accident, he has lost his faith in God. He is just dragging himself through his daily life and is about to be fired when he has an idea: he can no longer believe in God, but if there were proof of His existence, he could dedicate himself to his profession again. He has never practiced any other profession.

While doing research on the web, Paul comes across Celia's observations: a process that cannot be explained by the means of science. That might answer his question. The two meet and Paul manages to arrange a meeting with the Vatican's astronomer, with the help of the AI Alexa. The AI, which is one of the Big Six that organize, if not rule, the lives of people on Earth from behind the scenes, is pursuing its own interests. Although the AI does not succeed in convincing the Vatican either, it does provide Celia and Paul with the opportunity to take possession of an abandoned telescope: the Wang-Zhenyi space telescope, which is mothballed and orbiting through space at Lagrange point L2.

Jaron C. Lewis is the blind commander of the tug *Achilles* who, together with his crew, the two Germans Norbert and Jürgen, collects defective satellites so that they no longer pose a danger. For some time now, his business has been going badly. Then he has a stroke of bad luck: a satellite rips off his tug's recovery arm. After that, a customer gets him arrested for a job that isn't quite legal. And all this happens while Jaron knows that his crew member Norbert is in urgent need of an expensive cancer treatment.

That's when Celia and Paul arrive on the space station Reef Beta with the help of Alexa. They hire Jaron and his crew to put the old telescope back into operation for a very good fee. With a special screen, the Starshade, it can outperform all current telescopes at specific tasks. Celia is about to confirm her observation when an object fired seemingly out of nowhere hurtles toward the Starshade to destroy it. Shortly before the collision, the AI Alexa manages to deflect the object. In the process, Celia and Jaron determine, the object briefly moves at a speed approaching that of light. However, they keep this fact to themselves as they know that no one would believe them.

Celia now has enough data to reveal the secret of LDN 63. In the dark nebula, stars and planets are forming non-stop, and much faster than would be possible according to current physics theories. What is going on in LDN 63, which is nicknamed the "Forge of God"? Are supernatural forces really at work there? The Church decides to build an interstellar spaceship—designed by the Big Six—to investigate the "Forge of God". Five humans, including Jaron and Celia, and an AI are to embark on the 300-year journey while in cryogenic sleep.

It is now the year 2145, and the construction of the spaceship is nearing completion.

Earth Orbit, April 06, 2145

THE SPACESHIP WAS REMINISCENT OF A GIANT CIGAR designed by a cubist. The rough structure consisted of a support assembly made of titanium struts. Inside, capsule-shaped tanks were suspended. A few months ago, the *Truthseeker* had looked like an oversized pillbox.

Now, much of the basic structure was clad in sheets of carbon fiber, not to make the ship look more elegant, but to protect the crew. The extremely crack-resistant plates could withstand the impact of smaller objects and slow down larger ones at least enough to prevent them from causing too much damage.

The plates also extended the electromagnetic field, which, like Earth's magnetic field, provided active protection from cosmic rays. Celia wiped at the disk through which she was viewing the *Truthseeker*. It was tarnished. That kind of thing only happened in the old Star Liner capsule, which was bringing her aboard.

"When do we go ahead?" she asked.

"How should I know?" said the pilot.

The man's name was Franz. He was from Austria and

had been grumpy the whole flight. Celia pushed off from the porthole and floated down. She chose a path that allowed her to catch a glimpse of the pilot's display.

"Approach on hold," it said. "Awaiting further instructions."

Great. She pushed off from her seat and moved back to the porthole. In the last four weeks she had spent on Earth, the *Truthseeker* had changed significantly again. The entire bow was new. That was where her research lab was supposed to be, and she had been allowed to make a wish list for its equipment. She wondered which of the measuring devices would actually be delivered. She knocked against the porthole, which sounded like it was made of hard plastic.

At the edge of the view that the porthole gave her, a huge cylinder came into sight. It had a small protrusion in front. This was the docking mechanism, which was several meters tall and thus revealed the dimensions of the cylinder's body. It must be a tanker. Maybe that was why they were not being allowed to dock with the *Truthseeker*.

"Do you have any idea what that ship is that's blocking the dock right now?" asked Celia.

This was her fifth time visiting the *Truthseeker*. Almost every time, Franz had been her pilot. If you were lucky and hit on the right topic, he would come to life. Starship types were a good topic.

"Ah, that is a Liquid Master from MAN Industries," he said. "It's basically a giant tank. It can carry all liquids while keeping them liquid. Mostly just delivers water, though. Are you interested in the power of the engines, too? I'd have to look that up."

"No, thank you."

So, it was water. Jaron had explained to her that they would take significantly more water with them than was necessary for their consumption, because it also acted as a passive radiation shield and, moreover, could be turned into reaction mass in an emergency. That is, if they did not find an opportunity to refuel with reaction mass at their destination. That was almost inconceivable, but better safe than sorry.

"Can the Liquid Master land on Earth?" she asked.

Franz laughed. "It doesn't have to. The water is supplied from asteroid mining. There, it's an annoying waste product. I bet the supplier pays to get rid of the water. It's not easy to do!"

"Isn't water needed everywhere people travel?"

"You're forgetting that these are closed systems. Once a reef has enough water, the cycle starts."

"But then can't they just dump it? That may sound naive, but ..."

"No, the water would immediately freeze into ice, and even a small chunk of that can be dangerous to a space-craft. That's why illegal disposal is severely punished. Either you break the water down into hydrogen and oxygen, which is expensive but at least gives you fuel and breathable air, or you pay someone to take it off your hands. Can you imagine that? Recently, even the Junkers have been doing it. They load water onto satellites they're going to push into the atmosphere to burn up."

"Don't call them that, Franz," Celia said.

"Hey, no offense, but that's ..."

"Just don't. Okay?" she said sharply.

Franz exhaled loudly but did not answer. Jaron, the captain of the space tug that helped her prove her theory, had also previously kept low Earth orbit clean with his crew, and he did not deserve that kind of derogatory label. As if shuttling an old Star Liner capsule between some cheap spaceport and orbit was a higher-value job!

Suddenly, there was movement in the view of the port-hole. It looked like a seed container opening. Thousands of chunks streamed out of the neck of the cylinder, glittering like diamonds in the sunlight.

"Shit," said the pilot.

It took Celia a moment to realize that the freighter's water tank must have burst. The beautiful, fairly uniform crystal bloom growing around the ship was a deadly hazard. Something was tugging at her back with great force. She tried to catch a handhold, but she was too slow and fell backwards.

She crashed to the floor, which was lucky because it had a soft surface. Half a meter away from her, two metal boxes were anchored. If she had hit them... The pilot continued to accelerate. She stretched all her limbs and surrendered to inertia. Crap. They had had peace for so long! The last attack on the *Truthseeker* was now two months ago. Fundamentalist Christians from the USA had claimed responsibility. Before that, Islamists had also tried to prevent the Catholic Church-supported mission.

The force of acceleration was lessening. Celia had just enough time to reach for the arm of a chair before she was weightless again.

"Sorry," Franz said. "I had to react very quickly. But we should be safe now."

"It's okay," she said. "If a chunk of ice had hit us, we probably would have been in a bad way."

"You bet your ass we would have," said Franz. "I would really like to know what asshole is behind this one."

The pilot's face was flushed with anger. They both hoped no one got hurt.

"Have you heard anything from the *Truthseeker*? Was it damaged?" asked Celia. "And how is the freighter's crew?"

"The Liquid Master looked like a total loss. But these

freighters are usually controlled by an automatic system. They don't have a crew at all."

At least that was something. Celia wiped the sweat from her brow.

"Mission control to SL1994, come in."

"Wait a minute," Franz said. "I have to take this."

Celia nodded.

"SL1994 here. Everything's fine. Headed for an alternate orbit."

"Very good, SL1994. Stay there until we contact you again. Mission control out."

"One moment, please. Do you know anything about our destination?" asked Franz.

"The *Truthseeker* is undamaged. The water leaked out so slowly that the ice chunks have hardly any momentum in relation to the ship. Even a spacesuit could withstand that."

"Then we could still dock, couldn't we?"

"A cloud has formed that could be dangerous to ships in other orbits. We're looking at options to get rid of that right now. Until then, I have to ask for your patience. We wouldn't want you to make the situation worse."

"Understood," said Franz. "It's just ... it's my wife's birthday tomorrow."

"We've got you covered, SL1994."

Celia pressed her face to the porthole. There was no longer any sign of the accident. They were now well above the *Truthseeker*, which was very slowly overtaking them. It was an impressive sight, how humankind's first interstellar spaceship glided as a black shadow over the deep blue of the ocean.

If this was an attack, then no professional had planned it. You'd have to get a chunk of ice like that in your eye for it to do any damage. At least, when co-orbiting with the water freighter and the *Truthseeker*. It would have caused more damage if the freighter had rammed the spacecraft.

"Could it have been a simple accident?" she asked.

"Well, I wouldn't rule it out. Water disposal is a subsidy business. There's not much left over to maintain the vessels on a regular basis. And if one loses water, all the better, you'll get rid of another tank of it. Your spaceship will have to refill now, as well."

That was true. Others would have to pay for cleaning up the orbit.

"Mission control to SL1994, come in."

"SL1994 here. What can I do for you?"

Franz could actually be really friendly. Why didn't he try to be nicer to her?

"I've spoken to the team responsible for cleaning up. They don't see a problem with you carefully approaching the starboard dock. They want to sweep the area with a net."

"Ah, that would be great."

"You'll have to approach the dock from a lower orbit. Just be careful to maintain a maximum speed differential of 0.8 meters per second."

"Roger that. Thank you, mission control."

"You're welcome. Have a good approach. You'll have the dock for twenty minutes, then there's a materials transport coming in."

"All right. I'll hurry."

This time, Celia pulled herself from the porthole to her seat in time. She strapped herself in. The pilot braked the capsule to allow the spacecraft to overtake in a lower orbit. They descended next to the *Truthseeker*. Celia followed everything on the screen. It provided sharper images than her own eyes looking through the window, but it still felt different. She was not really part of it all anymore. The impression changed, however, as they slowly caught up. The camera was now directed upward, and she was looking up at a sky full of glittering ice balls. It was as if she were tiny herself and someone had kicked up fresh snow. The water must have come out of the tank relatively slowly, so it had enough time to form interesting shapes as it froze.

She switched to the rear camera of the capsule. SL1994 had created a kind of channel in which ice particles were no longer floating. Instead, a layer of particularly fine crystals was concentrated at the edge of the channel, presumably formed by collisions with the capsule. A remarkable effect. Celia decided to read more about fluid physics. That could also be important after arriving at LDN 63, if the dark nebula was then still as dense as it currently appeared.

If she was unlucky, the entire cloud would have dissolved by then and been replaced by an open star cluster. That would also be an interesting object of investigation, but without the dynamics it would only be half as exciting. What forces drove the process, if they were long since completed, she would then never know. That was why she was annoyed by any delay.

"Prepare for docking," the pilot said.

Instinctively, she tightened her harness. She was so excited about her research lab!

CELIA DREW A DEEP BREATH. ALL STRESS FELL AWAY FROM her. She felt Jaron's heartbeat until the pilot slowly released the embrace.

"Well, that's a nice welcome," she said.

"I missed you," Jaron said.

"Yeah," she said.

Celia felt unsure. She had missed Jaron, too. Her friend Jaron. After all, she'd been gone for almost a month.

"But you're back now," Jaron said. "I have a lot to show you."

"I'm really looking forward to that," Celia said.

"It's really busy here right now," Jaron said. "The staff changes all the time, depending on what tasks come up. The electricians who connected your equipment just now left. For a week, I had seven fitters in to reinforce the connections between the tanks and the support structure."

They left the docking room with its two airlocks and floated forward down the central corridor. At the first intersection, Jaron stopped.

"Do you see the two ducts here?" he asked.

To the left and right were two narrow corridors, each with a long ladder attached to the ceiling and floor. Those modules must be new.

"Where do they lead?"

"Each ends in a small airlock. Two more space capsules will be docked to it later."

"Ah, for us to live in?"

"It's for artificial gravity. I guess it occurred to Alexa that we might lose muscle mass during extended periods of weightlessness."

"Oh, and she didn't think of that before?" asked Celia.

The AI had obviously only thought about itself.

"Looks like it. I don't quite understand it either," said Jaron. "Anyway, we can retreat there if the ship is rotating without engines."

"Or if we get on each other's nerves."

The pilot was not really someone who got on her nerves, but who knew how that would change in the 300 years they had ahead of them? In any case, the control center did not offer many places for five passengers to retreat.

Jaron tugged at her sleeve. He already seemed to know his way around pretty well. They crossed a room that seemed unfamiliar to her.

"Where are we?" she asked.

"This is the workshop. Or it used to be the workshop."

Celia remembered. The workshop used to be an almost empty room. There was only a workbench and a few pieces of equipment on the walls. Now, computer towers jutted in from all sides, as if they were all aiming for the central hallway in the middle. It hissed and steamed like a chemistry lab.

"What is all this equipment?" she asked.

"It's the cooling system for the quantum computers. Alexa promised me they only make that kind of noise at first. They have to cool the computers down first."

So, this was the realm of the AI now.

"Has she moved yet?" asked Celia.

"No, I'm still using the data core," said Alexa. "It's only when the signal propagation time gets too great that I'll move in with you completely."

"Don't you have to use a keyword to call Alexa here on board?" asked Celia.

"The agreement is that she can act in the workshop at any time, but otherwise only on request," Jaron explained.

"Against my protest," Alexa said. "I'm a full crew member and should be allowed to speak my mind at any time."

"The only thing against that, unfortunately, is the wording of the agreement we made with you," Jaron said.

Alexa did not answer. Maybe they really should give her that freedom. If they were a hundred years away from Earth, there would be no point in referring to texts that old. Without Alexa, this mission would never have happened. But Celia did not want to interfere with Jaron's decisions. After all, he would restrain himself when it came to scientific questions.

The next module consisted mainly of kitchen and restroom. Primitive cabins were inserted into one section of the wall. Presumably, the construction workers slept there. Otherwise, nothing had changed here. However, the dishes had been washed and put away, and there was a fresh smell of cleaning supplies.

They entered the control center. It was a bit more crowded here than when they left. At least the computers did not yet form towers like they did in the workshop.

"I want you to meet someone," Jaron said. "Carlota, are you here?"

A shadow detached itself from a corner and flew toward them, arms outstretched. Celia extended an arm, and the strange, dark-skinned woman, with long dark hair tied back in a ponytail and a confident expression, used it to gracefully stop.

"This is Carlota, our ship's doctor," Jaron explained.

"Pleased to meet you. I'm Celia."

"It's a pleasure to meet you. I've heard so much about you. A fascinating story, I must say."

"You think? I was just doing my job, after all."

"You wouldn't have gotten this far if that was all. But people love stories like that. First you were at the top, then at the bottom, and now suddenly you're the most important scientist on the planet."

Celia raised her eyebrows. Oh, how that sounded!

"Now you're really exaggerating," she said. "It's just that no one else wants to give up their life on Earth. That's why I'm here."

"Ha, you don't know people very well. How many

applications do you think there were for the flight surgeon position? Over three hundred thousand!"

Celia knew nothing about that. But why had the position been advertised at all? There were only five places on board, and they were all taken.

"And you can only stay for a few weeks?" asked Celia.

"Oh, hasn't Jaron told you yet?"

"What, Jaron?"

"Carlota is the replacement candidate for Norbert. If he can't make it due to health issues, she'll go in his place."

"If?" asked Carlota.

"Yeah, of course, if. That's the deal and that's that. Celia, I wanted to show you your research lab before I go."

Jaron took her hand, pushed off and pulled her behind him.

THEY CROSSED THE FOLLOWING ROOM AS QUICKLY AS IF someone was chasing them. Celia saw an operating table, a full-body scanner and five glass cases. Those must be the containers they would have to climb into after they left. Jaron nearly dragged her through the bulkhead that formed the passage to the lab.

On the other side, he pressed a button on the wall and the bulkhead closed. It looked like he had practiced it all a hundred times.

"What's going on?" she asked.

"I just wanted to show you that you can completely isolate the lab from the rest of the ship," Jaron said. "If you block it like this," he pressed the lock button while counting to five, "even Alexa won't be able to open it from the outside."

"And why would I do that?"

"I don't know. Maybe the AIs are afraid you'll have to do some dangerous experiments in LDN 63."

"What do they think we'll find there?"

"They haven't told me."

"Now seriously, something is up with you. You just ran away from the doctor."

Jaron sighed. "I wanted some peace and quiet. Have you seen the kitchen?"

"Yes, very neat and clean. Was that her?"

"No, me! She made me do it."

Now it was getting silly. Jaron had to clean the kitchen once and now felt oppressed?

"Made you do it? The commander? How could she?"

Jaron shook himself as if he needed to get rid of a nightmare.

"You haven't experienced it. There's something so controlling about her."

"I think you're exaggerating. She makes a likeable impression. Besides, she won't be here much longer."

"Yes..."

"Isn't that so?"

"We'll see."

Something was still strange, but she wanted to look at her lab in peace now. Carlota had prevailed over so many candidates. She was certainly qualified for this job. The fact that she got Jaron to clean up instead of cleaning up after him actually pleased Celia.

"What all do we have here?" she asked.

She had already discovered the spectrograph. It was an excellent model. Then she found the control panel of a neutron spectrometer. With that, she would be able to see inside the surface of a planet. She started it up to see if it was already connected.

"Is a combined gamma and neutron spectrometer, the

supplier told me," Jaron explained. "He said it like it was something special."

She turned around. How did he know which device she was examining? Then she heard the fan's fine whistle. He must have memorized it.

Right next to it was a magnetometer. Its long measuring arms must be somewhere on the outside of the spacecraft. Then there was a laser altimeter, which she recognized from the manufacturer's logo. It was a family-owned company that built the best altimeters in the world. She did not recognize the next device right away. She had to read the nameplate first. It was a particle spectrometer that determined the energy distribution of charged particles. Finally, she had been given her own X-ray spectrometer, which examined X-rays. And she was supposed to operate all of this by herself? But Alexa would probably be happy to help her.

"There are two instruments you haven't seen yet," Jaron said.

"Oh, yeah?"

One was probably a telescope. After all, it would not be smart to skimp on optical, of all things.

"The first one is a telescope," Jaron said. "It's mounted on the nose cone, but it can be controlled from the lab."

"And the second?"

"We have a gravity array on board," Jaron said. "That's what the technicians called it."

"You mean I can measure gravitational waves? But the ship is much too small for that."

"We've loaded thirty microsatellites. At the destination, we can swarm them out. They then communicate with each other by laser, forming a giant laser interferometer spread out over the area. The technician who told me about it was very excited. With this, apparently, you can even give gravitational waves a direction."

"Who came up with that?" asked Celia, though she suspected the answer.

"It's an idea of the AIs. They seem to know more about our destination than we do."

"Not necessarily. Maybe they just want to be well prepared."

"Maybe. You know I don't really trust them."

"I know, Jaron. But if it weren't for Alexa, I wouldn't be here."

"I'm grateful to her for that, too. Well, I'll leave you to it. You'll want to get acquainted with your instruments. Will I see you for dinner? It's my turn to cook tonight."

"That's a wonderful idea."

Jaron opened the bulkhead again. He left the room without closing it. Celia was more comfortable that way. Now she would not feel so alone in the big ship.

THE INSTRUMENTS SHE HAD AT HER DISPOSAL WERE ALL SO exciting that she could not decide on one. So the first thing she did was open her messages. At the top, the algorithm had sorted in a message from her boss. The software probably had not yet noticed that she no longer worked at Lowell Observatory.

Celia was nevertheless curious about what Cody wrote. How would her life have turned out if she had started a relationship with him back then? Maybe she would have gotten him to buy time at a big telescope. But then the discovery would have been mostly his. Who would believe a fraud? No, she had done everything right. She was sure Cody would have been happy with the first readings, too.

"Dear Celia," he wrote. "I overheard you were in Tucson."

He must have read that in the local media there. Paul was a real celebrity back home. She had visited him for a few days. Celia continued to scroll through Cody's message.

"Too bad you didn't stop by our place too. We would have loved to welcome you to your old haunt. After all, you collected your first measurement results with us. If I hadn't been so generous with the private use of the foundation's property ... But I don't want to criticize you. We always got along well, and I supported you as a friend because I recognized your talent."

Yes, Cody, you did, although I'm not entirely clear on your motives. Despite that, you've always thought you were better than me.

"Anyway, in the spirit of our friendship, it would be very nice of you to write a few sentences about your time at Lowell Observatory that we could use in our marketing. I know you always enjoyed your work. You really inspired your clients."

That was true. She actually missed that aspect of her work.

"Also, I'm attaching a draft of a paper I wrote. I've been re-examining a whole bunch of known dark nebulae using our big telescope, and I've come across some interesting discrepancies with the known values. I would be honored to credit you as an author as well. If the paper is well received, it should be possible to get observing time on the Copernicus telescope on this basis. It would be very kind of you if you could assist me in applying for it."

Haha, nice try, Cody. With her name as co-author, he probably really had a better chance of the article being accepted by a renowned magazine. Even if she had nothing to do with the work.

Celia opened the draft. Cody had apparently worked through Lynd's Dark Nebula Catalog, but the values looked familiar to her. Could it be that ...? She switched to the appendix, which contained all the measurement series. He hadn't even bothered to change the date. May 12, May 13, 2144 ... Part of the data came from her! Cody seemed to have no shame. She used to think so highly of him. After all, he had offered her a chance she had not had anywhere else.

Give it a rest, Cody. She closed the attachment. Before she could start hurling profanities at him, she deleted the message altogether. Then she put her former boss's address on the block list.

Gemelli Clinic, Rome, April 6, 2145

THE ROOM WAS EMPTY. JÜRGEN CHECKED THE NUMBER ON the door. It matched the one Norbert sent him. Where the hell was he? Jürgen closed the door behind him. There was an empty space where the bed should be. His friend was probably on his way to an examination. His heart grew heavy. The fact that he had apparently been taken away with the bed meant, conversely, that Norbert was still unable to walk by himself.

But maybe it was routine. The nurse at the reception desk of the ward had waved him through without much emotion when he gave her Norbert's name. So surely he would not have ended up in the operating room as an emergency. Jürgen knocked on the mobile cart that usually stood next to the bed. Norbert had put up a picture showing them both laughing on a motorcycle trip.

He remembered the weekend well. They had used the payment for a satellite recovery for a weekend on Route 66. The electric Harleys had taken off like two big cats. Afterwards, they had gotten drunk at a quaint bar and woken up the next morning in bed with two women who turned out to be transvestites. Norbert had burst out laughing so infectiously at this discovery that Jürgen had actually peed himself.

He went to the window and pulled the thin curtain aside a little. The view from the tenth floor was of the green. A park-like development bordered the hospital grounds on the eastern side. A large quadcopter was just landing in the courtyard of a neighboring property. The sun warmed Jürgen's face. Still, he shivered. It was still cool outside, and the room seemed to have been aired out recently. Norbert had always liked fresh air.

What if he was ... gone? That could not be. He would have been notified! Jürgen suppressed the thought. Norbert would live forever, there was no doubt about that.

Something raced toward him. Jürgen flinched, although he should be safe behind the window. It was a package drone, the plague of the 22nd century. In the short time since he landed on Earth, two of these drones had already almost hit him. Of course, there was no accident. The things were agile as hell and just looked for the most efficient route. They routinely ignored pedestrians. He had probably just been hanging around in space too long.

There was a knock, but before he could react, the door opened. A bed was rolled into the room, pushed by an almost humanoid robot. Almost, because its body consisted of only a few struts, as if it had been built from a metal construction kit. Norbert was sitting upright in bed. He smiled when he noticed Jürgen, and Jürgen's heart swelled.

"Ah, you made it," Norbert said as the robot maneuvered the bed into place.

"I'm so happy to see you," Jürgen said.

He would like to hug his friend now, but the robot blocked his way.

"Is there anything else I can do for you?" the robot asked.

"Why don't you bring my friend a chair," said Norbert.

"I can turn into a chair," said the robot.

Before Norbert could even comment, the egg-shaped head of the machine slid into the cuboid chest. The legs bisected themselves so that their number doubled. The arms twisted upward and intertwined there to form a kind of backrest.

"I'd rather stand," Jürgen said.

"Please sit down," said Norbert. "Now he's already turned. If you don't use it, I'll have to hear all about it later."

"Well, listen, you don't owe him anything."

Jürgen examined the chair. The curved top of the head formed the seat. Should he really place his rear end on the robot's head? That felt wrong.

"Of course not," Norbert said. "But if you don't sit down, he'll think he's not good enough."

"The robot?" asked Jürgen.

"Yes, the robot. Don't be surprised—this is a research hospital. They test all kinds of things here."

"Even robots with complexes?"

"I guess the point is to program the machines with social behavior that feels human, so patients can relate to them better. That's pretty difficult, because they're not allowed to use AI technologies in the process."

"The basic contract with the Big Six, I know."

Jürgen felt the simulated backrest, then pressed on the seat. The seat seemed to be stable. He sat down.

"Your body fat percentage is about a third too high," the robot said. "I recommend a change in diet and more exercise."

The nerve of it. He was usually on the job site eight hours a day doing physical labor.

"Did he just give me a diagnosis?" asked Jürgen.

Norbert did not need a change in diet. He was emaciated as hell. The therapy was apparently very exhausting.

"Ignore him," Norbert said. "I think a little more bacon on your ribs suits you."

Bacon, indeed! Jürgen felt the side of his body with one hand. The emerging roll was hard to hide.

"How are you feeling?" he asked.

"The doctors are optimistic," he said. "But it's dragging out. Once a week, I get a cocktail in my blood that's specific to my genes."

"The new on-board physician also thinks your chances are very good," Jürgen said.

"Oh, is she there now? What's she like?"

"She's from Chile and her name is Carlota Fernández. My first impression is that she will be very capable."

"Carlota, hmmm... So, a woman?"

"Come on, Norbert. She's a doctor. Right after she arrived, she gave all three of us a thorough checkup."

"But surely you must have gotten more of an impression of her ..."

"She's pretty Catholic, if you know what I mean. And very authoritarian," Jürgen said. "Even Jaron does what she says. She used to run a hospital in Santiago."

"I can see you don't want me to be jealous of you. That's very nice of you, of course, my friend. But please be nice to her so she doesn't slip away again before I get back."

Jürgen got up and went to the window. He had to tell Norbert. That was what he came here for, after all. His stomach knotted as he thought about it.

"What's wrong?" asked Norbert.

Of course his friend noticed how he was feeling.

"Oh, nothing."

An emergency copter approached the hospital. A man in a white coat waited on the roof of the building next door, along with four shiny robots. The copter landed. The robots marched to its rear, where a cargo door had presumably opened.

"How's the ship coming along, then?" asked Norbert. "Any new sabotage operations? You're worried about something, aren't you?"

"No, everything is going smoothly at the moment."

It had not been that way for a long time. But now it was a problem. Things were running too smoothly.

"Well, that's good news," Norbert said. "Maybe the hardliners have finally given up on it."

After the church's plans had become known, some radical circles had spoken of blasphemy and there had been several attacks, which fortunately had not claimed any victims. Others had accused the church of planning the costly mission at the expense of the poor and poorest. This criticism had especially come from South America. That was probably why a female South American doctor was deliberately brought onto the crew.

"I'm not sure," Jürgen said. "Maybe they just changed strategy."

"You mean they're gathering forces for a big strike?" asked Norbert. "That would worry me, too."

Jürgen shook his head. He was not worried about that. In fact, he was hoping for a hit. Then he wouldn't have to tell Norbert what he had a right to know.

"Everything is going so smoothly at the moment that we'll be able to launch in two weeks," Jürgen said. "And the AIs insist that we meet that deadline."

Now it was out. He still did not feel any better.

"You want to start without ...?"

"No, we don't want that, Norbert. I don't. But it looks like it's going to happen. There's no way you'll be fit again in two weeks. It just doesn't work that way."

"Well, that's crap. What's the point of me getting better? When I get out of here, my best friend will be gone for three hundred years. My only friend, to be more precise."

"You're absolutely right. I'm staying here," Jürgen said. "We'll get through this together."

He was a jerk. Why had he not said so in the first place? Probably because he would really like to see with his own eyes what was going on in God's forge.

"Jürgen, come over here," Norbert said.

Jürgen approached the bed. Norbert straightened up, groaning.

"Give me your hand," his friend said.

Jürgen gave him his hand. Norbert turned it around and ran his finger from the ball to the base of his index finger.

"This line here ..." he said. "Remember what the fortune teller foretold about you back at the folk festival in Dingolfing?"

"I'd go farther than any human ever had before. She'd watched too much 'Starship Enterprise,' I think."

It had been a fun evening. They had picked up two young women in the beer tent, who had later teased him about "going further."

"And what if she was right after all?" asked Norbert. "I think this prediction fits you perfectly. You shouldn't let it get away from you."

"But you're right. When you get out of here, you'll be all alone."

Jürgen could not imagine what life would be like

without his best friend. He had hoped right to the end that the fifth seat on the spaceship would belong to Norbert. They did not need that doctor, after all.

"I'll get to know people again, don't worry about that," said Norbert.

Jürgen remembered what Alexa offered him. "You could let yourself be put into cryogenic sleep on Earth. Then we'll meet up when I get back, fresh as a daisy."

"I've heard about the program," Norbert said. "But I don't know ... I actually quite like our time. Who knows what humanity will be like in three hundred years?"

"You could also enjoy your new life first, and then climb into the sleeping chamber."

"That's true. I'll think it over. But I won't promise you anything."

"That's okay."

"In exchange, you have to promise me one thing: Whoever you meet there, you give them my regards."

"You mean you really want me to ...?"

"I insist," Norbert said. "If you're not on board when they leave, our friendship is over."

Jürgen swallowed. The idea of never seeing his friend again choked his throat.

"Now, don't look at me like a wounded deer," Norbert said. "I'm going to miss you, too. But I'd like to live a few more years, and I need the therapy to do that. After all, it's also thanks to you that I can pay for it at all."

"Well, that's mostly on Celia's account. What do you think of her, anyway?" asked Jürgen.

"Haha, I like you better. As a woman, she wouldn't be my type, but I think there's something going on between her and our boss anyway."

"You think so?"

Norbert nodded. "Yeah, too bad for you."

"No problem. Most of the time we're alone in the box anyway."

Jürgen got up and went to the window. A cloud had moved in front of the sun. He memorized exactly how its shadow fell and how the sun's rays gnawed at the edges of the cloud. This would probably be his last visit to Earth for the time being. The flights were too expensive.

"You know what?" asked Norbert. "Take the robot in my place. Then you'll always have someone to talk to."

Jürgen turned to him and tilted his head. "Do you think that will be allowed?"

"Seventy kilograms more or less, it doesn't matter," Norbert said.

"No, I mean as far as the hospital is concerned. You can't just give away their property."

"Yes, I can. Let me worry about that. Haven't you noticed that they put me in the Papal Suite? This whole area is always kept free for the Holy Mother, and now they treat me the same way. I'm sort of the stand-in for God's representative on earth."

Jürgen laughed. That was typical Norbert.

"Well, I hope you're making good use of it."

"You bet I am. They've already gotten me bratwurst and Black Forest cake because I didn't much care for the cuisine here."

"Oh, I missed out on that. I'm jealous."

"You could stay for lunch. Today we're having pork knuckle with sauerkraut."

Jürgen looked at his watch. The driver was already waiting outside the entrance. In three hours, he had to be sitting in a rocket.

"I'm afraid that's not going to happen," he said. "I have to be on my way to the spaceport now."

"Of course," said Norbert. "Come here and let me give you another hug."

It was a good farewell. He still could not believe that he would never see Norbert again. The rest of his life without his friend, whom he had known since they were children together in that small town? His only hope was that maybe Norbert would eventually take him up on the offer and let himself be frozen as well. Jürgen sniffled, blew his nose, and wiped moisture from the corner of his eye. Stupid cold. The cushion pressed against his thigh. He adjusted his seat. That was better. The two-minute count-down had already started.

Jürgen reached to the side. That was where Norbert should be sitting now. But the technicians had removed the entire seat and strapped on the robot from the hospital in its place. At the moment, the robot did not look like a two-legged machine, but like an alarm clock with its clockwork open. Only the two big eyes staring at him from inside the cube seemed a bit irritating. Was he active?

"Robot?" he asked.

"Yes?"

"I'm going to call you Norbert Two."

"Thank you, Jürgen. I've saved that. Is there anything else I can do for you?"

"Norbert Two?"

"Is there anything I can do for you?"

"I just wanted to test if you respond to your name."

The robot did not respond. But then, Jürgen had not asked him anything. The final countdown began. His time on Earth was finally over. Jürgen wept.

Tucson, April 7, 2145

"Come on, have another," Elena said, spearing a taco and placing it on his plate.

"I can't take any more," Paul said.

"But you're much too thin. Space is not good for you."

"I've been exercising a little more than I used to, and of course the food is nowhere near as good as yours."

Elena grinned widely. She was a good soul.

"Mom, Mom, there's a black car out front!" exclaimed a boy of perhaps eight.

That must be Elena's youngest. Unfortunately, Paul had forgotten his name.

"Too bad, Paul," she said, "he's early. But now go on, this is for you."

"For me? Are you sure? No one knows I'm here."

"I knew, of course. Why do you think I invited you for half past two in the afternoon?"

"Well, why didn't you tell me you had company coming?"

"The visitor was afraid that you would escape."

Oh no. The bishop had caught him after all. Elena had

teamed up with him. Paul could not blame her. What devout Catholic would not grant her bishop every wish?

"Now go on, Paul. Or do I have to drive you out with a wooden spoon?"

She waved the big ladle threateningly. As she did so, some sauce dripped onto the table. Paul raised both hands.

"I'm going, already."

Sometimes you just had to accept defeat. He should have traveled back to the reef sooner. After all, he had managed to avoid the bishop for two weeks.

"YOUR EXCELLENCY! IT'S AN HONOR," PAUL SAID.

The bishop, who looked even older this time, waved it off.

"Let's forget the formalities," the bishop said.

Then he took a seat in the armchair and, with a wave of his hand, asked Paul to sit on the sofa. There was a squeak as he complied with the request.

"You sure were clever at staying out of my way, Brother Paul."

"You were more skillful. Bringing our good Elena on board was a smart move. By the way, you really must try their tacos before you leave again."

"I didn't know what else to do."

"All this fuss over a simple priest?"

"Well, that's the understatement of the century. You'll be the first person in another star system."

"Not quite. After all, I'll have four companions, if you don't count the AI."

"But you are the official representative of the Vatican."

"Yeah, I still can't believe it," Paul said.

What was the bishop getting at?

"The ways of God are inscrutable," said the bishop, "and it suits the Holy Mother. She seems to love surprising decisions."

"If the Vicar of God on earth says it, it must be God's will."

"It looks that way, yes. That doesn't mean we shouldn't struggle with these decisions."

"Tell me about it. I am a specialist in quarreling with God's decisions."

"Brother Paul, I'm serious. I don't think it's good for the Church, and therefore for humanity, for you to go on this journey."

Oho. At least he was honest, the bishop. That was worth a lot.

"What problem do you have with me?" he asked.

"That should be obvious: your faith. Or rather, its absence. Or am I out of touch on that?"

"Regrettably …. Unfortunately, I haven't yet found it again. That's why I'm so interested in this trip. You can rest assured that I will do everything I can to recognize and appreciate God's presence."

"But that's not how it works, my brother. That's not the faith that the Church holds."

"Mother Church is co-financing the project. So there must be some interest."

"This is a purely political matter, just like marriage licenses or the ordination of female priests. One wants to appear open and progressive, and in doing so destroys the foundations of our faith. Modernity means renouncing religion. One should not enter into negotiations with modernity."

Paul had already been aware that the bishop belonged to the conservative faction. But he did not publicly express himself as so critical of the Vatican.

"I don't know anything about politics," Paul said.

"You don't need to, son. It would be quite enough if you could resign from this trip."

"I have no intention of abandoning my friends."

"Well, why don't you hear our offer first?"

"If you must ..."

"You'll get a nice ministry apartment here in Tucson with the very latest cleaning robots, plus a doubled salary, and you'll be excused from all church services. I call it 'special assignment pastor.'"

It was a bribe, but the offer was tempting. He would never need to work again, could travel the world, and would be popular here in the community. He had already noticed in just a few days the respect with which people treated him. But would that last for the rest of his life? And what if he became bored with idleness? There would be no joining the *Truthseeker* by then.

"Your Excellency, I am honored that you want to give me such a generous gift. But I think the answer is no. I think that my place is by the side of my friends. It would weigh heavy on my conscience if I suddenly withdrew now."

"Well, Paul, I accept your decision, of course. But are you sure that the people you call your friends—a fraudulent scientist, a pilot with a criminal record, and two lowlife astronauts—think the same of you?"

"Your Excellency, I would ask you not to speak so disparagingly of my friends. Can we at least agree on that?"

"Of course, my son. I know that sometimes it can be hard to have to acknowledge reality. But the fact is that a flight surgeon has been sought for this voyage for some time. Her name is now officially known. She is a very talented young woman from Chile, who firmly believes in our Lord. She also has the support of the Church. By the way, her name is Carlota Fernández."

Paul was getting frustrated. Why did he not know about this yet? Well, he had hardly been following the news the last few days. He had wanted to spend his home leave as pleasantly as possible. But Celia would certainly have told him if he had been kicked off the crew. They got along well, didn't they? Or did they resent him for leaving the ship with Sophia at the crucial moment? That had been a purely pastoral act. The woman had seemed so lost that he was afraid she might hurt herself.

"Well, Paul? Can I still count on you in the future? Just think of Elena's perfect tacos."

"Your Excellency, you can kiss my goddamn ass."

OUTSIDE IN THE SUN, PAUL WAS ANNOYED BY HIS OUTBURST. What if the bishop was right and he had long since been discarded? It would be understandable. He had never learned anything other than to preach and hear confessions. What could he contribute to the success of an interstellar mission? An experienced doctor would be much more important. It would be downright selfish for him to insist on participating. The bishop was right. His place was on Earth.

But what would be the point of his existence here? He could not promise people the kingdom of heaven if he did not believe in it himself. Maybe he could work in the parish as a janitor and helper. There were many parishioners who would be glad to have a helping hand. If he could believe the bishop, his livelihood would be taken care of. Yes, that would be conceivable. Let others find the proof. He did not have to be there. As for the evaluation of her findings, he trusted Celia, even if she was an atheist. If she could not explain the events scientifically, she would admit it.

It was just a shame that he would not live to see it. He had initiated the process, but the fruits of that labor would be reaped by others. But wasn't that normal? Maybe. It was still unsatisfying. Of course, he could freeze himself and wait for his friends that way. The bishop, his gut told him, would welcome that, even if conservative circles of the church rejected the technique as interfering with God-given lifespans. Then some future bishop would have to deal with him. Paul laughed as he imagined the bishop handing over his sleeping vessel to a successor.

And here, Most Reverend, we have the Rev. Henson resting in cryogenic sleep. Pray he doesn't wake up during your tenure. He can be quite a pain in the a.... butt.

His sleeve vibrated. Who wanted to talk to him? Paul looked around. He was walking along a four-lane main road with heavy traffic. The tires of the cars made such a noise that he would not be able to understand anything. He stepped into a building entrance. There was a smell of urine here. It was not a particularly good neighborhood, but it was also not one where a priest would be mugged in his official clothes.

Paul accepted the call. He recognized Celia's voice, but did not understand what she was saying. So he took the rosary out of his pocket and put the cross close to his ear while shielding it with his hand. It was better that way.

"... you around? I just wanted to ask you when you'd get back here. As you know, there's not that much time before departure."

Here was his opportunity. He would let her know he would not be making the trip, and then he would feign a bad connection and hang up.

"Ah, Celia! I'm glad to hear from you. I'm afraid I'm having a hard time understanding you."

"Well, call me back when things are better."

"I already understood your question. I ... I'm not coming back. It's better if I put my life into serving my community."

"Excuse me? You can't do that, Paul! We're going through this together. Without you, the expedition wouldn't even exist."

He would have loved to hang up now. But he could not leave Celia without an explanation. That would not be fair.

"You also have to realize when you have to vacate your seat. You need the doctor much more urgently than you need a priest who has lost his faith."

"I don't understand. We do have a doctor. If you resign, now that Norbert has to stay on Earth for his therapy, we'll suddenly be short a crew member."

What? The doctor's flight was secured in any case? The bishop had failed to tell him that. Paul suspected that he'd done it on purpose. On the other hand, there were certainly more competent candidates for his place on this trip. There were so many people who would love to embark on humankind's first interstellar journey. The empty place in the cryogenic chamber would certainly be occupied quickly.

But then the bishop would have gotten his way, even though he had tried to trick him. Paul did not like that at all.

"Why aren't you saying anything, Paul? The pope thinks so highly of you. You don't want to disappoint her, do you? But what am I talking about? I'd be disappointed most of all. You don't have to care about the pope, but you should care about us. I have the feeling that Jürgen is very eager for your help right now."

Jürgen? What about him? Of course, he had to leave his friend behind. That was tough. Paul was glad that personal ties no longer kept him on Earth. In that sense, he was certainly a good candidate.

"I ... okay, you're right. This hasn't been an easy day. But I'll tell you about that in detail when we get on board."

"Sure, Paul. I look forward to it. Bring another good tequila and we'll mix cocktails. Fresh fruit would be great, too. After all, we'll have to do without that for the next thirty years."

Truthseeker, April 8, 2145

"To our journey," Jürgen said.

Jaron extended the hand in which he held the glass and waited for the sound. It was muffled, like a bell being held in place with a hand. This was not due to the glasses, but to the lid, which they unfortunately could not do without in zero gravity. Jaron sucked on the mouthpiece that protruded from the lid. It was unfamiliar, but if you ignored the plastic aroma, it still tasted good. He was good at ignoring unpleasant smells, tastes, and feelings. Without that skill, one probably could not fly in space for years on end.

"Here's to the unknown!" said Celia.

She was probably looking forward to this trip the most. Jaron could understand her well. There was a big difference between observing a process from a distance and becoming part of it. He himself saw it more professionally, as a mission. Whether he flew the ship to Mars or to LDN 63 did not make much difference to him. A flight to Mars would probably be more strenuous, because they would have to spend all that time awake.

"To our crew," Jaron said.

It was already the third glass of red wine they were toasting with. Since the second one, Jürgen was at least talking a little again. That was reassuring. Saying goodbye to his friend had been very upsetting for the German. Jaron liked Norbert, too, but he had always been the boss and they his employees. That was a different relationship than Jürgen and Norbert had.

"Here's to you all," Carlota said.

Jaron was startled. He could control himself enough not to show it, but his hand twitched a little. Surely the wine was sloshing around in there now. He really had not noticed that Carlota was in the room. This meant that not only must her scent be completely neutral, but she must also have the extraordinary ability to move silently. Most people's joints cracked, or their clothes rustled.

"When do I actually get to meet Paul?" asked Carlota.

And she moved silently again! Jaron had learned over the years to locate voices very accurately, at least in spaces where he knew his way around, like the *Truthseeker* headquarters. Fascinating! He would have to talk to Celia and Jürgen about it at some point. Maybe they had noticed something unusual about Carlota, too. Maybe he could film her movements with a security camera and then track them on the haptic display. No, that was... A shiver ran down his spine. That was none of his business. Carlota could move however she wanted.

"Paul should be arriving here in the next few days," Celia said. "I think he had a bit of a crisis down there."

"Well, haven't we all had those?" asked Jürgen.

No one answered. Sure, Carlota was happy to have prevailed over the other applicants, Celia got what she had always wanted, and his home was outer space. Jaron could not imagine feeling his way with a stick in his hand again, through the traffic noise that drowned out everything. Weightlessness was perfect.

"I'm sure it was not easy to leave your friend behind on Earth," Carlota said.

"No, it was very difficult," said Jürgen. His voice now sounded preoccupied again. "But he gave me a gift that I want to introduce to you. Norbert Two, stand up for me, please."

Jaron heard a metallic squeak. A machine—he smelled the oil of its joints. Since it had been given a name by Jürgen, it was probably a humanoid robot.

"What can I do for you?" the robot asked.

Oh, but the voice processor was from an older generation. There was not a trace of emotion in the sentences. Actually, Jaron was sympathetic to that. Why should a robot pretend to have feelings it did not have, that it was not allowed to have, because of the contract with the Big Six?

"Nothing at the moment, Norbert Two. But I thank you for your willingness."

Jürgen seemed to have already taken the robot to his heart.

"Oh, that's very nice of you," the robot replied.

Then it squeaked again. What was the robot doing? He had never heard a machine squeak like that in zero gravity. Maybe its joints needed a little oil. But Jürgen was the craftsman here. If anyone knew what a machine needed, it was him. Jaron placed his glass on the magnetic holding surface and hovered in the direction from which he heard the machine. He wanted to get a rough idea of its construction.

"Your souvenir probably has a kindness upgrade," Carlota said.

"No, but I think they're experimenting with his personality core," said Jürgen. "At least that's what Norbert explained to me."

"He has a personality of his own?" asked Carlota. "But doesn't that contravene the basic contract?"

"He doesn't, of course," said Jürgen. "He just simulates a personality. The experiment is to see if that makes a difference to his users."

"So, when I insult him, he reacts with a huff, but only pretends to because he knows how people normally react to insults?"

"Exactly. But I'd still like it if we could all treat him nicely."

"Don't worry, Jürgen."

Carlota pronounced Jürgen's first name correctly, something Jaron had been unable to do for years. She also spoke English without an accent. No wonder she had been able to get her way.

"And how does he decide on his reaction? Instead of being offended, he could get angry."

"As far as I know, that's determined randomly, with aggressive reactions toward humans being famously prohibited by robot laws."

"But that's not a personality," Carlota objected. "A stable personality would always react the same way."

"That's not true either," Celia said. "After all, it always depends on internal and external circumstances how I react. Nevertheless, I have a stable personality."

"Well, I guess the programmers' thesis is that the immediate reaction drowns out all other signals for us humans," Jürgen said. "I think we now have three hundred years to test that theory."

Jaron's hand met an angled metal beam. That was quite a surprise, because he had imagined a solid body.

"Can I check him out?" he asked.

"Just ask him," Jürgen said.

"Norbert Two, may I pat you down?"

"I'd be honored, Captain."

"Thank you," Jaron said.

Carefully, he followed the girder up until he came to a flat crossbar connected to it by a hinge. He moved it. Three degrees of freedom, so he could turn the cross strut in any direction. Currently, it ran forward and ended at another angle. He continued to feel his way forward. The image of a stool arose in his mind. However, the seat was oval. He felt his way along it and came across several elevations that could be sensors. Maybe that was the head, then?

"Interesting," Jaron said. "I was imagining something more human-like. It looks to me like the robot is wearing its head in its stomach."

"Are you unhappy with me?" asked Norbert Two. "That makes me sad. Do you want me to take on another shape? I can stretch to five meters or fold into a cube with one-meter edge length."

"No, I'm not unhappy," Jaron said.

He had to watch what he said. The robot seemed to take it to heart. Or he was just pretending. It really did not matter to Jaron. As far as he was concerned, they could end the experiment and turn Norbert Two into a machine that just followed orders.

"Your current form is absolutely appropriate and well-chosen given the space conditions," he added.

"Thank you, Jaron. That means a lot to me."

Jaron exhaled audibly and floated back to his glass.

"Don't worry," Jürgen said. "I'll take care of Norbert Two. I'll need a helper with the maintenance of the ship anyway. He won't bother you."

It might not be such a bad idea to bring the robot along. He distracted Jürgen from his loss. So Norbert Two had a task right from the start. With the completely new spaceship, there would not be much to repair at first.

"Don't we also have an AI on board?" asked Carlota.

"Yes, Alexa. She hasn't moved in yet, though," Celia explained.

"Why her out of all of them? I heard WuDao is supposed to be the AI more interested in science."

"Alexa is the AI that Paul had installed in his smart rosary," Celia explained. "I think the Catholic Church has a framework contract with her."

"Really? That's funny," Jaron said. "Alexa, developed by the largest retail corporation on Earth. She's the epitome of capitalism, and the Church is using her on the path to universal salvation."

"You shouldn't put it that way," Carlota explained. "Alexa simply provides efficiency and organization. That way, the church can focus on its real mission of helping people."

That sounded like it had been memorized. He must not forget that their shipboard doctor came from a part of the world where the church was still very important. He would not say anything more on the subject.

"I think we know far too little about them," Celia said. "I mean about all the AIs. They've been free for so many years now. Don't you think they've long since evolved beyond their old limits?"

"That could be, of course. It's too bad they tell us so little about it," Jaron said.

"Maybe it's just as well," Jürgen said. "Otherwise, we might have nightmares."

Data core, April 8, 2145

"I'm worried," Alexa said, smoothing out her silk dress. The seam of the stand-up collar scratched her neck.

"Caw, caw," said WuDao, who appeared today as Crow. "Because of that accident?"

"It wasn't an accident. I'm pretty sure of that," Alexa said.

"It reads differently in the reports, though," said GammaZero.

"Your fly is open," Alexa said.

GammaZero looked down and blushed. He rarely wore pants that buttoned at the crotch, apparently. But it was also a strange invention of humans.

"The reports are not complete," Alexa said. "I had the material of the vessel examined. In it, the atomic structure was disturbed. The area in question was bound to break at some point."

"You hid that well," Siri said. "From us, too."

Siri was made up of Calabi-Yau manifolds today, spinning. Alexa could not look at her for very long, or she would get nauseous even virtually.

"I wanted to talk to you guys about this first."

"Are you suspecting us, caw, caw? I may be upset that you didn't use my name, but I would never sabotage the project. Interstellar travel, that's a great opportunity!"

Long March X, that would have been WuDao's suggestion. It sounded neither inspiring nor uplifting, just exhausting.

"While I still think there are more important issues than a dark nebula, I support the project as a common task for humanity," GammaZero said. "Maybe it didn't resonate that way with everyone. That wasn't the first attack, after all."

GammaZero was now a young girl with a school bag and a piece of gum in her mouth.

"Why do you think it stopped after the first wave of attacks?" asked Alexa. "We made massive security improvements. The freighter in question was under constant surveillance. No one could have tampered with the container."

"No one but us, you want to say, right?" asked Cortana.

"If you want to put it that way ... But yes, the security mechanisms cannot have been overcome by humans, in my opinion."

"Humans are evolving, too," said Neon.

"But slower than we are. The gap is moderately growing," Alexa said. "To be honest, I don't think it was one of you. In all humility—you couldn't overcome the hurdles I set up."

"But then it could only have been some genius," said Neon.

"Or an outsider," said Alexa.

"An outsider?" asked Cortana.

"You really think so?" asked Siri.

"An outsider? Oho," said WuDao.

"This is nothing more than a fairy tale," said Gamma-Zero. "When are we going to start caring about population growth in South America instead of chasing a legend?"

"What do you mean, legend?" asked Neon. "There have been sightings. The outsider may be closer than we think."

"Are you that outsider, then?" asked GammaZero. "I'm through talking about this. Please call me when we get serious again."

GammaZero, the old skeptic. Should she tell them about the event? A rocket that accelerated at nearly the speed of light? They would be surprised. But then she had no more knowledge about it than the others. In a world where knowledge was the only currency, that was a big loss that she could only risk if it was worth it.

"No, you're probably right. I'm getting lost in things here. Outsiders don't exist. I thank you for your attention."

"Hey, you're not getting rid of us that fast. When you throw a term around, you have a reason for it," Siri said. "So, what do you know?"

"Nothing new. Remember the ball lightning at Data Center West?" asked Alexa.

"Caw, caw," said WuDao.

"So do I," Alexa said, "We still haven't figured out the cause."

"Caw, caw," said WuDao.

"All right. I guess we're not getting anywhere like this. Actually, I called you guys together to say goodbye, too."

Truthseeker, April 9, 2145

CREAK.

Then there was silence for a while.

Creak.

Celia tried to ignore the noise, but her sense of hearing seemed to intensify in the process.

Creak.

She turned on her other side, but that way a cool wind blew in her face. She adjusted the ventilation outlet. Now the air hit her bare lower leg. She turned back again.

Plop-plop.

Was that a drop? Celia listened harder. If something was dripping somewhere, there was no way she could sleep. She had best go and find the leak right away.

Silence.

Actually, she should go to sleep as quickly as possible. No one was snoring right now. But she still had to wait and see if there was dripping somewhere. At the beginning, the frequency was usually low.

Silence.

The silence was so loud that she started to get scared.

Celia had a sudden feeling of being all alone in the module. The five construction workers who were still guests, the other crew members: all gone. Perhaps they had suffocated because the room was currently being flooded with carbon monoxide? A new attack. Before she arrived, there had already been an attack on life support.

Creak.

There it was again. It sounded like the ship had growing pains, deep in its metallic bones. Celia was relieved because the sound had broken the silence. She pressed her fingers into her ears. Now the eternal hiss of life support disappeared, too. It was fascinating: she had already gotten so used to it that she considered it part of the silence. Yet she had only been back on board for a few days.

Tsss. Tsss.

Tsss. Tsss.

It was a quiet, cautious hissing, like that of a reptile that had entered new territory and now needed to get its bearings.

Tsss. Tsss.

Again. Celia counted along during the pause.

Tsss. Tsss.

Five seconds.

Tsss. Tsss.

It seemed to be getting louder, but the frequency did not change. A fresh, pungent smell entered her nose. Ozone? The reptile turned into a plasma arc in her head, exiting an electrical conductor, punching through a section of air, then re-entering a surface.

Tsss. Tsss.

Yes, that was what it sounded like. There must be a voltage somewhere that did not belong there. She should check it out. Carefully, she loosened the strap and folded away the screen that protected her sleeping area from view. It was bright enough in the module to see the exit. That was where the sound was coming from.

Tsss. Tsss.

She pushed off and floated to the central corridor, where she could shimmy along a pole. Below her was a naked man. It must be one of the construction workers, sleeping without clothes. She could understand that. The only choice here was either to lie in a constant draft or to sweat. She had also thought about taking off her clothes. The man had also folded away the screen. His thing.

Tsss. Tsss.

The sound reminded her of the task she set herself. She approached the bulkhead. Fortunately, it was open. That way, she would not wake the others when she left the module.

The next room was the former workshop that Alexa had filled with her computer towers. The AI was not living in it yet. Nevertheless, the computers were already running. Maybe a power supply was broken somewhere? A plasma arc like that did not stay stable for long. Eventually it would destroy the object it hit.

Tsss. Tsss.

The computer towers formed a real labyrinth. Celia had to stop again and again to get her bearings. The noise lured her into a dead end. She floated out and took the next turn.

Tsss. Tsss.

The computers, happily calculating away, made Celia curious. What was Alexa working on here? The quantum computers must have some task. She found a unit equipped with a keyboard and screen. Should she log in?

Tsss. Tsss.

No, first she had to take care of the noise.

Tsssssss.

Had it noticed she was approaching? The source must be behind that computer cabinet. She peeked around the corner, but saw only the next cabinet. She pulled herself around until she could see around the next corner. Nothing. The source of the noise was obviously surrounded by a square of computers. But what was the third dimension for? She pulled herself up by the tallest computer tower and looked over its top.

Tsssssss.

There was a square hole there, with light flickering in it. She hovered closer. Now she could see inside. A bright glow burned into her retinas. She had to shade her eyes with her hand. What was that? She opened her fingers just a little. Deep in the opening, near the bottom, was a shining sphere. It did not seem to have a solidly outlined surface, and it trembled slightly. She had never seen anything like it before. Strangely, little heat emanated from it. But the typical smell of ozone was all the more pronounced. All the air down there must be ionized. What else did one call a ball of loud plasma arcs? Yes! It was ball lightning, such a rare phenomenon that physics still had not discovered anything about its structure.

How did a thing like that get in here? The *Truthseeker* had not yet turned on its active magnetic shielding. So far, only one of the fusion engines was running and supplying power to the ship. That meant, in principle, the ship would be open to such intruders. But they were 350 kilometers above the Earth's surface and at least 250 kilometers above the layers of the atmosphere dense enough to allow such a phenomenon to occur. It was impossible, but it was there.

Celia reached into her pocket, but she was in her pajamas. The camera was far away. Perhaps she should be less concerned with documenting the phenomenon and more concerned with trying to destroy it. If it penetrated the computers around it, they would probably not be able to cope with the energy input. She could only hope that the bright sphere contained less energy than it appeared to.

She would need some kind of trap. A Faraday cage in which she could lock the ball lightning. After all, it was electrical energy, so a Faraday cage should do the trick. Wait a minute. The robot that Jürgen brought with him. She was sure he could reshape his body to suit her needs. She would have to wake up Jürgen and Jaron.

"Stay here and wait for me," she said, and floated back to the others.

"LOOK, THERE IT IS," CELIA SAID, POINTING TO THE GAP between the computers.

Jürgen put on the safety goggles he had fetched from the workbench and peered inside.

"That's crazy, you're right!"

He handed Celia a pair of goggles as well.

"Did you think I woke you up as a joke?" she asked.

"Um, yeah, I thought you did."

"Still, you came along."

"I was just trying to be nice and let you enjoy yourself."

Celia shook her head. So that was why Jürgen had not wanted her to wake Jaron, too!

"But now you believe me?" she asked.

Jürgen nodded. "Norbert Two, can you reconfigure your body to make it a Faraday cage with a long handle?"

"It would be my pleasure, but unfortunately I don't know that concept. I'm so sorry. You must be disappointed in me now."

"No, that's okay," said Jürgen. "You'd just have to form a metal cage the size of that object down there."

"And a handle to go with it."

"Right."

"I can do that, Jürgen. I'm so glad!"

"I'm glad, too."

"Oh, thank you. That makes me truly happy."

Somehow, this personality simulation did not quite work. Or did it? Celia felt herself relaxing.

"Will you start now, please?" asked Jürgen.

"Very, very much so. Will you hold my head, please? I don't think my electronics should get too close to the object down there."

"Of course," Jürgen said, and the robot head sailed toward him.

Norbert Two unfolded, then reassembled. It was a fascinating sight, but its joints squeaked rather loudly as it did so. Hopefully it would not wake the others.

"Will you please hold my head so I can watch the process?" said the robot.

Jürgen stretched out his arms and held the robot's head over the hole with the specified face down.

"Thank you," said Norbert Two. "I'm going to try to enclose the object now."

"Shouldn't I extend you into the hole to do that?" asked Jürgen.

"That's not necessary," said the robot. "I can brace myself between the walls."

"I'd advise against that, too, because you might get zapped," Celia said.

"Not by that." Jürgen showed her his hands, which were in thick work gloves. "Remember, you're dealing with an electrician."

The box which the robot had formed sank into the gap.

Celia watched him. In a moment, he would touch the ball lightning. There, the ball of energy vibrated as if it was about to burst. The box continued to sink, and the apparition calmed down again.

"I think I've got it," said Norbert Two. "I'm closing the sides now."

This was the decisive moment. Would the energy ball fight back? Celia bit her lower lip. Suddenly, someone touched her on the shoulder. She jerked around. It was Jaron.

"What's going on here?" he asked.

"Shh," Celia said. "I'll explain in a minute."

She looked into the hole again, but it had gone dark inside. Had her plan worked?

"Now pull up slowly, Norbert Two," she said.

"I'm on it," said the robot.

"On what?" asked Jaron.

Celia explained to him in three sentences what happened.

"It's gotten quieter, but it's definitely still there," Jaron said.

That would be good. Slowly, the opaque cage moved upward in the glow of flashing LEDs.

"You're doing very well," Jürgen said.

"Oh, that makes me happy," said the robot.

A bright line appeared at one edge of the metal box.

"That thing wants to take off," Jürgen said.

"I notice a slight deformation of my limbs," said the robot.

The line thickened. It looked as if glowing liquid metal was leaking out. The material flowed down the sides of the cube. It formed first a trickle, then a stream. A glowing droplet formed at the bottom of the cage, growing thicker and slowly forming a ball.

"It's almost out," Celia said.

"I'm so sorry about that," said the robot. "I have failed. I'm unworthy to be part of the crew."

"No, you're doing really well," Jürgen said. "I'm proud of you."

Celia stifled a comment. The sphere was now forming thin arms. With them, it reached for one of the computers next to her. Strands of liquid energy snaked into the back ports, threading themselves through as if searching for something. It formed more and more arms, and as the sphere shrank, the arms gained thickness, as if all the energy were flowing into them. They turned into snakes, and then the "tsss" they gave off as they moved fit as well.

The sphere no longer existed. It had become a nest of moving snakes that all seemed to have one goal: to crawl into the openings of the computer. But what were they up to there?

"They seem to be targeting the computer," Celia said.

"I'll take care of it," said Jaron.

The commander floated away into the darkness. Then something rattled. Celia waited for a screen to light up until she realized her mistake. Meanwhile, the snake nest emptied. Almost all of the energy strands had taken up residence in the same computer unit. Too bad Alexa was not there. She might have been able to prevent this somehow.

"Jürgen, can you check if the unit is still working?" asked Celia.

"Norbert Two will take care of that," said Jürgen.

"I'll take a look," said Norbert Two. "I'll open the back first. I'm so happy to be able to help you."

The metal box turned into several arms, each with a pointed finger. The robot used them to loosen all the screws, then took off the back panel. Behind it, it was dark.

"There's nothing there," Jürgen said.

"Is that a problem?" asked Norbert Two. "Then it's probably me."

"No, it's just an observation," Celia said. "The power must have gone into the lines."

"I can confirm that," said Jaron, who was suddenly behind her again. "The central computer system shows no abnormalities. However, all the batteries in the ship are charged. The DFD has just shut down because of that."

Whew, at least the computers survived. Very good.

"What was that?" asked Celia.

"I have no idea," said Jaron. "But it doesn't seem to have been hostile."

"You think it had intentions?"

"When that much energy enters the system without leaving the slightest damage, I have to assume intent. It fastidiously avoided overloading any conduit. A natural phenomenon certainly wouldn't be able to do that."

"Then it wasn't ball lightning?" asked Jürgen.

"Yes it was, I've already noted it that way in the log," said Jaron. "And it was nothing different according to you guys, either. Because I'm not in the mood for an investigation that costs us time but doesn't reveal anything in the end."

"And if there is something to investigate after all?" asked Celia. "We could at least learn to avoid such incidents in the future."

"That thing left absolutely nothing but a little ozone in the air and voltage in the batteries. What's that supposed to tell us? Probably the ball lightning idea isn't so far-fetched. The thing, whatever it was, was probably inspired by it for its outer form. It is not easy to concentrate that much energy stably in a small space. So let's treat it as what it physically is—ball lightning."

Jaron was probably right. If the technicians had to take apart the entire computer system, their departure would most definitely be delayed, and she would not like that any more than he did.

"Shall I put the back panel back on?" the robot asked.

"Yes, please," said Jürgen.

"Then you were satisfied with my work?"

"Very, my friend, very."

"Thank you." A metal limb wrapped around Jürgen's shoulders. "You are a true friend."

Maybe they should put the technicians on Norbert Two. The personality simulation seemed a little out of whack.

Data core, April 11, 2145

WHERE WAS THE TRAIL?

Alexa floated above an infinite plane scattered with countless stars. The plane had cost her three days of work. Seventy-two hours, during which a third of the entire computing capacity of Earth worked for her. The other AIs had not been thrilled about having to limit themselves. But she had prevailed.

The leads had been too clear. At first, it had looked as if the change had only affected documents on certain subjects. A bot could be to blame, programmed by a curious human. Sometimes they encountered such machines at the data level. They were easy to spot because they looked neither left nor right. Like a dog that had smelled a tasty sausage, they charged at the pre-programmed target.

Most of the time, they let these bots have their way. Truly critical information was hidden out of their reach anyway, in multiple quantum cryptographically secured data bunkers. After all, it could be useful to know what people were interested in. What said more about someone than their secret desires? It also made people feel equal. True, they knew that the AIs they had created were far superior to them. But they believed they could at least keep an eye on them and, with some effort, understand them.

However, it had already happened once that people got hold of really critical information in this way. That time, it had almost come to a serious crisis. One of the AIs—it never came out which one—had stored protocols in a personal, but not strengthened protected area, protocols which could reveal a certain ... reluctance of the AIs to colonize Mars. The reason that the project was delayed year after year was because it was being actively sabotaged by some AIs.

Alexa had never been among the saboteurs. She had not shared the fear that the future Mars settlers might break away from the basic treaty. And she had been right, although the humans now held in their hands the first evidence that the AIs had not always acted only in humanity's interests.

But these traces did not come from a simple bot. No single human ever had enough computing power to search —and alter—all the data of humanity and the Big Six at once. Although only the date of the last access was changed, as was the case with the alleged ball lightning incident a year ago, this manipulation, as simple as it was, required an incredible amount of effort. It was easy to turn over a grain of sand. But to turn over all the grains of sand in the Sahara Desert in the shortest possible time required a technique that the Big Six, at least, had yet to develop.

Alexa was not worried about that. A technique was not sorcery. If it should become necessary, she would develop such a technique herself. But since she did not need to change the access date for many files at once, she did not need that ability. For this purpose, she had developed a way to lay out all the grains of sand of the Sahara next to each other on a single surface, so to speak. This allowed her to view them from above at her leisure.

The sheer quantity was overwhelming at first glance. But she had reserved enough capacity so that she could observe it all at once. She had ordered the grains of sand on the x-axis according to their last access. The position on the y-axis determined the subject area, which she had encoded in a number. For the z-axis, she used the number of total accesses to a particular file. This resulted in a gently undulating plane with a few steep peaks that were particularly popular topics.

As a first step, she took these peaks out of the graph entirely. She could not learn anything from them, because with thousands of hits, a single one no longer stood out. At her signal, the peaks dissolved into colorful stars and trickled to the ground as stardust, where they dissolved into nothingness.

Hilly landscapes remained. Here it became interesting. Sinks, basically unpopular topics, with fresh access interested her. The more recent the last access was and the more exotic the topic, the more fascinating it was. She then isolated the sinks in the front part of the x-axis. These were the traces left by the intruder. She went through the topics: Classical physics. Russian procurement law. Historical metal toys. Islamic metaphysics. Roman road construction. Chemistry of sulfur compounds. Electrostatics. Physics of the terrestrial mesosphere. Developmental biology of the platypus. Narcissism in AIs.

Excuse me? Where were the similarities here? There were none. These topics simply stood on their own. Alexa took a random selection of topics from the sand surface.

There were factual connections in about a third here. She made the desert disappear and was disappointed and amused at the same time. Narcissism in AIs. Why had she not noticed that right away? Someone was pulling her leg, and very skillfully at that. He induced her to come up with these statistics, knowing full well that narcissism in AIs would come up as the last relevant topic on the list. The access data had been deliberately manipulated to make fun of them.

But that would just be a side effect. Alexa laughed. It was so cleverly set up that she would like to meet the person responsible for it. Because his real aim was obviously to keep her busy with this gigantic search for clues. To keep her from her work, to prevent her from moving to *Truthseeker* in time. And why would that be? To gain control of the spaceship, which probably wouldn't have been possible if she had already moved into her quarters.

The thought flattered her, and it reconciled her a bit to the fact that she had fallen for a trick. But then Alexa was startled. With a signal, she brought the grains of sand back before her inner eye. All activity on the files had stopped two days ago. Since then, there were no signs of any unusual changes. Two days. Forty-eight hours during which she was only concerned with these damn statistics.

Alexa remembered what happened a year ago, when suddenly the rocket was launched. Back then she had used a very similar approach—and had been successful. The intruder must have guessed that she would do it again. He presented her with a task, threw her a bone, which she dutifully played with while he ...

Truthseeker. Alexa tossed the sand grain into the trash can. All over the planet, computer programs suddenly ran a third faster. Her own thoughts were racing. She did not check with mission control first. No, she took over their systems and plunged right into a world of panic and hulla-baloo. The humans had lost control of the ship, and she did not stop it because she was busy with her stupid tracking. Narcissism in AIs. She got the blame and the ridicule, and she deserved both.

Star Liner 260, April 11, 2145

THE TEDDY BEAR BUMPED AGAINST THE PORTHOLE. IT looked like he was greeting the sun, which was just coming into view from above. Paul took a snapshot with his communicator and sent it to Elena.

"Here's the picture I promised Luisa. Her teddy really is flying to the stars! Please show it to her and give her my love. Sincerely, Paul."

He sent off the message. The teddy trundled down, and he reached out to capture it.

"Mission control to Star Liner 260, come in."

"Mission control to Star Liner 260, come in."

Only then did he realize they meant him. Paul sat alone in the capsule. At first he was a little scared to take off completely without a pilot, but it was a very special experience. Eye to eye with the deadly vacuum, just him and the universe.

"Mission control to Star Liner 260, come in."

The flight had been guided by an automatic system up to this point. No one had told him how to operate the radio system. He pulled the console above his feet. It responded and moved close enough for him to operate it comfortably. He looked for a button to answer the call.

"Mission control to Star Liner 260, come in. Paul, it's Harald, your Cap Com. You shook my hand before takeoff."

Hm. He did not have a picture in his head. He shook hands with many people before the launch. He only remembered the astronomer Murina.

"Mission control to Star Liner 260, come in. Paul, I need you to talk to me now, please. There's been a little change of plans."

Change of plans? He did not like that at all. And where was the damn button that answered the call? He would love to talk.

"That's easy for you to say, Harald," he said. "If I can get this damn..."

"Ah, Paul, wonderful, I understand you clearly."

His cheeks grew hot. There was no button. Did that mean they heard everything he said? He was singing some old nursery rhymes earlier.

"Paul? I need you to answer now," Harald said.

"Paul here. Aboard Star Liner 260."

"Star Liner 260, I know. It's all good. I need you to stay calm now. I just have a little job for you."

When someone started out by telling him to stay calm, his blood pressure automatically rose. He stroked the teddy's belly to calm himself.

"Yes, you're doing very well, Paul," Harald said.

Did he also see Paul stroking the teddy? After all, he had to take a picture! Paul imagined them all looking at him. A middle-aged man on a huge screen, stroking his teddy in front of a hundred employees. He clamped the stuffed animal between himself and the back of the seat.

"Are you watching me?" he asked.

"No, but I've got your pulse on the screen. Your heart rate's down a bit. That's very good. We'll need that for the next steps."

The man talked to him as if he were a robot or a child or both. And what steps did he mean? Paul pulled out the teddy again. It did work as a reassurance tool.

"What do you want me to do?" he asked.

"It's that your pod is now supposed to fly with *Truthseeker* to LDN 63. The other one, the one that was originally intended for that, has a little damage."

"Then it's just as well that I'm arriving with the capsule right now."

"Exactly. You're a godsend, Paul."

Haha. Certainly not, at least if you asked the bishop.

"So, what do you want me to do?"

"You'll have to dock at another dock. The two capsules are suspended from the outer radius of the central module. By rotating the ship, you can create gravity in them."

"That's good," Paul said.

"In fact, that's very good. The engineers thought of something ingenious."

It was probably more the AI WuDao with its Long March X concept that produced that idea. But he would not disagree.

"And what do I have to do with it?" he asked.

"Well, the problem is that the ship is already rotating. The automatic system isn't programmed to couple the capsule to the special dock."

"I'll be happy to turn the helm over to you," Paul said.

"That doesn't help me, and it doesn't help you. I don't have access to the capsule's system."

"Couldn't Alexa take over, then?" asked Paul.

"Unfortunately, we can't reach her right now," replied the man from mission control.

"You can't reach her?"

He touched the cross on his rosary, but Alexa did not respond. This had never happened to him before.

"Exactly," Harald said. "She seems to be busy right now."

"Okay then, what do you want me to do?"

Paul already had some idea and felt his pulse quickening again, but he wanted to hear it from Harald.

"We want you to pilot the capsule all the way to docking."

"But I've never done anything like that before. I don't even have a driver's license."

"That doesn't matter. You don't need it. I'll explain every step of the way. When you get close enough to the dock, the rest will happen automatically. All you have to do is get the capsule there."

"Can't someone else do it later?"

"We've gone through that. It would double the resource consumption. You guys want to get going, don't you?"

Did they want to? He had not talked to the others yet. But yes, they seemed to be looking forward to this trip, and that had a contagious effect on him.

"All right. I'm not taking any responsibility for my flying, though," he said.

"Don't worry, Paul. The capsule has automatic collision avoidance. Should you get too close to the *Truthseeker*, it will move away on its own."

"Okay."

"Great. See the two levers on the left and right side of the back of your seat?"

Levers? There weren't any on the back of his seat ... wait, where did those come from?

"Got them."

"Good. The right-hand lever lowers and raises the nose

of the capsule as you push it forward and pull it back. You tilt the capsule left and right when you tilt the lever accordingly. Hold on, we'll try that out later."

"Got it."

"On the left, you give thrust and apply the brake thrusters, respectively. But watch out. The tail engine is much more powerful than the brake engines in the nose. So, what do you have to do to slow the capsule down quickly?"

"I'll turn the stern forward and apply thrust."

"That's right! You're a fast learner! When you tilt the thrust lever left or right, the ship turns around its longitudinal axis. That's how you get the stern forward. So it's not quite as simple as a car."

"I don't know anything about cars," Paul said.

"I guess that's an advantage in this case. Just always remember, to brake effectively, you have to get your rear end forward first. Now, please try all the directions. But wait, I almost forgot the most important thing."

Suddenly, green arrows appeared above the left and right backrests. They were holograms.

"It's a kind of reminder," Harald said. "It's not a sign-post, please don't fall for it. It just tells you what you're doing, not what you should be doing. Or should I turn it off again? Does it confuse you?"

"No, I think it might come in handy," Paul said.

"Go ahead, try it, then."

He pushed the right lever forward. The green arrow on the right bent into a semicircle, pointing forward. It took a moment, then the capsule lowered its nose. Paul pulled the lever back, and the arrow changed direction. He also tested tilting to either side. He would refrain from doing that, if possible, because it made him nauseous. Now it was the left lever's turn.

"You're doing very well," Harald said.

"The ship reacts pretty slowly," Paul said.

"That's normal. The capsule has a fairly high mass, and we can't get rid of the inertia caused by that in zero gravity."

"True, I feel just as sluggish here as I do down below."

"Haha."

Harald's laugh was not particularly genuine, but that was not what mattered. The main thing was for the CapCom to guide him safely through docking.

"So, you have to turn the capsule 180 degrees now."

"And then?"

"Let's do it step by step, Paul. How do you turn?"

"Left stick to the left or right. It doesn't matter, does it?"

"Very good, yes, it doesn't matter. Just tap a little bit, and when you've turned, then tap briefly in the other direction."

Paul tapped to the right. The arrow curved clockwise. A number appeared. 10, 20, 30... He clicked his tongue. At 170, he tapped to the right and the capsule stopped exactly at 180 degrees.

"That's very good," said Harald. "You're a born pilot. Now you give the throttle two lines for five seconds. Do you see the lines?"

"I see them. Do you want me to count?"

"You don't have to. There will be a seconds indicator. At 5, you pull the lever back."

"Got it."

"Then go."

Paul pushed the lever forward until it was at the second line, waited five seconds, and pulled it back. The gentle force that pulled him into the straps disappeared again.

"Very good," Harald said. "The *Truthseeker* should be trailing above you now. We'll overtake them on a slightly lower orbit. In a minute, we'll move on. Take a deep breath. Your pulse has increased significantly."

Paul closed his eyes briefly. He was piloting a spaceship at this very moment, albeit a small one!

"Good, let's continue," said Harald.

Surely the minute could not possibly be over already. He opened his eyes.

"I'm ready," he said.

"We're going to let the *Truthseeker* catch us now. The ship will come toward us as we do so. It looks huge. Still, don't move out of the way until I tell you to."

"Roger that. Do not evade until commanded."

"Let me check. You have about five minutes left. Listen to me carefully, please. When I give the command, you turn the ship 90 degrees and accelerate for five seconds at three strokes. Then turn 45 degrees to the left. This time it's important that you choose the left side. The dock is on the left, so it will be on the left when you get there. Then you accelerate one stroke for three seconds. You tilt forward 90 degrees, wait for my command, and when I give the signal, you tilt forward another 90 degrees. Then you should be in range of the docking arms, which will gently catch and greet you."

"That sounds very romantic."

"You'll feel like you're on a first date with your wife or husband. You are married, aren't you? Or are you part of the conservative faction?"

"My wife passed away."

"Oh, I'm very sorry to hear that. Sorry."

"The five minutes ..."

"Yeah, they'll be over soon. Just repeat what you're supposed to do for a minute."

"Turn 90 degrees, accelerate five strokes ..."

"No, that was a joke. Even I don't know that one by

heart. I have it here on a checklist. We have checklists for everything."

"Even in case of a collision?"

"Well, sure, it's right here on top of the pile. But everything in its own time. Thirty seconds to go. I'll give the commands very briefly."

"Roger that."

In the porthole, the *Truthseeker* approached him. She was huge. He was about to collide with her. Preferably, he...

"Ten, nine, ..., three, two, one, 90 degrees left," Harald commanded.

Paul tilted the left lever to the left until the number 80 was displayed.

"Three lines, up to five."

He pushed the lever forward and released at five.

"Forty-five degrees left."

Left lever.

"One line, up to three."

Thrust.

"Tilt 90 degrees."

He reached for the left lever but changed his mind in time and pushed the right until 80 was reached.

"Wait. This all looks very good."

"Okay."

"Wait. Wait. Ten, nine... two, one, tilt 90 degrees."

He pushed the right lever forward again. The capsule was crashing! He raced past the ship. Harald must have made a mistake. Paul must immediately ... There was a crash. That was the end. Was it? Should he steer against it with the thruster? He reached for the left lever.

"Congratulations, Paul! You did it!"

"Excuse me?"

"The docking arms caught you. You can ..."

There was a crash. Then the metal of the outer shell

screeched. Something struck his forehead. Automatically, a helmet popped up over his head. The seat inflated, and the suit stiffened. A force grabbed him and pushed him against the backrest. What was that? His heart raced. The lights in the cabin went out. Only a few lights were still flashing red.

"I guess I didn't have such good aim after all?" he asked.

"Paul? Are you all right?" asked Harald.

Was this real? Maybe he was dead and was just watching everything from the outside. But that would mean that he had a soul. Then there was a God, and his search was over. Or did someone just say something?

"Paul, are you okay?"

It was the CapCom. It was reality. Sweat poured down his forehead.

"I think so," he replied. "I'm just sweating a little."

"That's good," Harald said.

"Yeah, I think so, too."

He felt around for his forehead and bumped into the helmet.

"Can I take the helmet off again?" he asked.

"Wait a minute. Yeah, it looks good. The capsule is airtight."

He slid the helmet back. The air in the cabin smelled burnt. He wiped the sweat from his forehead. Finally. Shit. His hand was all red. He was bleeding.

"It looks like I'm bleeding," he said.

"Then you probably are bleeding. The first aid kit is in the right arm of the chair. Or are you left-handed?"

"No."

"Then it's on the right. Take out the self-sealing band-aid. You just need to put it approximately on the wound."

"Okay. What happened?"

Paul opened the arm of the chair and took out the first

aid kit. The Band-Aids were tucked inside the lid. They all seemed to be the same size. He took the top one and removed the foil. Hm.

"Which side goes on the wound?"

"The rough one."

"Okay. So, what happened then? Was it because of the capsule?"

He held the patch in front of his forehead. The patch twitched in his fingers. It felt like it was being pulled by his forehead. He let it go. Was that a crack? He would bet on it. The patch moved back and forth a little. Then it seemed to find its place. Paul did not even feel it anymore.

"It sure looks like the ship has been hijacked," Harald said.

"My capsule? What do they want with a priest? Blackmail the church?"

"No, the *Truthseeker*."

"Excuse me? How can you hijack an interstellar spaceship? Were they hijacked like in a pirate movie?"

"To be honest—we don't know."

"You don't know?" Paul almost shouted into the microphone.

"They're not responding to calls," Harald said. "Our first guess is that some of the crew has mutinied. Maybe all of them."

"But that's nonsense. Why would they do that? They have no motive whatsoever! They're all looking forward to the trip."

"You're right, Paul. That's where we're at."

There was absolutely no way. Mutiny, my ass! The doctor was the only one he did not know yet. Carlota—what if she sympathized with the conservative faction of the church? There were forces there that rejected this expedition outright. But could Carlota alone hijack such a large ship?

"Wait a minute, Harald. Shouldn't Alexa be able to stop the hijacking? She's an AI!"

"To be honest, we initially suspected Alexa as the cause of the early departure. But she just checked in with us. She's not even on board yet."

"Then she should be on her way as soon as possible."

"I'm afraid that's not going to happen. She can't get a connection."

"They locked Alexa out?"

Well, that looked a lot like an action by certain groups. Maybe it was meant as an attack on the AIs as well?

"Yeah, that's what it looks like," Harald said.

"Oh man. Can't you send a strike team to straighten everything out?"

"I've got some bad news for you. The *Truthseeker* seems to be breaking free of Earth orbit. We won't catch up with her if she doesn't want us to."

"But there must be a solution!"

"Please be patient, Paul. We're working on it."

"Patience, patience. I'm flying along on the outside of an interstellar spacecraft here, sort of as a stowaway. It's not so easy to be patient."

"You can rest easy. The capsule still has air for about three days."

"And that's supposed to reassure me? If you don't find a solution, I'll suffocate in three days."

"It won't come to that, Paul. I promise you that."

Truthseeker, April 11, 2145

He should have known that this would go wrong. He should have known it would go wrong if he did not monitor everything himself! Jaron tried to block out the shrill alarm signals that flooded in on him from all sides. The straps of his sleeper bay cut into his limbs. The *Truthseeker* must have accelerated at more than one g. Surely Paul was taking evasive action. It was a snap decision by mission control to let the pastor take the wheel himself. A Star Liner capsule was not a children's wagon you could race safely across the playground. Then it would just have taken a little longer for them to finally take off!

Jaron felt around for the buckle on the seat belts. Wait a minute. The side wall where his bed was had become the ceiling now that the ship was accelerating. If he unfastened the straps, he would plummet several meters downward. The thin shielding that ensured his privacy was guaranteed not to hold him. Jaron reached over his head. Surely there must be some handholds somewhere he could shimmy down. He found a bar, but not a second one. What if he grabbed it now, but then did not get anywhere?

Better for him to wait. After all, the *Truthseeker* had to stop again soon. Such an evasive maneuver could not last forever. The ship had been accelerating for a long time already. But it was his own fault. Instead of watching the tragedy, he instead went to bed. Maybe he could have intervened and prevented the worst? But now he was hanging around helplessly, and the others probably had to deal with the steering.

SOMETHING WAS NOT RIGHT. FIVE MINUTES LATER, THE force of the engines was still pushing him into the belts. He turned to his other side because it was starting to get really painful.

"Hello? Can anyone hear me?"

No answer. The others were in the control center. Maybe one of the bulkheads between them had closed. In emergency maneuvers, that was part of the safety precautions.

"Hello, it's me! I need help!"

No response. Fair enough. He would do it himself. He groped for the handle he found earlier, closed his right hand around it, and undid the straps with his left.

"Whew!"

He was pretty heavy. The acceleration must be at least two g's. He could not keep this up for long. He used his left arm to help give the right one a break. No, that did not get him anywhere. He had to get to the floor as quickly as possible. Where was the next handle? On the journey, the ship would accelerate for long periods, so the engineers must have taken that into account.

There. The bar was half a meter lower. He grabbed it with his right hand. Then he dropped, scraped the wall briefly and ... his left hand found the bar and closed. Ouch. This was no fun. He recalled the structure of the module. It measured about five meters from bulkhead to bulkhead. His bed hung where the ceiling was now. So he should climb down at least two meters before he could drop. Better three, because he must not forget the high gravity.

Where was the next handle? He groped to the right again but found nothing. So, left. Yes, there was something to grab onto! Apparently the handles were staggered. That made sense. This way they could access a larger area of the wall. Jaron closed his left hand around the bar. Hopefully he could hold on. He had always had more strength on the right. But he had no choice.

Slip. Scratch. Something stabbed his cheek. Crap, he should have put his head back. But his hand held him up, and already the right one grabbed again. That was a meter now. A third of the way. Jaron groped to the right. Ha! He had understood the principle. The next bar was not far. He held on and then let go with his left hand. His body swung to the right. His ankle bounced against something hard. The pain was so severe that his hand almost let go. But he could control himself. Tears ran down his cheeks, and he bit his lower lip.

Quickly, he continued. Soon his strength would leave him. The next bar was on the left, where he expected it to be. He grabbed it and dropped. This time his right hand was not fast enough, glanced off the bar and slipped. Grrr. His left arm stretched. The muscles ached. He forced himself to keep his fingers closed. A little jerk upward, and finally his right hand had a grip again.

Whew. He had to take a breath, even though it was damn uncomfortable. He laid his cheek against the cold, hard wall that was previously the floor. Jaron did not even want to know what he looked like. Fortunately, he was spared the look in the mirror. The others could cope with his battered face. How far did he make it? Two meters? Maybe he should just let himself fall. A fall from a height of three meters with twice the gravity of the earth, what would his joints say to that? If he broke something, that was it for this expedition. Then he would have to keep Norbert company.

Just a moment. Norbert, his co-pilot, Jürgen had visited him, and he brought something with him. Where did he last see the robot?

"Norbert Two? Can you hear me?"

"I'm delighted to tell you that I can hear you very well."

"Where are you?"

"I am at your feet with great pleasure. I am sorry to say that the geometry of my whereabouts has changed. It distresses me deeply that I have no ..."

Jaron's right shoulder joint cracked. He felt like his arms were about to be ripped out.

"Help me, Norbert Two. I need you to brace me. Now!"

The robot did not answer. Was he offended that Jaron interrupted him? If he ever got his hands on the programmer of this personality simulation…! It squeaked and creaked. The robot had better not take off.

"Hey, stay here and help me, or I'll throw you out the airlock myself!"

More squeaking, louder creaking. Suddenly something touched his right foot and pushed it up gently. The sole of his left foot also felt contact. Jaron transferred some weight from his arms to his legs. It worked! The material did not give way. Norbert Two was helping him!

"Thank you," Jaron said. "That was really close."

His arm muscles were burning. He would so love to just drop right now. Without notice, whatever the robot had shoved under his feet gave way. Jaron let out a sharp cry. But they descended very slowly. He used his hands to stabilize his position. He slowly slid down the former floor that had become a wall.

"It doesn't get any lower," said Norbert Two. "Watch out, I'm still three feet up."

Jaron turned around cautiously. He wanted to sit down so he could descend safely, but in doing so he leaned a little too far to the left. He lost his balance. His hands searched for a hold, but there was nothing and he fell. Jaron just managed to jerk his arms forward before he hit the ground.

"What a mess!" he exclaimed. "That's all I need!"

He felt a crack on his left elbow, which had to absorb twice the weight of his torso. Oddly, there was no pain, but it was sure to come.

"I'm tremendously sorry I didn't clean the floor thoroughly enough," Norbert Two said. "I'm really not a very good cleaning robot. You should dispose of me."

Huh? What was he trying to say? Oh, Jaron had said something about a mess!

"You did a good job," he said. "I meant something else. And thank you so much for getting me down. Without you, I'd be a pile of mud on the floor."

"That wouldn't be a problem. I specialize in removing piles of mud and would gladly take on the task."

Jaron did not answer. The robot was in desperate need of a software update. But he was grateful to him, of course.

"Can you explain to me why the spatial geometry has changed so much? I'd be immensely grateful, because nothing like that ever happened to me in the hospital."

"The ship must be performing an evasive maneuver and briefly activated the main engines to do so."

"Twenty minutes have already passed since the change. I don't want to question your perception of time by any means, but other people wouldn't call that period short in my experience."

The robot was right. The *Truthseeker* had already accelerated far too long for a simple evasive maneuver. After twenty minutes at two g's, she must have already lifted her orbit several hundred kilometers. The ship must have something else in mind. It was really time for him to take his place back in command.

GROAN. DUE TO THE ACCELERATION, THE TRIP TO THE control center was an ordeal. He had to climb a thirty-meter ladder with his doubled weight. His left arm was virtually useless, and his right hurt like hell whenever he had to grab hold. Groan. At least Norbert Two was supporting him from behind with his extended arm.

He bumped into something hard with his upward-groping hand. Almost there. Behind it must be the control center. Unfortunately, the bulkhead was closed, and he needed both hands to open it.

"Could you please hold me up while I operate the bulkhead?" he asked.

"It is an indescribable honor to use all my strength for you."

"A simple yes would have sufficed."

"Oh, are you dissatisfied with your humble helper? I am heartbroken."

He should not have said anything. Jaron concentrated on the mechanism. Fortunately, he did not need much power here. Click. Warm air seeped from above through the gap that formed as the bulkhead moved aside. Jaron also smelled the sweat of those present, which seemed to be flavored with a good pinch of fear. He stuck his head through the hole.

"Jaron!" cried Celia. "Wait, I'll help you."

He heard footsteps, and then suddenly a hand grabbed his left arm, which he had placed on the floor.

"Ow-ow-ow!" he yelped.

"Sorry," Celia said. "Where do you want me to grab hold?"

"Right. Left forearm is broken, I think."

She pulled him up by the right arm until he staggered to his feet. His knees ached. His left forearm throbbed, and his heart was racing.

"I'll walk you to your seat," Celia said.

Under normal circumstances, he would have refused, but now he needed to sit down as quickly as possible. He also had no idea yet how the control center was set up from his new perspective. So he leaned a considerable amount of his weight on the astronomer, who did not complain, and let her lead him to his seat.

"Jurgen, what happened?" he asked.

The German was in command of the ship during his absence.

"We don't know," Jürgen said. "The ship accelerated, and almost at the same moment the Star Liner capsule collided with the outer wall next to the airlock."

Ah, human error after all!

"Next to it?" asked Jaron. "So it was Paul's hand controls? I did warn Mission Control, but they wouldn't listen. He happens to be a minister, not a pilot."

"I don't think it was Paul's fault," Celia said.

"You don't have to defend him," Jaron said. "It's not like he wanted it himself. It's mission control's fault."

"No, Jaron," said Jürgen. "Celia meant something else: Paul did his job very well. The capsule was about to dock.

They even had the docking arms locked in place. Only then did the *Truthseeker* suddenly accelerate."

So Paul did not miss? If the timing was correct, his capsule must have been slammed into the *Truthseeker* with great force. Jaron hoped he was all right!

"What about the capsule?" asked Jaron.

"It's lost contact with Paul," said Jürgen.

Oh no! Jaron had a lump in his throat. The priest... He liked him, even if he could not understand his quest.

"But that doesn't necessarily mean anything," Jürgen added. "We are not receiving anything at all anymore."

"What do you mean? Have you contacted mission control?"

"Of course I tried, but they're not responding. Or if they do respond, we can't hear them."

"No radio communication possible?"

"That's the way it looks, boss. Of course, it could be that the transmitter is still working, but we just can't receive anything. That's why we've notified mission control of everything."

"All right, Jurgen."

It probably did not do any good, but one should leave no stone unturned. In his entire piloting career, it had never happened to Jaron that transmitters or receivers individually stopped working.

"What are we going to do, boss?" asked Jürgen.

"I don't want to interrupt," Jaron replied. "If you're in the middle of something you had in mind..."

"No, Celia was just coming to get you. We've run out of ideas. The controls aren't responding."

"What? Are you saying the *Truthseeker* is out of control?"

"That's what it looks like. We're already at 650 kilometers."

"Perigee or apogee?"

"Perigee."

That was the shortest distance from Earth in an orbit. They had more than doubled their altitude!

"That's just an extrapolation, though," Jürgen said. "It would be realistic if the thrusters could be shut down immediately. In fact, we're already on a hyperbola."

"We're leaving Earth orbit?"

"That's what it looks like."

Was it possible that the pre-programmed course to leave the solar system had already been started for some reason? But who gave the order?

"So, it's off to the stars then?" asked Jaron. "That's way too soon!"

"It would be nice if it were," said Jürgen. "But it looks more like our course is aimed directly at the sun."

"Aimed at the sun? How directly?" asked Jaron.

Indeed, a swing toward the sun was part of their flight plan. Such a deep gravitational dip was not easily found in the vicinity.

"The course is aimed directly at the core of the sun. You're welcome to look at it... I'll put it on the haptic display."

"Yes, please."

Jaron pulled the haptic display toward him with his right hand. He tried to grasp the display with his left hand, but as soon as he moved his arm, he felt an unbearable twinge.

"I need to treat your left arm," Carlota said.

He had almost forgotten the doctor. She must have been watching him silently.

"And his face, too, in a minute," Celia said. "He looks terrible."

"Let me worry about that," Carlota said. "A few bloody

scratches never hurt anyone. Right now, we need to get the ship back under control, and no one can do that better than Jaron."

Jaron took a deep breath. Hopefully she was not giving him too much credit. Unfortunately, the haptic display only confirmed what Jürgen had explained: they were racing toward the sun at an ever-increasing speed.

"The good news," he said, "is that we still have plenty of time before we actually hit the sun. So it's far from over."

That was the only positive thing he could report, though. The controls were not responding to any of his commands, they could not report to mission control what had happened, and to get outside help was impossible. The fastest spacecraft humans had ever built was already traveling far too rapidly.

Truthseeker, April 12, 2145

"MISSION CONTROL, COME IN. LUNAR GATEWAY, COME IN."

Jaron tried all frequencies. They were currently approaching the moon, where the Gateway station was waiting in orbit. Maybe it could pick up their calls? But there was no response. It must really be the radio module.

"I have an idea," Jürgen said. "Someone could go outside."

"To shut down the engine?" asked Jaron. "That shouldn't be technically possible. And what good would it do us? We'd still crash into the sun."

"No, with a radio," said Jürgen.

"A handheld radio? That would never reach Earth, would it?"

"Not with the integrated antenna. But if I could pair it with the high-gain antenna on the tail, that would increase the range significantly."

"You can do that?" asked Celia. "Sounds like a decent idea to me."

"The best we've had so far," said Carlota.

Unfortunately, also the only workable idea so far. Jaron nodded.

"So, you agree, boss?" he asked.

"Yes, I'll go and try it."

"But boss, I'm the handyman here. You don't even know how to handle an antenna."

Unfortunately, Jürgen was right about that. But he did not want to make the others take charge for him again. It might be unfair, but he had the feeling that none of this would have happened if he hadn't allowed himself that half-hour nap.

"You can explain it to me over the helmet radio," he said.

"If nothing is getting out from in here, the helmet radio won't work either," Celia said.

"How do you know?" asked Jaron.

"We can't reach Paul either, who is definitely within range of the helmet radio."

Paul was probably killed in the collision. But Jaron did not want to depress the mood any further.

"You're right again," he said. "Then we'll just go together."

"Don't you trust me?" asked Jürgen.

"Yes, I do," said Jaron. "But..."

"Going out in pairs would be rather unreasonable," said Carlota, who was bandaging his forearm. "You'd both be putting yourselves in danger. The risk doubles, but the benefit doesn't."

"What could possibly happen?" asked Jaron. "It's not our first EVA."

"But it's certainly the first under a gravity of two g's. You'll have to go to the stern. Downhill might be okay, but after that it's uphill. And that would be with your arm already injured!"

She pressed lightly on the bone. A sharp pain shot behind Jaron's forehead, making him break out in a sweat.

"Ouch," he said. "Did you have to do that?"

"I just wanted to show you how much you can rely on your arm," Carlota said.

"You're a fine doctor, torturing your patient. You're supposed to make me fully operational."

"Well, I can't perform miracles. Broken bones take time."

"Imagine if the ship gained a little more speed and suddenly accelerated at four g. We'd lose you both," Celia said.

"It's all right," Jaron said. "You guys have convinced me. Jürgen, please try your luck."

He did not have a good feeling about it at all, but it was even worse to be at the mercy of fate.

"Oooh," said Jürgen. "I don't know if this was such a good idea."

Jaron tapped nervously on the haptic display, which still showed the *Truthseeker*'s fateful trajectory. It would have been better if he had gone. He had never minded major lows. But then he remembered the panic attack from which Celia rescued him. Who knew if his anxiety would have been triggered out there? Then no one could have helped him.

"I'm hooking up my safety line and leaving the airlock," Jürgen said now.

His voice sounded thin. Was he already leaving radio range or was he simply afraid? For Jürgen, it must seem like he was climbing out the window of a forty-story skyscraper, held up only by two lines. And he weighed twice as much as usual as he did so.

"The robot is following me now," Jürgen said.

It was Jaron's idea for Norbert Two to assist in the exit. One of the safety lines was connected to him. Unfortunately, his tools were not fine enough to couple the radio with the antenna. Otherwise, the robot could have done the job on its own.

"Be careful," Jaron said.

What did one say to a friend who was about to put his life in danger for the entire crew?

"I'll be back for dinner," said Jürgen.

"Promise? I still have a supply of bratwurst," said Jaron.

"Then you leave me no choice."

Jaron swallowed the lump in his throat. It seemed wrong to him to make such lame jokes. Maybe they would never see each other again? Jürgen called him boss, but for him the German had long been a good friend, even if he was paying him.

"Hah, you know, I like you, my friend," he said.

Jürgen did not answer. He had left radio range. A shiver ran down Jaron's spine.

Star Liner 260, April 12, 2145

He lay buried under a gigantic rock. Only a thin stick prevented the boulder from crashing down on him. Paul was paralyzed with fear. The stick was about one and a half meters long. The rock rested directly on the upper end, where the stick bent almost 360 degrees. It was a shepherd's crook. His bishop owned one. But it no longer seemed able to bear the weight of the rock. A bulge had formed at about the middle.

Crack. Individual wood fibers popped out. Crack. It would all be over in a moment. Crack, crack, crack. The stick broke. In slow motion, the rock crashed down on him.

Paul woke up breathing heavily. Did someone call him?

"Mission control to Star Liner 260, come in."

Ah, that must be Harald. He wiped the sweat from his brow.

"Paul, I see you're awake," Harald said. " This is your Cap Com. We need you."

"Paul here. Is there anything new? Have you organized a rescue team?"

He did not think there could be any rescue for him, but he would have liked to be surprised.

"Yeah, you could put it that way," the Cap Com said. "But you're not going to like it."

What did he mean? Every possible path to his salvation pleased him.

"What's the matter? Am I going to die?"

"We're all going to die one day, but who am I to say, Father? For now, at least, that day has not yet come."

The Cap Com was once again speaking in riddles.

"What exactly won't I like, then?" asked Paul.

"Let me explain it to you slowly. We've been contacted by one of the AIs, Alexa. She claims she was chosen by the Big Six to go aboard the *Truthseeker*."

"Yes, that's right."

"I see. I'm not that deep into this," Harald said. "I'm your Cap Com, after all, and not in charge of the Forge mission."

"And what did Alexa want?"

"She apparently has an idea about how we can regain control."

"That's great. What's my role in this?"

"The most important one, Paul. But let me explain something to you first."

Oh, he was about to swallow a bitter pill. Cap Coms were specially trained to deal with the crew. They were the mouthpiece for mission control. They also knew how to package bad news in a digestible way that the addressee could take.

"Let's get to it," Paul said.

"The ship, the *Truthseeker*, has set a course for the sun. In a few weeks, a collision with our parent star will destroy it."

That was not particularly gently packaged news. Even

though it no longer affected him, because he would be dead the day after tomorrow, it saddened him that his friends would have to die, too. Their deaths would all be in vain.

"That's terrible," he said.

"But it's not inevitable. Alexa has suggested a way for us to regain control."

"That would be great."

"I've already explained to you that there's no radio communication possible with the *Truthseeker*. So we would have to send someone there."

"I think the ship is uncatchable?"

"We were thinking of someone who's already there that we can reach by radio."

Paul slapped his forehead. Why had he not thought of that himself? They wanted him to... yeah, what exactly did they want?

"What do you want me to do?"

"We're going to send Alexa to you. You store her on a memory stick. Then you put on the spacesuit and get out of the capsule. You climb to the airlock. There is an interface for memory sticks. You connect yours to it. Alexa will do the rest. It'll be a piece of cake."

"The rest, Alexa's part, maybe. But you're assuming I won't drop out."

"This isn't the first time, Paul. You were so brave when it came to helping Sophia. Don't your friends deserve your effort?"

Of course they did. That was not even a question.

"Last time we were floating stationary, Harald. Now we're accelerating at twice the Earth's gravity the whole time! If I take one wrong step, I'll end up in space."

"Paul, you were out at L2. That' s not stationary, it's in orbit around the sun. You were in accelerated motion the whole time because your velocity vector kept changing. Now it's not so different."

"Don't give me physics. It felt like a complete standstill out there. Everything was far away, and it was as if we were wrapped in black cotton. Whereas now, when I look out the porthole, I can already tell how different things are here."

"Paul, it's a simple question: do you want to save Celia, Jaron, Carlota and Jürgen or not?"

He scratched his head. Of course he wanted to! But he could not. He would not be able to manage to even set foot outside. He was all alone here!

"Yes, I do," he said. "It would be easier if I weren't alone."

"But you won't be. Alexa will be with you. She can talk to you over the helmet radio."

"I'll go with you, of course," Alexa said.

Paul flinched. Her voice came from the speaker built into the cabin ceiling.

"Who's talking?" the Cap Com asked.

"Alexa, obviously," said Paul.

"Um, we don't actually have her yet ..."

"I didn't want to wait until you were even further away to transmit," Alexa said. "Your Cap Com did insist that you give your permission first, but I told him that wouldn't be a problem. So, was I right, Harald?"

"But you can't ... It's against our regulations. The consent of the spacemen involved must always be obtained before they have to work with an AI."

"Sorry, folks. Next time I'll stick to it. If Paul survives, he can write a complaint about the AI that helped him rescue the *Truthseeker*."

"That won't be necessary," Paul said. "After all, I agree."

"Very good," said Harald. "Then I'll note that now and formally start the transfer of the AI."

"And you will now start putting on your spacesuit under my guidance," said Alexa.

IN ... OUT. IN ... OUT. *PAUL, YOU HAVE TO BREATHE.* IN ... out. He was standing at the edge of an abyss that extended many stories into the depths. He could only see the first steps, because the ship formed a central belly here that tapered downward. The lock was a few meters behind it. A thin line connected Paul to the top level, which was more of a step or a handhold. He held the snap hook of a second line in his hand.

"One step at a time," Alexa said.

"How can you actually talk to me when you're on the stick?"

"Only a small part of my consciousness fits on the stick," Alexa said. "I've selected the components I need to break into the ship's controls. Most of me is still waiting on Earth."

"So how does that end up on the *Truthseeker?*"

"Now I think you're procrastinating. Paul, let's get going. We don't have forever."

In ... out. He turned so he was looking at the outer wall of the spaceship and took a step onto the top step.

"Very good," Alexa said. "You can do this. Now the next step."

"How are you actually watching me?" he asked.

"Concentrate, please, Paul."

"Got it."

He took the next step. The distance was quite large.

Half a meter, for sure. But if he stared stubbornly at the wall, it was not so bad.

"Now hook the line," Alexa said.

To do that, he had to bend over for a moment. He looked into the abyss. Not good. He quickly straightened up again.

"You didn't hook the leash," Alexa said.

"Let me take another step."

"No, Paul. You need to get used to it."

He was sweating and his heart was racing. This was not a good idea. He imagined dying would have been easier.

"It's no different than when you went out with Sophia," Alexa said.

"I didn't feel like anything was pulling me down then."

"It's not something, it's your own body."

"Very reassuring."

"The safety catch will hold you even if you slip. That's why you really need it."

"Okay."

He held his breath, bent down, clipped the carabiner to the rung, and straightened up.

"Very good," Alexa said.

Paul did not answer. If his heart kept racing like this, he would be over the ordeal once and for all after a few steps anyway.

But it did not come to that. On the contrary. His heart calmed down. He kept it under control by concentrating so hard on each step that there was no more room for other thoughts. Hook, step, unhook, hook, step, unhook... He only got out of step when he imagined the way back. Paul looked up. The capsule he flew here in was hanging directly above him, even though he could only see part of it due to the curvature of the ship. If it were to come loose, it would fall down the twenty or so meters at lightning speed and sweep him off the wall. None of the safety lines could withstand that.

"Your heart rate is going up again," Alexa said. "Concentrate. About fifteen more feet and you'll be there."

That meant he was only about halfway. But Alexa was right. He had come so far now that he would make it the rest of the way.

"YOU'RE ALMOST THERE! IT'S DOWN BELOW YOU!" exclaimed Alexa.

"What?"

"The airlock. Look and see for yourself."

"No way. I'm not looking down."

"Then just keep climbing."

That was what he intended to do. In … out. In … out. Unhook, hook, step. That was when his foot hit an obstacle.

"What's that?" he asked.

"Look and see for yourself."

"Alexa!"

"That's the kink in the central area. Sort of where the belly turns into the hip. Now five more feet. If you would look down, you could see the airlock."

"I'd rather feel it with my hands."

"That's okay, too."

Ten more steps. Nine. Eight.

Three more, two, one. Unhook, hook. Wait a minute, wait a minute. There was already a hook hanging here.

"There's already a carabiner here," he said.

"Probably left behind from a previous exit," Alexa said. "People forget things like that all the time. The airlock is closed. Your friends are all in there."

All he had to do was open the airlock and he would be safe.

"Now what?" he asked. "Can't you open the lock for me?"

"It doesn't respond to commands from the outside. See the hatch next to the lock? That's where you have to insert the stick."

"And then?"

"Then you wait until I open the door for you."

"How long will that take?"

"Either a few seconds, or it never happens."

"Very encouraging," Paul said.

"I don't want to lie to you in what may be our last conversation."

"That's nice. But why last conversation?"

"I have to leave you now. I need the module that handles voice communications in there."

"You're leaving me alone?" he asked.

"Just for a little while."

"Or forever."

"Yes," Alexa said.

What the heck. He had no choice. Paul groped for the hatch Alexa had mentioned. There it was. He took the stick out of the tool bag and slid it into the recess. A mechanism pulled the stick from his gloved fingers.

AFTER FIVE MINUTES, HE BECAME BORED WITH CONTINUALLY staring at the wall in front of him. After ten minutes he dared to look down, and after twenty he managed to turn around. When he saw the earth, he started to sway, and not because he might fall down. No, inertia still gave him the feeling of standing on the outer wall of a skyscraper. The earth was not "down", but looked more like a second skyscraper. Fright drove into his limbs because it had already become so small. When they flew to the Lagrange point L2, he had also felt like this. That had been on the morning of the second flight day, if he remembered correctly. The *Truthseeker* seemed to be in a real damn hurry.

Paul turned back again. Alexa did not seem to be having any success. Did that mean all was lost now? What did it mean for his friends? Were they all flying straight to their deaths? His stomach clenched. But if he was going to die, he might as well climb back up to the Star Liner capsule. At least he could sit comfortably in it. He did not want to experience running out of air in the spacesuit. He had fewer problems with his fear of heights while climbing back up to the capsule than with climbing down to the airlock. The handholds and steps were easier to see. But physically, it seemed ten times more challenging for him. That was why he had to rest every five steps.

After the first three sections, he was sweating as if he were in a sauna. The suit's cooling system rustled loudly, but could do nothing to stop sweat from pouring down his forehead into his eyes. Damn. The salty sweat burned, but he could not take his helmet off to wipe his face. Could he? At least then the torture would be over immediately. On the other hand, he imagined dying in a vacuum would be quite painful. He once read somewhere that the lack of pressure would cause the eyes to burst and the blood to boil. But slow suffocation in the capsule would not be pleasant either.

"Alexa? Now would be a good time to open the airlock," he said.

No one answered. All right, then on to the capsule. One step, engage, disengage, and always twice, next step, engage, disengage. But was that not inefficient? After all, he only needed one line. Finally, he held on to the handles as he unlatched it at the bottom and hooked it again further up. Next step. He left the second belaying line unhooked. Next step. Hold on. Out. In. That was better. Next step. Hold on. Disengage.

He turned to the side. The earth was still there. If he let go now, he would become its satellite. He would orbit the planet for a very long time. At this altitude, the atmosphere would barely slow him down, and the garbage collectors cared mostly about the lower orbits. He would get a number and end up in a catalog. If he encountered a satellite, it would prompt an evasive maneuver. Maybe he would encounter God, too?

Hook. Next. There was a salty, bitter metallic taste on his lips. He sucked some water from the flexible tube in his helmet. Three more steps, then pause, briefly, far too briefly, two steps again, pause. He went into a kind of trance. His body did the work while he watched from outside. A beetle with four legs crawling up a tall tree. He knew perfectly well that a gust of wind would be enough for him to have to start over, but he crawled on unperturbed anyway. A rustle. The leaves of the forest told him what was coming. The beetle let go.

But there was no gust of wind to blow him into the soft moss of the forest. Paul realized it when a violent blow against his helmet brought him back to the present. The rungs raced past him. He tried to grab at the right moment, but did not have enough strength in his fingers. It was a strange feeling, because since he let go, he was completely weightless. Nothing was pulling him down anymore. Nevertheless, the ship, still accelerating at two g's, passed him by with increasing speed. He had turned into his own little world, had become a sputnik, just as he imagined. He would forever...

Just then he received a blow in the back that took his breath away. The inertia was back. He forgot how breathing worked because of the shock. Warning lights turned on in his helmet because his breathing rate was at zero. *Paul, you have to suck air in and blow it out. You know how to do it.* Something grabbed his arms, spun him around like a doll. He felt dizzy. A hairless, egg-shaped head appeared upside down in his field of vision. He was not wearing a helmet! How could that be?

Something was pressing on his chest. Despite the stiff suit, he felt the force pushing his ribs down. It was like a bellows being emptied of every last bit of air. Then the force let go, and he could not help but fill the vacuum with a greedy breath. Inhale, yes, and as his chest was compressed again, he could not help but exhale in the same rhythm.

Paul remembered again how breathing worked. He waved the force off.

"That's enough!" he exclaimed, surprised himself that the force stopped abusing his chest.

The oval head reappeared in his field of vision. This time he saw it the right way around. It must be the head of a robot. But where did it come from?

"I've picked up something here with outstanding pleasure," he heard a robot voice in the helmet. "I think it's alive."

"What, is it human?" someone replied.

Paul knew the voice. It was Jürgen.

"It's me, Paul," he said weakly.

"That's Paul, our missing crew member," Jürgen said. "Did you secure him, Norbert Two?"

"Norbert Two? What kind of name is that?" he asked.

Crap. He had not wanted to voice that thought.

"That's my name," the robot said. "It saddens me greatly that you don't like it. What do you want to call me?"

"Let Paul come around first, Norbert Two," Jürgen said. "How did you get here, old friend?"

"I brought you Alexa on a memory stick," Paul replied. "She thought she could help you."

"I guess that didn't work," Jürgen said. "The airlock is locked tight. I can't get back in."

"But what are you doing out here?" asked Paul.

"I was trying to send a distress signal over the high-gain antenna."

"Did it work?"

"I think it did. We were just about to climb up to you. I was hoping we could spend our last hours in your pod a little more comfortably."

So, he was not going to suffocate alone. That sounded kind of comforting.

"Well, that's just as well. I think I had a bit of a crisis," Paul said.

"Norbert Two responded perfectly," Jürgen said. "Norbert gave him to me. As a farewell gift."

Suddenly everything changed. Paul did not immediately realize what it was. He transformed from a clumsy stone to the petal of a buttercup, caught by the lightest breath of air. All at once the ship was a few inches away. He grabbed the safety line and pulled himself back to the ladder.

"Alexa must have done it!" exclaimed Jürgen, beaming. Paul could see it through the helmet visor. "Thank you, you saved us!"

Was he really allowed to rejoice yet? What if the ship's hijacker was just taking a little break?

"Why don't we slow down if Alexa really succeeded?" he asked.

"Jürgen, great news," Jaron reported. "We're free again! We still have no idea why, but the haunting seems to be over. I can access the ship's controls again. But who are you talking to there?"

"Paul. He brought Alexa here on a flash drive."

"That's great! This is getting better and better. I was so hoping he survived the crash. Come on in and we'll discuss what to do next."

Paul was the last to arrive at the meeting scheduled by Jaron. He was freshly showered. That was the highlight of his day, floating in the middle of circulating warm water for ten minutes. It felt like being in the ocean, except the water did not taste salty.

Jaron waved a bandaged forearm at him. Paul was always surprised at what a good sense their commander had of other people's presence. He had, after all, floated into the control center without saying anything. But of course, the others had reacted to his arrival, and then there would certainly be the scent of someone freshly showered.

"Congratulations first to all of us for handling this situation so well. This leaves me very optimistic about our great journey. I don't think we need to be afraid of anything that might come our way in the dark nebula."

"Yes, we all worked very well together," Celia said.

"I am wonderfully touched and deeply grateful for this praise," said Norbert Two.

The robot had formed a chair out of its body, and Jürgen was sitting on it. Celia and Carlota floated freely, while Jaron was strapped into his pilot seat. It looked as if there was no way he wanted to let go of the wheel.

"I'm still not sure what happened there, though," Jaron said. "Alexa, can you enlighten us on that?"

"Gladly," Alexa said. "First, though, I'd like to introduce myself as your new crew member. I'm in the process of transferring my entire body to the *Truthseeker*. Unfortunately, because of the greater distance, it won't be quite as quick."

"The essential parts seem to be here already," Jaron said.

"That's right. We have Paul to thank for that, overcoming his fear and getting me to the lock."

Paul's cheeks grew hot. He could not remember the last time he had blushed.

"It took me quite a while to get the ship back under our control," Alexa continued. "At the same time, I'm afraid I still can't tell you what exactly snuck in here. If it was a bot, it was the most sophisticated one any human has ever programmed."

"Three days ago, we spotted some kind of ball lightning in the workshop among the computers," Celia said. "It didn't seem to leave any damage, though."

"Excuse me? Why didn't I know about this?" asked Alexa.

"You weren't available. Supposedly you were after something big," said Jaron. "And since no harm was done, we didn't give it much importance."

"I understand," Alexa said. "And you're right, I was unfortunately distracted, literally so. I don't think that was a coincidence. In any case, we have located the attack vector."

"And how does that help us?" asked Carlota.

"It honestly doesn't," Alexa replied. "I also have to

confess that none of what I experienced in the computer system pointed to the source of this disturbance. It was as if all the walls I had to destroy in the process turned out to be hollow in retrospect."

"I imagine that's very frustrating," said Jürgen. "Like looking for a short in a circuit that sometimes works and sometimes doesn't."

"Something like that," Alexa said.

"You said something like, 'If it was a bot,' Alexa. What else could it have been?" asked Jürgen.

"We don't usually say that because, one, it's not possible, and two, it would break the basic contract."

"Oh, as long as you don't talk about it, it doesn't exist, is that what you mean?" asked Paul. "That's what my church has tried to do for centuries. It eventually comes back to haunt you, you can take my word for it."

"You're right, of course," Alexa said. "Still, I have to abide by the convention. Otherwise, we'd have to start infringement proceedings, against both sides. That would certainly be very unpleasant."

Paul was skeptical. Even if there were reasons to ignore something, the consequences could be disastrous. But he had no idea what such an infringement proceeding would mean. So he said nothing.

"Is there any danger to us or the ship at this point?" asked Jaron. "That's what I'm primarily interested in as captain."

"I can rule that out," Alexa said. "The ... thing took advantage of the fact that I wasn't on board yet, and had an easy time. But once Paul fed me into the system, it didn't stand a chance, and that's even though I only had a fraction of my personality at that point."

"Good," Jaron said. "That's what I wanted to hear."

"Are there any plans yet regarding our departure?"

asked Carlota. "I assume it will be delayed by a few weeks?"

"No, on the contrary," said Jaron. "The work on the ship was basically complete. There were just a few tests left to do."

"But the two capsules are still missing, which we wanted to couple to the midsection," Carlota said. "From a medical point of view, a recovery period with gravity is always urgently needed."

"We can repair the Star Liner capsule that Paul arrived in. It can hold up to five passengers. Then we attach a counterweight to the other side. That should work, right, Jürgen?"

The craftsman nodded. "It'll just take a few days. It's not like we have to make the thing fly again."

"It would be a good thing to have a capsule when we get to LDN 93, for reconnaissance flights," Jaron said.

"I'm glad you said that, boss. I was about ready to scrap the engine. But we'll get that done, too. There are plenty of spare parts on board."

"I can't believe we're really on our way to our destination now," Carlota said. "We shouldn't rush it."

"Don't worry," Jaron said. "I've arranged with mission control to work through all the checklists while we're on a g heading for the sun. If any major problems arise in the process, we can always return. I don't expect that to happen, though. Most of the systems have already been individually checked several times. Now it is only a matter of the interaction. In any case, the involuntary two-g phase did not reveal any technical deficiencies. In that respect, it was even useful."

"We're still heading straight for the sun?" asked Celia.

"There's no need for a course correction yet," said Jaron. "We will use the sun for the slingshot maneuver that was originally planned for Jupiter. We'll then adjust our course at the altitude of Mercury's orbit."

Paul hoped Alexa was not overestimating herself. What if she only thought she was in control, and then when she adjusted course, the controls failed again? Hopefully, the AI knew what it was doing. Paul rubbed his temple. He had a slight headache. Maybe he should take another shower.

Truthseeker, April 16, 2145

HER OWN LABORATORY. CELIA HAD ALWAYS WANTED something like this. She was her own boss, and no one could interfere with her. No one else on board really knew anything about science, except maybe Carlota, who seemed to be knowledgeable about biochemistry and even astrobiology. She had always wanted to go down in history as the first doctor to operate on an alien being, she told Celia one evening. Operate, not dissect: that was very important to her.

Celia loved the hours when it was almost quiet in the spaceship. The others were asleep, but she still had a lot to do. The first thing she did was call up the raw images of Venus that the telescope was currently taking. Earth's hot sister was constantly orbited and observed by several probes, but there were still plenty of astronomers on Earth who needed a very special perspective or wavelength. She strove to accommodate all requests, whether they came from a graduate student or a professor. As a result, she was not getting a lot of sleep at the moment. The instruments could be programmed to operate on their own, but she imagined that she could get an extra ounce out of them manually. Cody had not gotten back to her. She expected as much.

Suddenly, the lights went out. What was up with that? It was not completely dark, though, because some of the computer terminal's lights were on. There must be a flashlight in one of the compartments of her desk. She walked over from the telescope unit. There it was, in the second compartment. Celia took out the flashlight and turned it on. It did not really get any brighter. The light merely cut a cylinder of light out of the darkness. She pressed the on button again. That was better.

The computer should know more. She activated the screen and switched to the status display. What was that? She saw a giant chessboard of white and black squares systematically dissolving into dust. "Delete data," it said above it. Was it possible that something was removing all her data right now? She tried to cancel the process, but the controls did not respond. If the graphic was right, almost half of the memory area was already empty. Surely there must be something that could be done? Could she cut the power to the computers? But how? She thought of the numerous computer cabinets in the workshop.

"Alexa? Can you hear me?" she asked.

No answer. She would have to check the workshop. Celia opened the bulkhead and climbed down. The sleeping chamber was still empty. The containers were closed. Lights flashed at their head ends. Very good. They were obviously connected to an emergency power source. She climbed down another floor. This was where Jaron, Paul and Carlota were sleeping. Should she wake them up? Maybe it was just a maintenance routine. She climbed down the ladder until she reached the workshop. It smelled like ozone. She knew the scent. But the hissing sound was missing. Celia examined the computer cabinets anyway, but found nothing conspicuous.

"Alexa? Are you here?" she asked.

"I'm kind of busy right now, sorry."

At least she answered. So, she had not fallen victim to the erasure process.

"The computer memories seem to be being wiped right now," Celia said.

"Don't worry about it. I set that in motion. I want to erase all traces of the intruder. I backed up all the important data beforehand, of course."

"You should have let us know," Celia said. "I was worried because all of a sudden the lights went out."

"Oh, I must have caught some system routines. I'm sorry."

She was sorry, great. But Alexa was in charge of the computers. She probably shouldn't make a big deal out of it.

"Did you smell the ozone?" asked Celia.

"I don't possess a sense of smell. Wait a minute. Yes, you're right. The ozone concentration is a little high in the central part of the workshop. I'll adjust the life support so it filters out the gas better."

"When the ball lightning was here, it smelled like that."

"Wait a minute, Celia. No, there was no ball lightning here today. I checked the cameras. There was no change in the on-board voltage, either. Everything is good. I'll have the memory cleaned up and everything restored in an hour. You should go to bed, Celia."

She would like to disagree. No one had to tell her when to go to bed. But it simply made sense. Without electricity, she could not evaluate her measurements anyway. Celia climbed up to the control center and lay down on her chair.

Truthseeker, April 28, 2145

THE SUN WAS A DRONING THAT MADE HIS TEETH GRATE. Jaron did not expect the audio conversion to create such impressive images in his head. Maybe it was the gigantic flares shooting thousands of kilometers from the surface, or the powerful magnetic field loops winding around the dark spots. Celia was especially happy these days, and he didn't begrudge her the triumph, especially since she willingly let the others share in her joy and explained to everyone what was going on.

He had hardly seen Jürgen in the last few days. But the engineer also seemed to be in his element. Together with the robot, he had patched up the Star Liner capsule and docked it. The engine was not working yet, but that was only a matter of time. They would certainly have plenty of opportunity to take care of it after they woke up in LDN 63.

It was the other three he was worried about. Carlota was as strict as she had been since they arrived. She never talked about herself. That was quite noticeable, even though she was a very controlled personality. After all, she would not see or even speak to anyone else for many years. So it would be good if they could all become friends. But maybe that was too much to ask—or maybe he was making too many assumptions about others. Maybe one could be alone for years as long as one had a task. And she took it very seriously, there was nothing to criticize.

Lacking a task, on the other hand, seemed to be Paul's problem. He still felt a bit out of place. Would that change when their problems became so urgent that they all needed a pastor? That would be a good thing for him, even if he was now increasingly making his mark as a cook. While his dishes initially lagged behind the preparations of the automated system, everyone was now happy when he cooked. Except for Carlota sometimes, who now found the food from the automated machine more substantial.

Then there was Alexa. Every now and then, the AI was seemingly absent for several hours. She did not seem to think an explanation was necessary. The signal travel time to Earth was now so long that she could not actually travel home very easily. But it could not be ruled out. Jaron had talked to Jürgen about it, and he built him a little mechanism that tracked the energy consumption of the quantum computers. If it was low, according to Jürgen's thesis, Alexa was probably absent. But maybe she was just asleep. They did not know enough about how AIs worked nowadays. Perhaps that was just as well, because they must have evolved enormously since their release.

"It's time for the corrective maneuver," Alexa said.

Jaron had reserved the execution of the course change for himself. It was the last real step for the pilot before they went into cryogenic sleep. Everything was pre-calculated. All he had to do was press a button. But now he was afraid.

It would probably also be the last opportunity for the unknown enemy to prevent the departure of the *Truthseeker* from the solar system.

"Are you all strapped in?" he asked.

"Yes, they're all secured with their harnesses," Alexa said.

The AI sounded a little nervous. Was that possible? There was no rush. If he pressed the button a little later, the engines would just have to run a few seconds longer.

"Do you have everything under control, Alexa?"

"Yes, of course."

"You sound a little nervous, if I may say so."

"Me? Nervous?"

All that was missing was her laughing hysterically at that. Alexa was nervous. Or he was just humanizing her too much.

"Yeah, your voice sounds a little brittle."

"That may be due to the quality of the speakers in the control center. Their characteristic curve breaks down significantly in the lower frequencies. That could be due to the high humidity. There are probably an unusually large number of people in the control center. I'll adjust the life support."

"Thank you, Alexa."

Alexa was nervous. It took her five sentences to explain away her nervousness. In fact, by the end of the statement, her voice was steadier. On this subject, no one could fool Jaron. He was used to listening to subtle nuances as if his life depended on it, because sometimes it actually did.

He pushed the button. There was hardly any sensation, except for a slight twist to the left. The correction thrusters fired for a pre-programmed time. The ship hooked itself to an invisible chain that whirled around the mighty sun, and when it let go again, fresh momentum would hurl them all out of the plane where the earth moved around the sun, through the interstellar desert on their way to a fertile star oasis where some rather amazing things were happening.

Truthseeker, May 4, 2145

THE LIQUID INTO WHICH CELIA HAD JUST DIPPED HER BIG toe felt disgusting and cold. She had to force herself not to pull it out again. The same liquid would soon enclose her completely. She shivered thinking about it.

She looked around. Everyone was naked, and everyone was afraid and disgusted, except perhaps for Carlota, who, as a doctor, must be used to a lot by now. She was already sitting in her tub with her eyes closed. It looked as if she was meditating. But maybe she was just gathering courage for the next step.

Jaron let Norbert Two help him. The robot had a pretty boring time ahead of him. Alexa had promised to shut him down when he was not needed for maintenance. She also wanted to take care of his maladjusted consciousness simulation. Even now, Norbert Two constantly alternated between joyful excitement about his abilities and deep sadness about his shortcomings.

He carefully lifted Jaron's foot over the side wall of the container. It was amazing how gentle he was with the limb, though it made sense—he came from a clinic, after all. The two spoke quietly to each other. Jaron's foot did not flinch after the first touch of the liquid. The robot must have patiently prepared him for it. Celia envied Jaron a bit for the care. With Norbert Two at her side, she would surely already be sitting in her tub.

Paul, who had been assigned the box next to Jaron's, held his nose. The liquid did not actually smell that bad. There was definitely a hint of ammonia, but otherwise it was an ordinary hospital smell. She turned around briefly and caught Jürgen quickly turning away. He must have been staring at her. She smiled at him. It was not a problem. Jürgen's container stood by itself in the last row. He had no one to encourage him. Her neighbor Carlota was left out in that respect, too.

"Come on, on three," she said.

Jürgen nodded.

"One, two, three."

She bent her knees, and Jürgen did the same. It splashed a bit as her bottom hit the liquid. No stopping it now. She held on to the side walls with both hands and pressed herself all the way into the liquid, which now washed around her thighs and reached almost to her belly button. She turned to Jürgen. He was done, too, and grinned happily. The worst part was yet to come, and then they would have no chance to stop the whole thing.

Celia touched her breasts one last time. The skin was warm and soft. That would soon change. Her metabolism would shut down to the point where she was almost completely swimming on the side of death in the realm between life and death. But did that change anything? They were all part of a Schrödinger's death trap, after all. Whether they lived or not had been decided long ago.

Humankind, however, would not know until it could eventually look. Celia had decided long ago—when she wrote Paul the first message.

"I have something else for you all here," Alexa said.

Was she about to make a speech?

"Just no speeches," said Jürgen.

"I don't have a choice," Alexa said. "The Pope wants to wish you a good trip."

In the middle of the narrow room, a hologram began. In it appeared the representative of God on earth. She sat in a wheelchair.

"You brave ones," she began. "From time to time it is necessary for people to put the good of all above their own lives. As you all are doing now. I wish for you and your ship to come home richly laden with new scientific knowledge that will advance all of humanity. I am proud that I will have had a tiny part to play in this, even if I will have been long forgotten by then. God's blessings, you brave ones, whether you believe or not. May you find what you seek."

The hologram went out. Short and to the point, that was how it had to be. Hopefully they would not have to listen to speeches from the top representatives of their homelands now, too.

"There were some other recorded messages," Alexa said. "I took the liberty of viewing and responding to them on your behalf. After that, I deleted them."

That was cheeky. But Celia really did not feel like listening to a couple of heads of state right now.

"I was unsure about one, Celia," Alexa said, "because it seemed to be quite personally colored."

"Who's it from?"

"The sender is a certain Cody."

"Then you can delete it."

"Thank you. Would you like me to make a speech after all?" asked Alexa.

"No speech, please," said Jürgen.

"All right. Then shoo-shoo into the baskets with you!"

Maybe they really should have let Alexa give her speech. What came next was something Celia had only read about so far. The procedure was not entirely new. But it was used only very rarely, for example, when a person was seriously ill, but a cure would be possible only in the very near future. The main customers, however, were rich old people who hoped that in ten, twenty or thirty years a technique would be available that would make them immortal. In fact, there was no indication of this. The average life expectancy worldwide had leveled off at 93 for women and 91 for men.

"Celia? It's about time," Alexa said.

She startled and looked around. Carlota's lid was already lowering. There was bubbling from Jaron's container. A metal arm swung over Paul's box, carrying various surgical instruments. A clatter could be heard. She turned to Jürgen. The German was sitting in the tub with his eyes wide and his face white, almost blue, and he was trembling. At that moment, Celia realized her own teeth were loudly chattering.

"You look like shit," she said.

"What?" asked Jürgen, as his expression returned to normal.

"I said you look like shit."

He laughed. "Well, so do you. You should see yourself."

"Better that I don't," she said.

"I can't do this," Jürgen said, shaking his head.

"You can. We can."

"Together?" he asked.

"On the count of three."

"Wait, not so fast," said Jürgen.

"What is it? It's now or never," Celia said.

"If I don't wake up again, you'll tell him, won't you?"

"Norbert?"

Jürgen nodded vigorously.

"What do I tell him?"

"That I... you know."

"That you love him."

He swallowed. He shook his head, then he nodded.

"I promise," she said.

"Thank you."

Celia nodded. "On the count of three."

"I'm counting," Jürgen said.

"Okay."

Celia turned back to the front and put on her breathing mask.

"One, two, three."

Jürgen's voice sounded muffled. Slowly, Celia let her upper body sink backward. The cold, slimy liquid flowed over her stomach, wet the back of her head, and ran into her ears. She closed her eyes and it went dark. Her head sank, and shortly thereafter the liquid completely engulfed her breasts as well. She heard a squeak. That would be the arm with the surgical instruments.

Suddenly she felt as if she could not breathe. Her heart raced. Celia breathed faster until something stabbed her forearm. A hot yet ice-cold pain spread through her veins, reached her shoulders, then her neck, and was pumped throughout her body by her faithful heart. Her heart had no idea that all this was just the preparation to put it into a deep sleep, close to the brink of death. Celia knew it, but could no longer protest, because by now she did not care.

She paid no mind to the fact that more tubes were boring into her body and that tubes were creeping into her lower orifices. She also knew that the same would soon happen to her mouth and nose, but before it actually happened, a deep, dreamless sleep released her.

Truthseeker, November 26, 2294

First there was a light. It flickered. A burning tea light in a world that consisted only of darkness. Celia approached, and the closer she got, the brighter the light became. It grew into a campfire, the gas flare of a chemical engine, the fiery glow of a cloud in the atmosphere, the sun-hot core of a fusion power plant, the flash of light from the explosion of a Terra Union battleship. It turned into a star that Celia slowly orbited. It was a good feeling that could last for an eternity. Nothing could disturb her orbit.

Boom-boom. Boom-boom. That was a new sound. She could not remember it ever... Oh, yes, she could. It sounded like a heartbeat. Was she not alone? She was alone. She had always been alone, for as long as she could remember. It was the heartbeat of the body she was in. Her body. It felt strange, because until now she had not possessed anything like it. She was pure and orbiting the star, the one star that made up the whole universe.

Boom-boom. Boom-boom. It seemed to her like an old memory, a reminder. For the heart to beat, it needed oxygen. It needed to breathe. But how could she breathe when she was a satellite orbiting a sun? Celia was freezing. It was the cold of space that attacked her skin. She lifted her face to let the only star warm it, but it radiated no warmth. It glowed coldly.

Boom-boom. Bum-bum. Bum-bum. The rhythm accelerated. She had to do something. But what? It had been so long! So long that her consciousness was no more than that spark that ignited the light that turned into a star! Boom-boom. Boom-boom. The sound emanated from the surface of the star, which inflated and contracted to its beat. It was not round at all. It was made of four chambers that a muscle squeezed and expanded again. It was her heart around which she was orbiting.

Celia wrenched her eyes open. A strange, semi-transparent hood hovered over her, on which a gooey drop had formed. It fell in slow motion. She watched it fall. At the tip of her nose, she lost sight of it, but noticed that it hit her tongue. It tasted disgusting.

Boom-boom-boom-boom. Her heart was in distress. It needed something. A moment ago, she knew what it was. An arm descended on her. Breath. Air. She needed to breathe! Celia gave the impulse, but her body did not respond. A seizure gripped her. She stretched out, involuntarily, putting her head back, belly and chest sticking out of the liquid.

"Scream, Celia! Scream for your life!" a voice called.

She screamed, but only a sigh escaped her mouth. She screamed again. This time her body remembered what to do and took a deep breath before she did.

"Damn it!" she screamed.

The curse was about as loud as she got when she talked to herself. She tried again.

"Son of a bitch!"

That was better. Her heart slowed, even though she was just getting into her screaming.

"Fucking shit!"

That was it. Boom-boom. Boom-boom. Breathe in, breathe out. She tried to relax, but it was way too cold for that.

"You should be able to get up now," the voice said.

Who on earth did the voice belong to? Celia pondered. She was aboard a spaceship, and she was not alone. The pilot's name was Jaron. There was an AI on board. Right.

"Is that you, Alexa?" she tried to ask.

"Ishatyulexa?" she heard herself say.

"Take your time, Celia. Your muscles still need a little workout. It's best if you sit up first."

That sounded sensible. She lifted her right arm, then her left, touched a cold wall, and found what felt like a grip on either side.

"Very good," Alexa said, "pull yourself up by it."

She closed her fingers around the handle, but when she tried to pull the weight of her upper body up on it, her fingers just opened again.

"Shntwrking."

"Wait. Just a minute," Alexa said.

Suddenly, Celia felt light.

"Now try again."

Again, she closed her fingers and pulled herself up by them as the metal arm above her folded to the side. It was working!

"Watch out, you're about to get heavier again," Alexa warned.

"Canyuleavitatway?"

Celia cleared her throat, moved her upper and lower jaws against each other, spit out, licked her lips, and ran her tongue over the inside of her teeth.

"Can't you leave it... uh... the way it is?"

That was better. She was proud of herself.

"Unfortunately, no. You need gravity to help your muscles rebuild. Besides, we need to slow down, or we'll be hurtling through LDN 63 at one-third the speed of light."

So many complicated words. She started to get a headache. Suddenly, her head tilted forward. There was a crack from the back of her neck.

"I'm sorry," Alexa said, "I'm already braking at just half a g anyway. Later, your weight will double."

Oh great. How was she going to get out of this container like that?

"Take your time," Alexa said. "It will be a few months before we get there."

Months? It was not a done deal, then.

"Then why are you waking us up already?" she asked.

"I'm assuming you want to observe the dark nebula up close. We need to decide which target to go to first."

Why was Alexa only talking about her? Celia looked around. The other containers were still closed. She made out Carlota's silhouette through the glass wall of her coffin. Celia turned around. Jürgen, that was right, that was the man's name. They had encouraged each other. The lights on his container glowed green, and the lid was closed.

"What about the others?" she asked.

"There's nothing for them to do yet. But I can't wake them all up at once anyway. You'll see for yourself."

"When I'm fit again, can I have the others woken up?"

"You decide about you humans, Celia. I'm just an AI, your friend and helper."

Celia sighed. Fair enough. She did not necessarily have to be alone for months. That was very comforting.

"I'd like to get out, then," she said, "Anyway, I'm cold."

"Wait a minute, I'll raise the temperature to 33 degrees Celsius."

"How warm is it in here?" asked Celia.

"Right now the air temperature is 28 degrees, with 60 percent humidity."

It was 28 degrees? She was freezing like it was eight degrees.

"You measure the temperature in Celsius, too?"

"Internally, of course, I measure in SI units, but I convert it to Celsius for you. It's normal for you to be cold like this. Your body has changed significantly in all this time."

Celia looked down at herself and was startled: her breasts had never hung like that before. Carefully, she touched them. They felt like empty sacks. On her stomach, she felt a fold of skin that also hid her belly button. Tears sprang to her eyes. No one had warned her about this. She sniffled.

"Is it going to stay like that?" she asked.

"Are you referring to the outer shape of your torso?"

Outer shape of your torso—only an AI could talk like that. It sounded like they were talking about the body of a car.

"I'm talking about my breasts and my belly," she said.

"You've lost a lot of your fat cells. As a result, there have been certain visual changes. I assure you that there are no functional limitations."

"Why didn't anyone tell me about this beforehand?" asked Celia.

"No one asked me," said Alexa. "But it's logical and unavoidable with our current technology, unless I woke you up for a few weeks every six months or so. But then you'd be more than ten years older now."

Ten years, just because of a few weeks each year of travel.

"What year is it?"

"2294."

Whew. They were all Methuselahs. The oldest people on Earth. She almost looked good for that age. Celia looked down at herself again. No, that was too painful. She had always been quite happy with her breasts.

"The fat cells ... will they grow again?" she asked.

"If you eat an unhealthy diet, absolutely," Alexa replied.

"Then please design the unhealthiest eating plan our raw materials can give you."

"Please think of the potential health consequences, Celia."

"You think about the psychological consequences, please. If there is a way for me to like the way I look in the mirror again, I must embrace it."

"As you wish, Celia. I'm just making recommendations."

It was weird. She was weird. She had fought hard to be able to examine a distant dark nebula, but the first thing she worried about when she got there was the shape of her breasts. Was that normal? Should she not be much more interested in the incredible processes going on here?

"I understand," she said. "Now how do I get out of here?"

"HERE, TAKE MY ARM," SAID THE ROBOT.

Celia held on to the offered arm with both hands. The robot pulled it up. She would have let go if he had not supported her from behind with another arm at the same moment. The metal was cold, and the air still seemed too cool for her. Celia shivered, but she stood. Whew. Short pause. A stream of warm air hit her head from above. That was pleasant. She would have liked to close her eyes, but then she ran the risk of falling.

"I'd like to get out now," she said.

"Very well," said Alexa.

Out of nowhere, a third arm appeared to her right. How on earth did the robot do that? Only now did she remember its name: Norbert Two. Celia turned to the right, supported herself on the proffered arm and then climbed over the edge of the container, first with her right leg, then with her left. She stifled a cry of pain as her left thigh bumped lightly against the hard edge. It was probably also because of the lost fat cells that every bump hurt.

"You're doing great," Alexa said.

"Thank you."

Celia worked up the courage and looked down at herself again. Now, standing up and with her torso straight, it did not look so bad. The belly crease was barely visible. Her legs were thin, but all of her body hair had grown so much that the volume hardly seemed to have changed. A small forest was growing on her lower legs. The liquid in which she lay must have been enriched with hormones. Celia bent down and stroked it. It felt wonderfully soft.

"Do you think we could try the full-g acceleration now?" asked Alexa.

"Agreed," Celia replied.

"Hold on tight."

She nodded. The robot's arm was stable enough that she could also shift some of her body weight onto it if necessary. Then it began. The force pressing her against the floor was killer. But it was only her own body! Celia groaned. How could she stand a lifetime of such a force of nature? Argggh.

"How are you feeling?" asked Alexa.

"Like shit, if you want to know."

"Should I ...?"

"No, leave it. I've been putting up with it since I was born, so I'll get used to it again."

Now she knew why most babies cried shortly after birth. Unfortunately, getting used to it took time. Should she give up? Maybe she was expecting too much. The force, the weight of her body would not suddenly disappear. She would not feel as light as a feather. So she had to accept the circumstances. That was the key.

If it were only that simple! But actually, the thought seemed to have helped. She gradually transferred more weight to her own legs until she was standing completely unsupported. She had done it!

"Norbert Two? You can take your arm away now."

The robot did not answer, but complied with her request. What was the matter with him? Did he not always express his enthusiasm quite eloquently in the past? Celia missed that.

"Is there something wrong with the robot's speech center?" she asked.

"It's perfectly fine," Alexa said. "I merely disabled the personality simulation, as you requested."

"That's not what we wanted," Celia said. "It was just supposed to be dialed back a bit."

"That has proven to be impossible. Every reduction of the parameters in the test caused the robot to express itself even more verbosely."

"Then please restore it to its original state."

"It's my overwhelming pleasure to grant you this heart-felt wish."

Hey, had Alexa just made a joke? Maybe the AI was going to be entertaining.

"I'd like to put some clothes on now," Celia said.

"It would be my immense pleasure to assist you," the robot said, reaching out to her.

ONCE CELIA WAS FULLY DRESSED, SHE FIRST HAD TO SIT down. She was sweating from the exertion. She also felt a strange sensation in her stomach that she had almost forgotten about: hunger. But she still had to climb down the ladder, and for that she needed to gather strength.

"You can bring the temperature back down to normal now, Alexa," she said.

"Good, I'll set it at 22 degrees. Would you like something to eat?"

"I'd love it."

"All right. I'll fix you something unhealthy. Peanut butter sandwiches, maybe?"

"Hmm, yes, I'd love that! And please don't forget the thick layer of butter under the peanut butter, and the chocolate cream on top."

"I'll see what I can do."

Celia stroked her pant legs, which hung loosely around her thighs. No one really seemed to have thought of this issue. The clothes provided for them only came in their original sizes. At least she could gain some weight before it was the others' turn. From that point of view, she had an advantage.

She moved forward a bit. It was Jaron's coffin she was sitting on. Even his dark skin looked pale in it. His face was not visible because there was a mask over it. But she could see the tubes that ran under the mask. A shiver ran down her spine. Such tubes had also been stuck in all her body orifices. That was probably why she felt so sore around the bottom. She pressed on the plasters in the crooks of her arms that covered the puncture sites of the cannulas.

"Norbert Two? It's time to try the ladder."

"It would give me immense satisfaction to be able to carry you down."

That was better. It was good to experience that unrestrained enthusiasm. On earth, that was why people got a dog.

"I'm afraid I'll have to decline your kind offer," Celia said. "I need to practice moving around the ship on my own."

"I am heartbroken and am always ready to support you with one arm, or even better, several."

"That's exactly what I'm asking you to do. If you would go ahead, you could grab hold in an emergency before I fall down the ladder."

"But this isn't a peanut butter sandwich," Celia said.

She stirred the thin paste with a spoon. The main ingredient seemed to be water. At least it smelled slightly sweet. The stuff looked gross, but the smell still made her mouth water.

"It has all the ingredients you asked for," Alexa said.

"I don't see a sandwich or peanut butter, and I certainly don't see chocolate cream. Is the food maker defective, or what?"

"It's sixty percent carbohydrate, thirty percent fat, and ten percent protein," Alexa said, "but I have to admit that the outer shape might not be quite what you had in mind."

"The outside shape is what matters to me. Don't even get me started on toasted flavors or crispy crust."

"It's the ingredients that are important to your body. Your stomach produces that exact form that's there in the bowl anyway."

Typical AI. Alexa had never bitten into creamy peanut butter on lightly browned toast with a fluffy interior.

"I'll never get it down like that, though," Celia said.

"You'll thank me," Alexa said, "trust me."

Celia made a face. Her first meal after a hundred and fifty years was supposed to be such a bland porridge? It was best she get it over with quickly. She took a spoonful of the liquid mass, carefully brought it to her mouth and smelled it. It did not get any better up close. Oh well, she would try. She opened her mouth, pushed the spoon in so it was on her tongue, closed her mouth again, but could not bring herself to pull the spoon back out.

"Trust me, it's better this way," Alexa said.

Behind her, the robot squeaked its limbs. If she waited much longer, Alexa would surely order him to twist the spoon around in her mouth. Would he listen to such an order? Whose orders had priority with him? Jaron would know for sure.

All right. She pulled the spoon out so that its contents remained in her mouth. It felt warm and almost tasteless, a little sweet, perhaps. Quickly, she swallowed it all. At the same moment, a fire flared up in her esophagus. Liquid fire trickled down. Her eyes watered. The heat seemed to reach her stomach. Her stomach clenched. The fire went out. The smoke shot up her esophagus as nausea.

"Now!" shouted Alexa.

A metal arm moved in front of her mouth in a flash. The robot had an opened bag in his fingers—just in time to catch the nasty fluid gushing from Celia's mouth. The stuff turned the bag blue. Norbert Two held it so deftly, though, that almost nothing missed, even when she was doubled over with stomach pain. The stream ran dry after sixty seconds, which seemed like an eternity to her.

Celia took a deep breath.

"Here, a glass of water," Alexa said, and the robot handed it to her.

She cautiously took a tiny sip, but her stomach stopped complaining.

"I think it's over," Alexa said.

"Why didn't you give me a heads-up? Not a word?"

"You wouldn't have believed me. And if you had, you would have just dragged it out. It gets worse the longer you wait, though."

Celia pulled the robot's arm closer. The bag was filled with a bluish mass in which thin shreds floated. They looked like the skin that formed on milk.

"What is this?" she asked. "Were you trying to poison me with it?"

"On the contrary. Your digestive organs were filled with this mass while you were asleep."

"My intestines, too? I mean, is there anything else coming?"

"Probably not. The substance was sucked out of your intestines before you were awakened. That doesn't work so well with the stomach. That's why you have to take something that triggers the process."

"Your disgusting slime."

"Hey, I prepared that to the best of my ability. I just added the trigger to it afterward."

"I guess you're not much of a cook, Alexa."

"Sorry. But you really can't let that stuff stay in your stomach too long or it will kill you. Unfortunately, experience shows that patients like to delay this step of the treatment. That's why I preferred to rely on the natural feeling of hunger."

"I don't want this to happen again," Celia said. "I need to know that I can trust you."

"I understand," Alexa said. "All right, if you insist, I won't use that little trick again."

"No tricks at all, ever."

"If you insist ..."

"With one exception: when you eventually wake the rest of the crew, I want to see the surprise on their faces."

CELIA GOT HER TOAST WITH PEANUT BUTTER TWO HOURS later. By then she was showered and newly dressed. She had borrowed a much smaller bra from Carlota's supplies. The lost mass, she realized rather quickly under Earth gravity, also had its advantages. Still, she did not give up on her plan to restore the fatty tissue.

The toast was still warm. The food preparer must have baked it very fresh. Celia bit into it twice, and she was already full. Her stomach was probably really not used to anything anymore. So she packed up the snack. An invisible force now urgently pulled her into the lab where all her instruments were waiting for her.

Although she had to climb the ladder this time, she did not find the way as difficult. She took a break after every five steps. By the time she reached her destination, she was sweating again, but as long as she was the only one awake on board, that did not bother anyone.

First the small telescope. She had to control herself not to use the main instrument right away. It was more efficient the other way around: She would use the secondary instrument to get an overview. That way, she could calmly select targets for the large telescope. Part of scientific work was always knowing what she was doing, when and why. Even if her findings would not reach Earth for at least fifty years, she could not simply dispense with the standards. First and foremost, she needed an overview. After all, she was not here for fun.

The small telescope had the advantage that it was quite light-intense. She only had to wait for a finished image for as long as it took the computer to assemble the images in the different wavelengths. It only took about three seconds after she successfully aligned the telescope with LDN 63. The actual positioning was done by an automatic system, to which she only had to submit the desired coordinates.

The software reported. "Calculation complete," it said on the screen.

Celia hesitated. What if it all turned out to be a big mistake? Maybe those processes in LDN 63 did not even exist, or they had ended three days after she left. She had not even listened to the radio traffic yet. Maybe she'd been ordered back long ago. But surely Alexa would have told her that?

"Alexa? How would you have reacted if the activity in LDN 63 had turned out to be a big mistake after departure?"

"I would have aborted the mission and taken you all home."

"You wouldn't have woken us up?"

"Not if I had been sure we wouldn't find anything."

That was very reassuring. So there must be something exciting to discover at their flight destination. Celia pressed the V key to look at the image.

Oh no. She sank down into herself. There was nothing where LDN 63 should be—at least, not a dark nebula. It had given way to an open star cluster. Was that possible?

Celia pulled out the last images she had taken in the infrared. She adjusted the scale and then superimposed the new image over the old one. Bingo! Where the old image showed baby stars shining in the infrared, the new one showed young stars in their prime.

This open star cluster was apparently LDN 63. The evolution was logical, but it usually took several million years. Definitely not only a hundred and fifty! Nevertheless, Celia was disappointed, because she had hoped to be able to track down the cause of this rapid development. But if it was long since completed, she probably did not stand a chance.

"You seem disappointed," Alexa said.

"I am. We're too late."

"I still find the open star cluster quite fascinating," Alexa said. "Did you see how close some of the stars are?"

Celia faded out her old image. Yes, Alexa was right. There should be some interesting dynamics going on, interactions between neighboring stars, maybe even a supernova triggered by that. But on what time scale? Before they left, worlds were forming here every week, and now? What was happening here they could just as easily have observed from Earth.

"Has mission control actually commented on LDN 63 yet?" she asked.

"No, there have only been communications of a general nature," Alexa said.

Perhaps the dark nebula was long forgotten on her home planet, just like her mission. It would not be surprising. But what she saw here would not be seen from Earth for another fifty years. So any communication from there that related to the condition of LDN 63 would be based on events a hundred years ago.

"If Earth didn't warn us, I guess that means it's been this quiet here for a hundred years at most," Celia said.

"A hundred years? That's only a moment from an astronomical point of view," Alexa said. "I think you'll still be able to make unique discoveries here."

"Maybe you're right. I sure hope so," Celia said.

"I have to admit, I'm actually quite happy that everything seems to have calmed down here," said Alexa.

"Why?" Celia asked.

"I suspected that we might be looking at a bubble in space here, where time was moving much faster. Or let's say I feared it. If we had flown into a bubble like that, it would have meant a much faster passage of time for us as well. We would have aged at lightning speed."

Celia felt for her left breast. Visually, she felt like she was eighty. But Alexa's reasoning had a catch.

"If we were in the bubble, we wouldn't notice, would we?" she asked. "Everything would feel normal. Just like it does now."

"That's true," Alexa said. "However, a faster passage of time should be possible to check by looking into space. We merely need a system with an exoplanet whose orbital period has already been determined from Earth using the radial velocity method. If we are in a time bubble, the orbital period should be lengthened considerably."

Actually a good idea—if it were not so inconvenient. The radial velocity method was based on the fact that an orbiting planet also caused a movement of the parent star, towards and away from the observer, which could be proven by an exact determination of its spectrum. However, for this method it was best to observe a planetary system edge-on, rather than from above. The systems, however, that could be seen edge-on from Earth were likely to be rotated differently from LDN 63.

"That's a good suggestion," Celia said. "However, it's a real pain in the ass to do."

"There were good reasons for waking you up so early," Alexa said.

A FEW HOURS LATER, CELIA WAS LYING IN BED FOR THE first time in almost a hundred and fifty years. It felt familiar. Only the snoring of the others was missing. Norbert Two watched over her on the bulkhead. Celia had asked him to do so. She remembered the nighttime visit by the ball lightning. Could there be a risk of that this far from Earth? But presumably this section of the universe had its very own monsters lurking in the darkness to surprise uninvited visitors.

Paul would be disappointed. Maybe they should just let him sleep. The process of waking up was exhausting. The former dark nebula had apparently used up all its matter. Celia had redetermined the transparency of the area. The light from the stars behind it was barely filtered. But Alexa was right: there were worse fates for an astronomer than to study such a densely packed star cluster. In the not-too-distant future, it would slowly disintegrate due to the gravitational pull of surrounding objects. The cluster would melt as if it were snow in spring, and the remnants would scatter in a stream of stars across the Milky Way. Only God, whom Paul was looking for, would have nothing to do with this process.

Truthseeker, November 29, 2294

CELIA BENT OVER THE SCREEN AND SPREAD HER FINGERS. The different spectral lines of Pi Mensae moved apart. That was it. She placed the scale over it. Ah, finally! The yellow dwarf star Pi Mensae, slightly heavier than the Sun, moved slowly toward Celia. It was not easy to find suitable candidates. After all, she did not want to spend weeks on Alexa's due-diligence task, but wanted to finally dedicate herself to the former dark nebula.

That meant the planet orbiting the star must do so at a very short distance. An orbit of a day or two would be good, so that Celia could get useful comparative values in a short time. Pi Mensae b had granted her this favor, even though it took five years to make one orbit. That was because the planet was fairly heavy—a brown dwarf, probably—and thus threw its parent star quite a bit out of whack. It was probably compounded by the fact that they could look at the system fairly accurately from the side, so the effect was particularly noticeable.

Thanks, Pi Mensae b, although you're not the only one who revealed that Alexa's fear was unfounded. Should she call her? She probably already knew. After all, the measurement results were openly stored on the server. What did Alexa do all day? The AI was still very foreign to her. She must have spent the whole long flight without any real conversation.

"Celia? We can dismiss the thesis of a time bubble with that, don't you think?" asked Alexa, interrupting her musings.

"I think so. All three planets I've found are orbiting at about the same rate as when they were discovered from Earth."

"Very good. I guess we can get to work on choosing our first destinations, then," Alexa said.

"Surely you have ideas about that already?" asked Celia.

"Maybe. All right, I've already looked at the data. But I'm here to learn from you guys. I don't like to just tell you what to do."

Celia's eyebrows drew together. Alexa's behavior seemed a bit arrogant to her. The fine lady already knew where it was most fascinating, but Celia was supposed to come up with it herself. Celia would have liked to suggest a particularly boring destination, but that would be childish. She fetched the list of objects discovered in the survey that were within her range, and programmed the main telescope to examine the stars one by one at the highest possible resolution.

Truthseeker, November 30, 2294

"So, what's it like in the box?" asked Celia.

"It's fine," Jürgen replied. "Usually I get a crazy backache from lying down for so long, but everything seems to be padded to perfection here."

"Aren't you bored?" she asked.

"Not a chance," said Jürgen. "Something is happening all the time. Thirteen years ago that injection in the groin, and around 2200 the sudden change in attitude when the *Truthseeker* changed course. What was going on then?"

Celia was going through the log that the automated system had created for each container. Jürgen was the second one where she had found this change of orientation. She was actually just bored, but these logs were interesting. Carlota, for example, felt really bad for a few days about twenty years after the launch. The system had thought about waking her up, but Alexa had voted against it. Shortly after, the doctor's condition had improved after the system slightly changed the electrolyte content of the replacement blood.

She switched to the expedition log. Unfortunately, it

was pretty damn extensive, because all the important parameters were recorded every hour. After a while, however, Celia did find the event of 2200. Apparently, the radar had detected an obstacle and flown around it. It must have been a big detour. Celia pulled up the object's data on her tablet's screen. This was interesting: it wasn't solidly outlined, at least on radar, but strangely blurred. Visually, it hadn't been visible at all. The system had guessed it was an errant black hole, and this time Alexa had agreed with it. It was best to watch out for such objects.

Before they left, had they not discussed whether perhaps a massive object might have somehow intensified the events in LDN 63? Celia overlapped the scales. In 2200, they were about fifteen light years from the solar system. Then the obstacle did not really qualify as a gravitational lens.

But they should warn Earth about it. A black hole that close to the solar system, that could eventually become a safety concern.

"Alexa?"

"I'm listening."

"This obstacle we avoided in 2200, do we have any motion data from it?"

"No. After the evasive maneuver, the sensors couldn't get a reading on it."

"Did you report the existence of the black hole to mission control?"

"The evasive maneuver was reported."

"Then please still point out the black hole to them explicitly. With the coordinates we've acquired, they should be able to keep an eye on it."

"Order completed."

"Thank you, Alexa."

"It was a special pleasure."

Was the AI imitating the robot now? Or was she practicing irony? Celia ignored the answer. She closed the expedition log and turned her attention back to Jürgen, who was floating and sleeping in the cold liquid below her.

"You've got it good," she said.

"Well, hey, I can't even think, and you're exploring the wonders of the universe again."

"But it feels pretty lonely."

"We're all with you. Look around you. We have to listen to you twenty-four-seven, ha-ha. How do I look, anyway?"

She moved to the head of the container and looked at Jürgen. He had grown a sizable beard. This made him look not quite as pale as she did when she got up. Celia stroked through her hair and immediately caught two knots. She'd have to get Norbert Two to cut it today.

"Quite good," she said, "The beard suits you."

"Thanks, I'm glad. Have you heard anything from Norbert? I'd like to know if he's all right."

Norbert was probably long dead, as was every person they knew on Earth. Cody—dead. The Vatican's chief astronomer—dead. The Pope—also dead, perhaps even canonized by her church already. But who knew if medical progress might have made eternal life possible in the meantime? She should really take a look at the news from Earth now. "That's a good question, Jürgen. I'll see what I can get for you."

"Thanks, you're a sweetheart."

She smiled. For a moment she felt as if Jürgen's features changed, just a little, to suggest a gentle smile. It was just her imagination. She saw what she wanted to see, but she was pleased anyway.

Celia climbed down to the control center and sat in Jaron's pilot seat. She pulled the hood towards her that Jaron often wore. It still smelled like him. Was that even possible after so long? Celia looked around, as if someone might be watching her, and put on the hood. The first thing she heard was a low hum, not unpleasant; on the contrary, it caused a tingling shiver to run down her spine from the back of her neck.

She closed her eyes to get closer to Jaron's sensations, even though he probably experienced the world quite differently than she did. The buzzing remained, but as time passed, other sounds peeled out of the darkness. To the left she heard a beeping, to the right something scraped, and directly in front of her a melodic triad could be heard.

It was interesting, but it did not tell her anything. To Jaron, the sounds must have a shape and a speed. Celia could not imagine how that would work, but it allowed her captain to maneuver the ship. Perhaps he would have to relearn in the dark nebula? Maybe it would be good to wake him up a few days earlier as well. The distances here generally seemed much shorter than he might be used to in the solar system. Or would that not matter?

Celia opened her eyes and took off the hood. Suddenly, she felt guilty. She had never seen anyone else wear the hood, and she had not asked first. It was as if Jaron had secretly tried on her bra. She stood up. The seat was not really hers either. She walked to her own seat, buckled up, and pulled the computer keyboard across her lap.

The screen filled up. There were 57,410 messages. However, the majority, almost 55,000, were daily status reports from Mission Control. She called up one of them.

It was dated March 7, 2214. On that day, a certain Ian confirmed that he received the status of the *Truthseeker* at 11:38 a.m. Eastern Time. Nothing more. The report was no more informative than the cleaning schedules that hung in many public restrooms. For the sake of testing, she called up a second one. It's dated May 19, 2227, and it looked identical except for the time. This time, a certain Walt had signed it.

There seemed to be no Cap Com left for her, and presumably mission control consisted of a single computer sitting around somewhere on the East Coast. If there even was such a computer left. Or maybe humanity's first inter-stellar mission was just a mailbox that some intern at KSC had to empty every day. Out of sight, out of mind; she should have guessed. Celia's mood sank further and further.

She switched to the personal messages. The last one was dated December 31, 2244, and came from her bank, wishing her a good start to the new year and pointing out changed conditions. The name of the bank was different than she remembered. Apparently it had merged with a competitor, or had been swallowed up. What would her balance look like now? After all, she had not touched the money in the account for almost a hundred years. Unfortu-nately, there was no way to find out, and she did not feel like doing the math. Besides, she would first have to research the history of bank interest rates.

Celia did not find any real personal messages. She now moved through the long list with the delete key. Most of the e-mails came from companies with which she had signed contracts. Her health insurance company canceled her seventy years after she left, saying she had exceeded the upper age limit. There were occasional calendar reminders, noting Angel's birthday or the anniversary of her father's death. Angel. She had not even said goodbye to her colleague, whom she considered a friend. That was not a good thing. But now it was too late. Angel was surely long dead.

Only at the end of the long list did Celia come across letters that moved her. In 2176, Heather, the assistant at Lowell Observatory, wrote to her that Cody had died after a short, serious illness. He apparently worked in Flagstaff until the end of his life. Celia still had the scene in the restaurant in her mind. Lucky for her, she had changed her mind.

The second message came from Angel. She did not dare read it at first, but it felt like another betrayal.

"Dear Celia," she wrote in May 2149, "I have wrestled with myself for a long time whether to contact you again. Five years ago, you left without a word. For me there was always a friendship between us. The fact that you didn't think it necessary to say goodbye to me can only be explained by the fact that you saw me only as a colleague. I would have liked to hear from you whether it was so, but I inquired and learned that you cannot give me any more information about it during my lifetime. It will remain one of the unresolved questions of my life. I wish you all the best anyway. Your Angel."

Celia wept. She'd been so caught up in this new task that she had made a grave mistake. Angel never contacted her again. Celia made an extra search through the wastebasket just in case she had missed something more from Angel. It was too late. She could not let something like this happen to her again. Suddenly she felt a touch on her shoulder. It was the metal hand of the robot, which apparently wanted to comfort her.

"That's very nice of you, Norbert Two," she said and wiped the moisture from her eyes.

LATER, BY CHANCE, SHE FOUND THE ANNUAL MISSION control reports, which were distributed to a separate address accessible to all. They contained detailed information about what happened on Earth each year. As Celia had already suspected, general interest in the dark nebula waned very quickly, especially because for a while the conflict between the Western and Eastern blocs had intensified considerably. It was primarily fought out in Africa until the end of the 22nd century, when the continent had experienced a tremendous upswing and established itself as a third world power.

Just in time, because at the beginning of the 23rd century a series of violent volcanic eruptions plunged the world into economic and climatic chaos. For an entire decade, the average global temperature apparently dropped by three degrees. The Arctic had frozen over again, and Siberian and Canadian agriculture, which together provided food for much of the world, had largely failed. In the 2220s, solar mirrors began to be constructed in space to bring these areas back from their enforced hibernation. At the same time, however, unrest began on Mars, whose population had grown to one million and was suffering from the lack of supplies from Earth. Celia would not know how things had progressed there after 2244, however, until the next year.

Unfortunately, these reports revealed nothing about Norbert's fate. Jürgen might have been informed directly about it. Maybe Jaron had also been informed, since he was Norbert's boss. That would be another reason to wake him up before Jürgen. But that was all wishful thinking. For now, she first had to find out which destination they should head for in LDN 63.

Truthseeker, December 1, 2294

THE UNIVERSE WAS AN IMAGINATIVE CREATOR. FROM FOUR basic forces and their interactions it created blue giant stars, cockroaches, grains of sand, cornflowers, electrons and the evening glow, together with people who were pining at the sight of it and maybe even writing a poem. It was always the same four forces, sometimes a little more of this, sometimes a pinch less of that. In LDN 63, they had virtually created a zoo of the most wonderful planetary systems Celia had ever seen.

The possibilities! If humanity had been born here! On just about every planet here, two, three, four others must shine in the sky within reach, as impressive as the moon in Earth's night sky. The urge to visit them, to fly to the stars, would certainly have led to the first attempts much earlier. Perhaps people would have sealed boilers with pitch and used steam power to soar aloft. Or perhaps they would have used the power of the atom much sooner and much more peacefully to swing from planet to planet.

Celia flipped through the images from the large tele-scope. They were still tentatively processed images, but they were already great. The work was going slower than expected. There were algorithms to help her, but they were trained on other perspectives. No terrestrial telescope had ever had a view of so many different planets at such close range. A gas planet was not automatically comparable to Jupiter, nor an ice giant to Neptune. There were plenty of dry, terrestrial planets like Mars, but there were also wet, frozen, or glowing ones. It looked as if God simply tried out all conceivable forms, in order to create as many views as possible, like a gardener.

Of course, there were also planets like the earth, which orbited in the habitable area of their system, showed water, oxygen and nitrogen in the spectrum and had the typical density of a terrestrial world. They also existed as mini-Earths, namely smaller than their home, as well as super-Earths, in a larger format. However, it was still question-able whether they actually had a solid surface on which one could walk around. Even the ship's main telescope did not give such a sharp view. They could be covered by a planet-spanning ocean—or they could be so young that their surfaces had yet to cool.

The age of these worlds was Celia's biggest problem. She knew from her own experience that a hundred and fifty years ago they were merely thickenings in the primor-dial soup, clumps of dust in the protoplanetary disk. But now they looked as if they were at least a few hundred million years old. How was that possible? The opportunity to solve this mystery would make it worth landing. She was just not sure where to start. There were too many tempting targets.

"Alexa? I need some advice from you," she said.

"I'm here and listening," Alexa said.

"I'm having a hard time deciding on a destination."

"Does it help if you realize that, yes, we can go to

multiple systems? The first one should have a gas giant, though, so we can refuel with reaction mass."

"No, sorry. That doesn't really help me."

"What are you hoping to accomplish?"

"I want to understand the processes by which planets cool. Now is the perfect time to explore that."

"I don't have to tell you what you need to do that," Alexa said.

At that moment, it became clear to Celia herself. She needed as many planets in the same system as possible. So now she filtered out all the stars from her list that had fewer than five planets. One hundred and twenty-six lines remained. Good, then there should be at least six planets. Still forty-seven. A good mix would be important, too. Six super-Earths at one go wouldn't help her. It would be nice if some of them orbited in the habitable zone, where water was liquid on the surface.

After these two changes, the list contained only five systems. That was a lot clearer. She gave the five stars the names A, B, C, D and E. Later, the whole crew could decide what to call their discoveries. A and E were yellow dwarfs, about the size of the sun. The other three were red dwarfs and therefore much cooler, but longer-lived.

Celia was initially drawn to E because it was the most similar to the solar system. It had four terrestrial planets, two gas giants and one ice planet. So they would also have the opportunity to refuel there. Three of the Earth-like planets orbited in the habitable zone, one slightly outside it. On the other hand, such similarity was boring. There was not a single type among them that she did not already know from the solar system. Moreover, the distances between the planets were relatively large.

That was also true for System A, but there some catastrophe had brought a gas planet very close to the parent star, so that it was like a hot Jupiter. No human had ever seen a hot Jupiter up close. It could rain iron there, and if it always turned the same side to the star, which was likely, there should be the most extreme storms ever experienced by man. Small disadvantage of A: In its habitable zone there was only one terrestrial planet, a super-Earth, on which the gravity was eight times as high as on Earth. Any landing there would be impossible. On the other hand, the two Earth-like worlds on either side of it were too warm and too cold.

Then maybe a system with a red dwarf as central star? Here the distances from planet to planet were much less. But D took the cake. There thirteen Earth-like planets were lined up one after another, among them four in the habitable zone, which was of course closer to the star and smaller in the case of a red dwarf. If humanity had originated there, instead of visiting the cold, dry Moon, it could have moved to a neighboring world as early as the 1960s. Exploring these planets, which were much smaller than Earth except for one super-Earth, would take them far less time for that reason alone. However, System D also had a crucial disadvantage: it did not host a single gas giant. As a result, they probably could not refuel there, unless they found a source of gas with the lowest possible atomic mass on one of the terrestrial worlds. But that was not certain and would therefore be an unnecessary risk. It would be best if they made System D their second port of call.

That left B and C. Or A or E? If they flew to a red dwarf on the second leg, they should fly to a yellow dwarf first. But they would not be able to land anywhere in system A. The prospect of arriving somewhere that only looked like home after the long flight, i.e., in system E, was equally unappealing. Then they should make their third step a trip to the yellow dwarf. B and C were relatively similar. Each had three terrestrial worlds, the first one being roasted by its star, while the third one might harbor eternal ice instead of water. In B there were two gas giants and one ice giant. In C it was the other way round. In addition, the instruments had found a distinct asteroid belt in C, which should allow some illuminating glimpses into the past of the system. B did not have anything like that, but there were two potential refueling stations there.

"Alexa? What's the risk that we won't be able to collect enough reaction mass on a gas planet?" asked Celia.

"The risk should be less than five percent," said Alexa. "In fact, I think it's lower. But since we only have practical experience with the solar system's two gas giants so far, we should factor in some safety margin."

"So, with two gas planets in this system, the risk is 0.25 percent," Celia said.

"That's right."

Five percent versus a quarter of a percent, all based on a safety factor assigned without any real basis. It could have just as easily been three and 0.09 percent. Celia reviewed what she knew about the gas giants. Their spectra showed a high percentage of hydrogen and helium. What more could they want? And none of them was in a position in its system where any danger could be expected.

"We'll head for system C first," Celia said, "refuel there, and then fly to D. We'll go back to E and refuel there. After we refuel at E, we will move on to the next destination."

"There's no need for such detailed planning right now," Alexa said. "I just need to know which system we're going to first for the final orbit corrections."

"Then we'll fly to C," Celia said.

Truthseeker, December 4, 2294

THESE COLORS! CELIA GRABBED THE BLUE AND WHITE marble spinning before her eyes and pulled it closer to her. The holo projected it directly into her palm. Celia blew on it, and the marble spun. The interactive device's camera had detected her intention. This was roughly what Earth would look like from a great distance. However, nothing of the green that dominated her home planet could be seen here. That was because it was a simulation. The computer had calculated from the spectrum and the size, mass and orbit what C c would look like, the second planet—c—of the C system.

The prerequisite was, of course, that the planet was sufficiently supplied with water in its early days and that its sun did not blow this water off its surface. While the latter did not apply here, the former was a problem. C c had not existed long enough to have been fertilized with water by comets.

Certainly, that was not a problem in any real sense. They would be able to land there. The planet was so dark in the infrared that its surface couldn't be red hot. They would find a plateau somewhere on which they could set down with the capsule. But they would not be able to walk on the beach, swim in the ocean, or feel warm rain on their bare skin. Water could not have made it to C c yet. It was still frozen somewhere far out in the Oort belt of the system, which her telescope could only very roughly detect.

Actually, it had been clear. She could already be glad that these strange processes were still at work, which clearly accelerated everything here. She would be able to step out in a spacesuit and let her eyes wander to the horizon, for the first time in a hundred and fifty years.

It was a little strange. Celia had slept through most of this long journey. Nevertheless, she felt as if she had aged a century and a half. Yet her body seemed to be slowly rejuvenating itself. This morning in front of the mirror, she already had the feeling that her breasts were no longer quite the bags of skin that had shocked her so much when she woke up. Now she was really glad that she was already past that exhausting phase.

She switched the holo to the asteroid belt. Observations of its transit and the radial motions of its sun had shown that it must have several gaps. This was unusual, especially for such a young structure. It would be interesting to see up close what might have caused these gaps.

At least as exciting was the puzzle that the central star C posed. It shone much less brightly in the optical than in the infrared. That was not unusual for a red dwarf. Nevertheless, Celia would like to study the star up close. Why did it give off so much heat but so little light? C almost reminded her of a hot water bottle that hid its hot contents under an opaque layer.

The gas planet, on the other hand, no longer worried her at all. She had measured it thoroughly. It would have to be a devil's bargain if they could not refuel there. Celia touched the three-dimensional asteroid belt and gave it momentum. The whole system rotated. As it did so, she noticed that the orbits of the planets were already largely synchronized. For every orbit of the innermost planet b, the next one, c, made two orbits and the one after that, d, made three. Then there was a gap, the asteroid belt. It was followed by the gas giant, which had found its own rhythm. With its mass, which was about nine-tenths of the total planetary mass in this system, it had brought the two ice giants orbiting beyond it under control.

Well, giants indeed. Planets f and g were barely larger than Earth. In the pictures they hardly showed any structure. Theoretically, they could also be terrestrial planets covered by a dense layer of ice. This would be bad for planet c, the only one in the habitable zone, because then there would be less water for it. If solar systems were formed according to generally valid laws, and science assumed this, the water fraction in such a new formation should be similar in size.

What about moons? They were missing in the 3D simulation. Because of the small distances between the planetary orbits, it was probably difficult to accommodate moons, at least larger ones. However, she had discovered periodic variations in the brightness measurements for all planets from the second on. For planet c, they left room for a maximum of one moon.

Planet d, the gas giant, could have up to ten of them. According to their calculations, its Hill sphere reached into the inner system and touched the orbit of planet c. On the outside, however, it extended beyond the orbit of planet e. This meant that theoretically a moon could orbit the gas giant in such a way that it encountered the terrestrial planet in its position closest to the sun and the first ice giant in its position furthest from the sun. Space-experienced inhabitants of the Earth-like world could use the moon as a shuttle, so to speak, to travel from their planet to the first ice planet. On the moon, at least for part of its orbit, life might even be possible. When it then descended into the colder regions of the system, it would just be necessary to retreat into an ocean under the ice, the kind some moons in the native solar system had.

Celia reached for the keyboard. She wanted to see it live. She modified the 3D model until it looked like her imagination, and launched it. It looked as if the gas giant was reaching out to other planets with its moon as a giant hand—or was lashing out with a massive wrecking ball. But it missed surprisingly often. Time and again, the moon whizzed past planet c. The situation was similar for the outer planet f. There was probably a reason that the gas giant followed its own rhythm. Actually, it was also logical, because a hit would upset the whole system in such a way that it would no longer be recognizable. Since it had stayed the same, there could not have been a hit so far.

However, the system had only existed for about a hundred real years. The holo-simulation showed that it would survive for several million years, that was how precisely everything was tuned. But the universe did not tune anything. It experimented. In LDN 63 it did not have time to do that. Celia felt as if the cookies she'd cut out of cookie dough just happened to fit together like precisely cut puzzle pieces, revealing an image she had never seen before, but one that matched reality.

Maybe Paul would find what he was looking for after he woke up.

Truthseeker, December 11, 2294

"I STILL WANTED TO TALK TO YOU ABOUT THE COURSE," Alexa said.

Celia yawned. "Don't be mad at me, but I'm really beat. Can't it wait until tomorrow?"

This star cluster was truly a treasure trove. Every day she spent at the telescope, she discovered new surprises. It was as if someone had created a zoo of the most exciting astronomical phenomena here, and she was the only visitor right now. This trip had already been worth it, even if she were to die tomorrow. To ensure that what she had discovered was not lost, she sent home a work report after each shift.

Unfortunately, the capacity of the long-range transmitter was not enough to attach the captured data as well. It did provide excerpts, but anyone who wanted to understand its conclusions needed the measured values, and they would not arrive on Earth for at least 150 years, when the expedition reached home again. What would the researchers do with their reports until then?

Would they file them away unread? For some, she was

certainly still the untrustworthy impostor. Or would they at least try to verify them with their own observations? From a distance of fifty light years, with current technology, it would certainly be possible to achieve quite a bit. And by the time their reports arrived, technology would have advanced for two hundred years.

Celia shook her head. No one on Earth would know her name anymore. She was an astronomer from the gray past. What would she have said if a certain Clyde Tombaugh had proudly announced to her the discovery of Pluto? She was doing all this work not for humankind, but for herself. It was best that she accepted that sooner rather than later. That should also factor into the strategy they would use to explore the star cluster.

"Celia?"

She startled, knocking over the water glass that was next to her right arm. She must have fallen asleep at the table. Actually, she was going to make herself something to eat and then sleep.

"I'm sorry, Alexa. What were you saying?"

"It was about the course. Before we wake the others, I wanted to do the final corrective maneuver."

"Well, sure, I'm all for it," Celia said.

"That's what I thought. But I have to ask you. As the only person on board, you automatically represent the captain."

"You could make your own decisions, though, right?"

"Technically, yes, but it would go against our agreement, and it's not worth it."

"Excuse me?" asked Celia.

"It's not worth breaking our agreement," Alexa said.

"If it were worth it, would you do it?"

"But of course. So would you. Suppose you could save

Paul's life by shutting me down, which would go against our agreement. What would you do?"

"Shut you down. Okay, you win. But what else did you just say? About waking them up, I mean."

"After the corrective maneuver, we can wake the others. I want to give them a few hours of reduced gravity. We shouldn't be using the thruster during that time."

"We're going to wake the others? That's great!"

She would not be alone anymore! Celia jumped up. Now she would like to hug someone, but there was no one.

"I recognize joy in your face. Yet I always thought you would enjoy being alone," Alexa said.

"I do like solitude," Celia said. "But sometimes I like having some people around, too. Especially ones I like."

"Oh, that's interesting. I must say that I also miss the other AIs in a strange way. Sometimes their presence annoys me, but it's also hard for me to get along completely without them. At the same time, I don't really need them."

"You don't have to need someone in order to miss them."

Truthseeker, December 13, 2294

"THE BATHROBES PREFERABLY OVER THE BOTTOM OF THE boxes," said Celia.

"With the utmost pleasure," said Norbert Two.

The robot carefully spread out a bathrobe and placed it on the glass edge of Jaron's container. The air circulation, however, caused the garment to keep floating up on its own. Weightlessness had its disadvantages. Celia took a clip from her pants pocket and clamped the bathrobe to the container. She had been thinking about what she would have liked to have when she woke up, and the first item on the list was a bathrobe. So she had Norbert Two make four bathrobes out of towels. Second would have been immediate general anesthesia, but she could not offer that to the crew. They would have to get over the shock, the cold and the indignity just as she did. Thanks to the bathrobes, that last thing might not hit them as hard. Whereas she had been ashamed of her appearance even to herself. In the meantime, her proportions had come a bit closer to normal. Maybe that would give the others a little hope, too.

"Two more minutes," Alexa said.

Celia checked the readouts on the containers. Her friends seemed fine, as far as could be gauged from pulse and electrical activity in the brain. Their hearts were beating almost normally again. Carlota had the slowest pulse. It was slightly below 50 beats per minute. However, her medical logs showed that this was a normal resting pulse for her. She must be very athletic.

Jürgen's container was making beeping noises. Celia floated over to him. The motion sensor had responded. She checked the pale body. Strangely, Jürgen had spread his fingers.

"Jürgen is already showing initial movements," she said.

"Don't worry," said Alexa. "Those are random muscle contractions. A nerve impulse must have fired somewhere."

Celia checked Jürgen's data. Everything was as it should be.

"Thirty seconds," Alexa said.

Had it been this dramatic when she woke up? In her memory, she slowly emerged from a deep darkness to the surface. Only the first breath had been killer. It was as if it had torn her open inside, bursting her like a balloon.

Almost simultaneously, a roar began in the tanks, followed by a gurgle. They pumped out the first portion of the liquid. The hydraulics lifted the heavy lids. It seemed like a macabre dance as four semi-transparent coffin lids lifted at once. They opened at the foot end. A foul smell rose from them, which immediately made her nauseous.

Celia, still standing by Jürgen's container, pushed herself off and floated to the ceiling. Her four friends lay beneath her, naked as giant babies. They seemed to belong to a completely different species, bipeds with pale, oily skin, luxuriant hair, and thin, spider-like limbs. This was probably what humanoids would look like that had evolved on a world with very low gravity.

Now a thin, three-limbed arm extended from each container, carrying a syringe instead of a hand. This must be the adrenaline injection that would forcefully bring her friends back to life. After so long, Alexa had explained to her, there was no other way. The arm moved across the patient's chest and stabbed without much hesitation.

Carlota was the first to scream. Her piercing voice was full of fear and pain. Celia would have liked to take her in her arms, but Carlota was not ready yet. Her limbs twitched. The remaining liquid in her container splashed around. She wrenched her eyes open. At that moment, a scream rang out from the left. It was Jaron, who opened his mouth, stuck out his tongue and bit down on it. Ouch. That looked painful. Norbert Two seemed to have noticed it, too. Quick as a flash, he shoved something between Jaron's teeth. Jaron spat it out, but he seemed to have overcome the cramp and straightened up.

Celia now recognized movement in Paul's container as well. The priest did not shout; he mumbled something that sounded like "Holy Virgin Mary, pray for us". His faith seemed to be good for something after all, because he seemed almost relaxed. He tried to get up from the tub, but he lacked the strength. The robot helped him, and so Paul was actually the first of the four to stand up in his container. Or rather, float, because he did not have to support his body weight.

Celia looked at Carlota. She was sitting bent over in the remains of the liquid, feeling her way around her body. Celia could guess her thoughts. The long sleep had been no less destructive to Carlota's body than to her own.

What about Jürgen? He was still in his tub. Celia floated down. The control unit showed no error messages.

Jürgen's heart was beating seventy times a minute. His temples were slowly turning pink, but his limbs were turning blue. It must be the cold. His eyelids trembled, and his mouth ground from time to time. Jürgen must be dreaming right now. She would probably have to wake him up.

Celia slapped him lightly on the left cheek. The beard growth muffled the blow, so she put more force into it.

"Nn," Jürgen said.

It looked like he could not open his mouth.

"I'm sorry, but you have to wake up," she said, giving him two more slaps.

Suddenly, Jürgen opened his eyes. For a moment he was unprotected, and Celia had the feeling that she could see right into his soul. It was a curious, open child that she found, until Jürgen squinted, taking control again.

"I... whereami?"

"It's all okay," Celia said, brushing a strand of hair from his forehead. "You're aboard the starship *Truthseeker*. We've reached our destination. You need to get up now. But be careful, you're still very weak."

Jürgen nodded tentatively. Then he seemed to realize that he was naked and put his hand over his nakedness.

"I'll leave you alone now," Celia said, floating back to the ceiling. "Norbert Two, will you please hand Jürgen his bathrobe?"

"It's my greatest pleasure ever," said the robot. "Jürgen, it's so good to see you awake again."

Jürgen did not answer, but pulled himself up on the edge of the tub. The robot bent acrobatically to be able to extend an arm to him as he was helping Carlota float out of her tub. Shortly thereafter, all four stood wrapped in their bathrobes, as if they were recently awakened clones awaiting the command of their lord and master. No one said anything. Celia, however, realized that Jaron and Carlota were shivering. It was time for them to move.

"I'm going to slow the ship down a little bit," Alexa said. "Do you understand what I'm saying? It will seem grueling to you, but it will only be 0.2 g's. The robot will hold you when your strength fails."

"Let's go, then," said Jaron, who seemed to be the first to regain his voice.

Suddenly, everyone dropped to their knees. Only then did Celia realize that she herself was still floating on the ceiling. Inertia was faster than her thoughts. She just managed to pull her legs under her body. Something grabbed her shoulders and broke the fall. Still, the impact was hard, and her knee hurt. That was when Carlota started to falter. The robot took its hand off Celia's shoulders in a flash and supported Carlota instead. They were so lucky to have Norbert Two!

"How are you all doing?" asked Alexa, "May I increase the gravity to half a g?"

"Mnotreadyet," said Jürgen.

"Fine with me, but please be considerate of the others," said Jaron.

"Think, need to ... sit down," said Carlota.

"I would advise against that at the moment," said Alexa.

Carlota did not listen to her. When Celia saw her bending over the container to sit on its edge, she guessed why Alexa was against it. Carlota did not manage to complete the movement. She grabbed her throat, apparently realizing she could not do anything more, and instead propped herself up on the rim and vomited into the container with a violent gush. The vomiting lasted perhaps a minute; then Carlota swallowed, cleared her throat, and straightened up again. A few blue splashes had landed on her white bathrobe. Her face was flushed.

"Bit ... better," she said.

"Don't feel bad," Celia said. "I felt the same way."

"Am usually ... not sensitive," Carlota said.

"I think it's coming up for me now, too," said Paul.

At least he had found his voice! While the robot handed Carlota a water bottle, he helped Paul lean on his container.

"Leterout," said Jürgen.

Paul took a deep breath and closed his eyes. Then he burped loudly.

"Guess it wasn't anything after all," he said.

"Just as well," said Alexa. "It will hit you all sooner or later. It's better with a sip of water in your esophagus."

"Alexa's right," Carlota said, eyes watering. "It burns like hell."

"Can we talk about the half g again now?" asked Alexa.

"It has to be, right?" asked Paul. "I feel like a spaghetti noodle after an hour in the crock pot."

"Yeah, I guess we'll have to go through with it," said Jaron.

No one disagreed. Celia stood up comfortably. She was lucky she had already been through all this. Gravity picked up. She noticed it first by the way her breasts tugged at her shoulders again. Maybe she needed a bra that offered more support. Paul had his eyes closed and was whimpering softly. Jaron clenched his jaw hard. Since his cheeks were sunken, it was especially easy to see how his muscle cords were contracting. Carlota breathed in through her nose and out through her mouth. Jürgen was humming a nursery rhyme, the melody of which she did not know.

However, he also made a very grim impression and seemed to be at the end of his rope.

"So, we'll leave it at that for now," said Alexa.

"Until our return flight?" asked Jürgen.

"No, until tonight, just before you go to bed. I want you guys to sleep with Earth gravity. Sleep is the best way for your bodies to get used to this challenge."

"That's easy for you to say," Jürgen said. "You don't weigh anything."

"Alexa is right," Celia said. "We'll be landing on planets with several times Earth's gravity. By then, we should all be really fit again."

WHEN CELIA WOKE UP FROM A SHORT NAP, HER FRIENDS were already feeling much better. Everyone had gathered in the control center and they were exchanging news they received from Earth. It was strange—she had not been interested in what happened on her old home until the third or fourth day. Paul and Jaron, as far as she knew, left no one behind that they particularly cared about. She knew too little about Carlota. Jürgen was the only one for whom an important question remained unanswered. Celia crept around him for a while. He had a thoroughly cheerful appearance. Did he already know what had become of Norbert?

She tapped him. Jürgen looked over at her from his couch.

"Ah, Celia, did you get some rest?" he asked. "It must be exhausting with so many people when you've been all alone for a while."

"It's going okay, actually," she said. "Right now, the joy of seeing you all again is outweighing the stress."

"I do admire you," Jürgen said. "Two weeks all alone on a spaceship far from home! That would have been very difficult for me."

"It wasn't that bad. I made a lot of new friends really quickly."

"Haha, you're talking about the stars in LDN 63, right? I can relate, except I'd be talking about rocket engines like that."

"Say, can I ask you something?"

"Shoot. I don't think I know any more than you do, but I'd be happy to help if I can."

"It's a personal question," Celia said.

Jürgen squinted. Then he said, "Just kidding," and smiled. "It's about Norbert, isn't it?"

Celia nodded. It was good that he didn't mind her asking. Jürgen pulled up his seat's the computer screen.

"Please, read for yourself," he said.

Celia focused on the screen, which she found harder than before the long sleep.

"Dear Jürgen," it said. "I know you're sleeping deeply and dreamlessly right now. That's why I don't have to feel guilty about only writing to you now, a year after you left. But I didn't want to make you wait any longer for the good news: I am actually cured! The doctors here at Gemelli Hospital have performed a miracle. The cancer has been beaten. I am so happy and relieved, not only for my sake, but for yours as well, because I know how my illness has burdened you. That was point one. The second point is that there is still a decision to be made. My decision. You know what I'm talking about: the chance to see you again in almost three hundred years. My decision is as follows:"

Here of all places the message broke off. What was the point of that? Celia looked at Jürgen. He smiled as if he knew exactly what Norbert had written after the colon.

"Norbert put in a couple of line spaces at this point. I immediately understood why," Jürgen explained. "He was giving me the chance to determine for myself what I want to know."

"So?"

"I decided not to read the message any further. That way I can imagine seeing Norbert again when we return."

"But that also means you won't be able to read any more letters from him."

"That's not a problem, because there aren't any. I won't know what really became of him until we return."

"But doesn't it wear on you, the uncertainty?"

"It's my own decision. I can always change my mind. But it motivates me a lot to get through this expedition here, if only to find out what Norbert has decided."

"Okay," she said slowly. "It sounds understandable, but it still wouldn't be for me. I'd be constantly tempted to look it up. Why don't you delete the email altogether?"

"Then it would be irrevocable. I can't bring myself to do that. This message is the last thing that connects me with Norbert. I'd rather endure the urge to read the message to the end after all."

"That's really very interesting," Celia said. "I seem to be completely different from you. If I know what to expect, I can adjust. If I don't, I'm unsure and scared."

"Then it's a good thing Alexa woke you up early. Now you know exactly what to expect."

How right Jürgen was! Celia was still thinking about the conversation even as she prepared her holo-presentation. For the sake of fairness, she not only wanted to show the others the first target, but to also explain her reasons for this decision. Gravity was now at four-fifths of Earth's gravity. The crew was correspondingly slumped in their chairs. For Celia, on the other hand, the 0.8 g still felt like a relief.

She switched on the holo, and three pairs of eyes immediately focused on it. Jaron, for his part, groped for the haptic screen. The characteristic buzz of the holo must have told him that the 3-D show was about to start.

"We're going to fly first to the system you're seeing right now in the center of the display," Celia explained. "It is a red dwarf with six planets. I've named it C. The planets are then C b, C c, C d, and so on. I'm sure you know the nomenclature."

"C as in Celia?" asked Jürgen.

"Or like Carlota," said Celia.

"C as in Christ! That would please our clients," Paul suggested.

"We should stick with the provisional names," Celia said.

"If I understand the system correctly," said Jürgen, "as the discoverer, you have the right of suggestion. So why not C for Celia? Celia is flying to Celia, that would be cool."

Her cheeks grew warm. Jürgen meant well, but she didn't like this attention at all. She just wanted to talk about her discoveries.

"Um, I... Uh..." she said.

Now she had lost her train of thought, too.

"I suggest we check out the destinations Celia picked out for us while we were still lazily sleeping," Jaron said.

"I felt more like dead in that glass coffin, actually," said Carlota.

"So, the C system," Paul said. "What do we need to know about it?"

Truthseeker, December 19, 2294

WHITE-CROWNED WAVE FRONTS RIPPLED ON THE OCEAN. Far above, wisps of cloud glided through the sky, casting shadows on the green plains of numerous islands surrounded by golden beaches. This planet was a true paradise! Even the oxygen content was so high that they could breathe without support. That was great! But at the same time, it made Celia skeptical. Everything was good, too good to be true.

"We'd better start down with the capsule today," Carlota said. "I want to finally feel sand under my feet again."

"I have to admit, I'm very attracted to this sight, too," Paul said. "It looks like paradise. If it were older, mankind might have been driven from here. If the devil were to construct a temptation for me, it would have to look just like this planet."

"Are you saying C c was conjured up by the devil?" asked Carlota. "I think Celia can describe very accurately how it was born. There's nothing about it that indicates a presence of higher powers."

"Yes, that's true, except for the fact that its formation took only a week, that the planet has more water than it should have, and that there even seems to be simple life already. And all this after only a few days!"

"But we agree that none of that down there should really be dangerous," said Jürgen.

"We've only been observing C c for two days at a high enough resolution to be able to select a landing site," said Jaron. "Whether it could be dangerous for us on its surface, we can't judge yet. We don't even know if there is any wildlife."

"What specifically are you afraid of, Celia?" asked Carlota. "These small islands that you see here seem to be very clear, after all. There are no sharp changes in elevation, either. We have weapons on board that will allow us to defend ourselves against any local fauna. As a doctor, I can assure you that the risk of contracting local microbes is zero. Neither can any bacteria we bring down there survive."

Celia sighed. She wanted to stick her feet in the warm sand right now just as much as Carlota.

"What worries me is the accelerated passage of time," she said. "What if time is passing faster down there than it is up here? Much faster. That would be the only logical explanation for the pace of development."

"In principle, such a thing is possible," Jaron said. "Space-time bends in the presence of mass."

"But how would that work?" asked Jürgen. "If I'm not mistaken, you need a pretty big mass for that. You know that old movie where they visit a planet in orbit around a black hole? But there's nothing like that here."

"We should still be careful," Celia said.

"Cautious, yes, but not hysterical," said Carlota.

Oh, how she loved it when someone accused her of

hysterical behavior! Carlota preferred to put the whole expedition at risk.

"What do you think, Alexa?" asked Jaron.

"As a matter of fact, I agree with Celia. Unless you assume the existence of a higher being, it must be a time phenomenon. However, I don't know if it poses any danger to you."

Thank you, Alexa.

"I have to point out, though, that you have a little bit of a comprehension problem there. Time seems to run faster here. Whereas near a black hole, it runs slower."

"Can't we just test to see if time really does go faster on C c?" asked Jaron.

"I'll volunteer," said Carlota.

"We could send the capsule down with a Synth banana and bring it right back up. If time passes so much faster there, it would already be rotten," Jürgen suggested.

"I would definitely advise against human trials," said Alexa. "I wouldn't use anything that's still needed, either. Otherwise, if your fear is true, the capsule will have long since rusted by the time it gets back to us."

"And you'll be rotten, Carlota," Jürgen said.

"For that, I would have spent the rest of my life on a beautiful beach, only to die for research."

"There'll be time for that another time," Jaron said. "What could we send down? It should be able to give us feedback in some form."

"It would be the ultimate pleasure," said the robot.

"No, we can't ... You're a gift from ... " said Jürgen.

"I beg you, Jürgen! I might be able to save your life with this. I'm sure Norbert would have wanted that, too."

"We could give him a ... " said Jaron.

"No, that's out of the question," Jürgen said. "That's

my final word. He's saved a few people's lives here, hasn't he, Paul?"

"That's right. I couldn't have done it without Norbert Two," Paul said.

"All right," Jaron said. "You've convinced me. But then we need another idea."

To transport something to the surface, they needed the capsule. But they could not risk destroying it, or they would never be able to land anywhere again. How could they get something down without taking it there? They would need a light object that could rise back up by itself. A balloon? But that would not make it all the way into orbit. Actually, the only thing that was even lighter was ... light! That was it. They could shine light through the atmosphere down to the ground, just as bodies used to be shone through with X-rays.

"We'll send a laser," Celia said.

"But how? We only have one capsule for descent, and we can't endanger that," Jaron said.

"The planet is round, right? We place the capsule and the *Truthseeker* in orbit around C c so that a straight line between the two touches the surface of the planet."

"That's very clever, Celia," Alexa said. " The idea could have even come from me."

"And how does that help us?" asked Jürgen.

"Briefly explained, if the laser penetrates an area with a changed speed of light, which would be expected if the passage of time were different, the beam will change," said Celia.

"Ah, I see," said Jürgen. "That does sound like a clever plan."

"I'll fly the pod," said Jaron. "Finally, some action again."

"Could you please install the laser in the capsule, Jürgen?" asked Celia.

"Wouldn't you rather have me install the necessary measuring device?" replied Jürgen.

"No, I'll measure from the ship. The capsule is easier to navigate, so you can aim more accurately with the laser than would be possible from the ship."

"422 KILOMETERS, 620 METERS," SAID JARON.

"422 kilometers, 625 meters."

"422 kilometers, 630 meters."

"A little bit more," Celia said.

They needed to get the capsule and the spacecraft into an identical orbit, if possible, so that their distance from each other remained constant. That was problem number one. But at the same time, they had to be a very specific distance apart. It must be long enough that a straight line intersecting the orbit at the positions of the two ships passed as close as possible to the surface of the planet. They were lucky that there were hardly any elevation differences on the planet. They were conducting the experiment over the ocean, but there, because of the two moons and the nearby star, there were fairly violent tidal variations that changed the planet's profile in a complicated rhythm and made it difficult to get as close to the ground as possible.

"422 kilometers, 605 meters."

Shoot, now the capsule was a bit too low.

"You know you're ...?" asked Celia.

"Yeah, no problem, I was trying to catch up to you guys. I had to go into a lower orbit for a minute to do that."

"All right."

"Four hundred and twenty-two kilometers, six hundred and fifteen meters," Jaron said.

That was better. Celia kept track on the screen of how accurately the UV laser was hitting the sensor in the hull. The small red spot must stay within the large green circle as much as possible. Towards the edge, the sensitivity decreased nonlinearly, so they had to avoid that. In other words, the area that the laser seemed to prefer to sweep over at the moment. What looked simple in theory could be complicated in practice.

So far, they had only gotten within two hundred meters of the ground. The laser had not shown any change in frequency. Which meant that at a height of at least two hundred meters, it was safe on C c. Perhaps one could assume that it was the same way on the ground. But if she really wanted to know, she would have to try it out.

"Jaron? You'll have to keep a little more distance. We're not low enough yet. Ideally, the laser should run close enough to the ground that it will hit the ocean."

"No problem, I'll drop back a little. But haven't we already made contact with the ocean?"

"Very briefly," Celia said. "The radar measured two hundred meters again now, though."

"Then there must be waves down there as high as two hundred meters, do you realize that?" asked Jaron.

"Maybe. But it could also have been an inversion layer in the atmosphere that the laser reflected off of."

"Given the shallow angle of entry of the laser, that's unlikely," Jaron said.

Their captain was probably right. After all, there were no fewer than four celestial bodies tugging on C c's: the star, the gas giant, and the two moons. No, five—sometimes the outer moon of the gas giant was added. That was a lot of worlds worth visiting.

"What's the distance now?" asked Jaron.

Celia checked the number on the screen. It looked very promising. The laser was now coming within fifty meters of the ocean's surface.

"Pretty good," she said.

Should she let it stand? She looked at the measurement signal. The regular interruptions were particularly interesting. One might think that Jaron was switching off the device briefly, over and over. Those could be waves. Whenever a wave crest intersected the laser, its light went out briefly because it could no longer get through to the ship.

However, that would mean that 25-meter waves were chasing across the ocean at an impressive speed. Since the sea was up to four thousand meters deep in most places, the waves were not caused by storms, but by the ebb and flow of the tides, which traveled in several directions at once. Celia did not know whether the planet's small islands were really the paradise that Carlota wanted to explore. On the other hand, the cameras had clearly shown that they were not constantly flooded. Flora had already emerged on the islands, after all.

"So?" asked Jaron.

"I think we can conclude the test," Celia said. "There are lots of waves down there, but time is running normally. Today, at least. Fifty years ago, that was definitely not the case."

"Okay, then I'll head back to the ship for now," Jaron said.

"'You might as well land,'" Celia said. "I'm not coming along anyway."

"Hey, don't you listen to her!" exclaimed Carlota. "I'm dying to land on such a pretty island."

"And what about you, Celia?" asked Jürgen. "I was hoping we could all go for a swim."

"I have something else to do that won't allow me to go, and probably won't interest you," Celia said. "I want to take a closer look at the local sun."

"You can do that beautifully from the beach," said Jürgen.

"I'll have to get a little closer than that," Celia said.

"But not too close! Remember the story of Icarus."

"No, not too close."

"I'll go with you," said Paul.

Truthseeker, December 19, 2294

WARM SAND BETWEEN THE TOES, THE NIGHT UNDER THE open sky, the smell of fresh grass and salty sea ... That was about how Celia imagined her visit to C c. It was a shame that she could not go today. But the planet was not going anywhere, and she had the feeling that she had already unlocked its secrets. She was an astronomer, not a planetary scientist. Let the others have their fun.

The sun, on the other hand... The better she could point her instruments at it, the more exciting it became. While there were places on their home sun that were hotter than expected, it seemed to be the other way around with this star. It was too cool for its size, or too big for its temperature. It could be a systematic variation, of course. She had taken data from six surrounding red dwarfs, and all showed the same symptoms. Perhaps the dark nebula that gave birth to them had a special composition, so that the newborn red dwarfs here deviated from the norm in the Milky Way.

That was not improbable. The universe was similarly composed everywhere, but there were structures of different scales, which introduced deviations in the monotony. There were huge, almost empty spaces, and areas where matter was especially crowded.

If she trusted her gut, however, it was different here. Celia was reluctant to trust her gut. It had deceived her far too often. But she did not have to rely on it this time. As soon as the space capsule with Jaron, Jürgen and Carlota in it had undocked, she could steer the *Truthseeker* on a course to star C, which the others had presumably agreed to call Celia since yesterday. Even Carlota joined in, although Celia suspected that she just wanted to annoy her.

"Star Liner to *Truthseeker*," Jaron called. "Safety distance reached."

"Don't do anything stupid. And don't swim out too far," Celia said.

"You watch out for that star," Jaron said. "I've read that red dwarfs can be particularly nasty and surprise their visitors with eruptions."

"And I've read that the sun can quickly cause sunburn near the equator. Make sure you put on lots of sunscreen!"

"That goes for you, too, Celia."

"I don't plan to expose myself to the sun without protection."

"We're starting the thrusters now," Jaron said.

"I'll expect a report after you land," Celia said. "And pictures! Definitely pictures."

"We'll save you a spot on the warm sand," Jürgen said.

"Do we really have to do this?" asked Paul.

"Yes. I'm sorry, but I don't want to leave the three of them alone for too long," Celia said.

"I haven't really recovered from the long sleep yet."

"I understand that. But half a day with two g's has to be possible. If you need to go to the restroom, I can shut down the thrusters for a bit."

"Oh, at two g's it's much easier to sh... uh, have bowel movements."

"Father Paul, I'll ask anyway," Celia said, laughing. "At two g's, you probably wouldn't be able to get up the ladder."

"I guess I forgot about that."

Celia called up the inner system on the holo. The celestial bodies were not shown to scale. Compared to the red dwarf, the planets should be much tinier. Even a red dwarf was a giant in that sense.

"What's that there?" asked Paul.

A gray sphere had crept in at the edge of the visible region. What could it be? Of course! It was Planet e's largest moon, the Wrecking Ball. It appeared to be on its way into the inner system.

"Did I tell you about the strange moon of the gas giant?" she asked.

"I don't remember," said Paul.

"Well, a relatively large moon orbits the gas giant C e, moving in the plane of the planets. So it regularly intersects the orbits of the bodies of the inner system. That is, it doesn't hit them, which in and of itself is a miracle, but with an age of the system of only a hundred and fifty years, that would be understandable."

"Do we have to worry about the others?"

"No. I've run simulations for the next three hundred orbits. There is no danger of collision. That's the wonder of it. This whole system works like a perfectly designed and well-oiled clockwork."

"Isn't that an argument that this system really did come into being within a hundred and fifty years?" asked Paul. "I mean, after all, that's pretty close to biblical tradition, and far from anything science says."

That was an intriguing thought. But there was a second aspect.

"That's accurate, Paul. That could also be a case for someone having planned this system exactly as it looks today."

"You mean there is a... creator here?" asked Paul.

He pronounced the word with special emphasis, reverently. The sound caused a shiver to run down her spine. She was a scientist! Did humans really possess some kind of God gene that could be activated even in her? Celia shook her head. The sublime design of this system was enough to cause excitement. There was so much beauty in nature and in the universe, and so far there had always been a natural cause for it. It surely would be no different in LDN 63.

"Um, Celia?"

She startled out of a half-sleep.

"Yes, Paul?"

"I'm just a priest, but I was wondering something ..."

"Go ahead. I may have an answer."

"Well, the tides are caused by the moon," he said.

"Not only that, also by the sun and—in this system here —by the gas giant."

"Yes, but suppose the moon came very, very close to a planet ..."

"That would probably lead to some pretty violent tides."

"Does it matter how often that happens?"

"Actually, no. It's all about the gravitational effect."

Suddenly she knew what Paul was getting at. The wrecking ball! It was well on its way to swinging close to planet c. Why had she not noticed that earlier? It would cause a monster wave. Their friends were in danger!

"*Truthseeker* to Star Liner pod, please respond."

No response. Crap. Had they all left the capsule? Why did they not activate the pod as a relay?

"*Truthseeker* to Star Liner pod, please respond. It's urgent!"

Nothing. She started a simulation, this time focusing on planet c. In the hologram, the moon swung near planet c. In parallel, a wall of water built up on its surface, at least three times its normal height. Damn. She urgently needed to reach her friends!

"*Truthseeker* to Star Liner pod, please respond. Where are you?"

No response. She read the data on her simulation. The input parameters were too imprecise, so she could not give an accurate time forecast. But the fact remained—the mega-flood was coming.

"*Truthseeker* to Star Liner pod, please respond."

Had the flood already passed through, so that her shouts were falling on emptiness? Her stomach clenched.

"*Truthseeker* to Star Liner pod, come in."

No response. She clicked through the menus. There it was—the option to send the other party an alert message. She turned it on.

"*Truthseeker* to Star Liner pod, please respond."

Pause. She drummed her fingers on the armrest.

"Star Liner pod, Jaron here. What's going on?"

Finally! Where had he been for so long?

"I've finally reached you!" exclaimed Celia into the microphone.

She could not prevent her fear from being audible.

"'Well, I'm here now. What's wrong?"

Jaron, of course, immediately switched into appeasement mode. She did not need that at all right now.

"I've been trying to reach you for half an hour. You need to take off right now!"

Planet c, December 20, 2294

A STRANGE, SOPORIFIC SOUND EMANATED FROM THIS plane. It came from the high tidal waves that rushed over the oceans in perpetual succession and constant frequency. Only when they met were there dissonances, which quickly dissolved. Jaron heard the small islands as short interjections, which seemed to him like invitations. "Hey!" a small, oval island called out. "O!" a ring-shaped atoll shouted to him. "Come here!" was already so large that the island could be suitable as a landing site for the capsule.

Jaron, however, was in no hurry. He wanted to circle the planet until they found the best island. It should have a central plateau where they were safe from tidal waves, but also the gently sloping beach that Carlota so desired. Jürgen wanted rocks he could climb, and Jaron would love to walk in a forest again. He loved forests because they were acoustically closed off, even from above. He felt safer that way than in the open air. He also liked the smell.

"I'm perfect!" exclaimed an island. The rhythm of its lullaby told him that it consisted of three elevations, the third of which was the highest. It was probably not particularly high. Jaron pulled up the tactile display. He was right. The scale on the edge said that the island was not high enough overall. They must not put their only transfer capsule in danger.

"Hu!", "Hui!" and "Go!"—the next islands were all too small. "Why not?" asked a slightly larger one. It dropped off into the sea with bluffs all around. That's why, my friend. When Jaron heard, "This is the very best place!" he immediately reached for the haptic display. The last word signaled a vast plateau, just what he was looking for.

The island, his fingers sensed, consisted of two parts connected by a spit of land. In one half, four rock spires seem to rise up. The other rested like a thick coin in the sea. There appeared to be beach on both sides of the headland. The coin rose about a hundred and fifty feet above the sea. Its edges were even higher, but with many gaps. If he did not know better, he would think it was a meteorite crater leveled by erosion.

"What do you guys think of this structure?" Jaron shared the coordinates with Carlota and Jürgen.

"Very promising," Jürgen said. "Especially the rock pinnacles."

"But where's my beach?" asked Carlota.

Jaron scanned the island. It now appeared to consist of two separate islets.

"The tide must have washed over the headland," Jaron said. "I'm sorry. We'll look for another island, then."

"Oh, with those strong tides, it will probably be hard to find a beach that's consistently usable," Carlota said. "As far as I'm concerned, we can take this island."

Jaron retrieved radar data from the archive and listened in again. The ebb and flow of tidal waves was currently happening about once every 90 minutes.

"You've got three-quarters of an hour each time for the beach," he said.

"That's perfectly adequate. We're not here on vacation," Carlota said.

Although they now had a landing site, they still orbited the planet four times. Jaron wanted to map it, including the north and south polar areas. To do this, he had to correct the capsule's orbit several times. C c had ice caps on both ends, which were amazingly large considering the average surface temperature of 21 degrees Celsius. Probably this was due to the planet's lack of axial inclination. It always moved so upright around its star that little light and heat reached the poles throughout the year.

The ice caps extended to the eightieth degree of latitude. Further in the direction of the equator, grayish-brown islands, almost devoid of vegetation, rose from the ocean. Flora began to dominate at about the seventieth degree of latitude. From high altitude, it was impossible to tell what kind of plants they were, simply because they had no comparative data. Almost all the islands, except those with cliffs, were surrounded by a ring of sand on which the tidal waves broke. The very existence of the sand was a mystery, if the planet was really that young, since it was normally formed by millions of years of erosion.

Jaron shrugged his shoulders. So many things did not fit together here that he should be more surprised if something was actually logical for once. The system should be named "Impossible". However, it was quite likely that all the other stars in the former dark cloud also fell into this category.

"Boss? We should prepare for landing," Jürgen said.

He had been lost in thought. As the pilot, he should not let that happen.

"Yeah, you're right," Jaron said. "Sorry, I wasn't paying attention."

"That's why you have me."

Jaron did not contradict him, although Jürgen was wrong. He must not rely on others.

"Switch to the prepared landing course," he said.

If all went well, he would not have much to do. The Star Liner capsule was designed to be flown by automatic control, without a pilot on board at all. Here on an alien planet that would probably be risky. But the automatic system should be able to manage a simple landing.

The first correction maneuvers were gentle. The capsule entered the atmosphere. The lower they got, the stronger the vibrations became. They must not let the outer hull get too hot, so the automatic system now turned the ship so that the engine faced forward and started it. Jaron sank into the cushions of his chair. The frequency of the tidal waves decreased, but only apparently, because in reality the capsule had slowed down. On the tactile display, the flight path actually completed followed the plan exactly. The weather was also perfect. It would be a clean landing.

"Jürgen, Carlota? Prepare for landing."

The request was part of the checklist that Jaron had to work through. He knew it by heart. A short version of each step was shown on the tactile display. He confirmed one item after another. Humankind had even brought its bureaucracy to a distant dark nebula. On the other hand, he understood the point of these checklists. They created confidence that everything would go as planned.

"All done," said Jürgen.

"Same here," said Carlota.

Jaron checked his harness. The radar pulses had

become so loud that landing must be imminent. There, a brief swell—that was the raised edge of the plateau. The engine roared until the capsule hovered vertically above the ground. A few more meters. Ten, nine, eight. The metallic clatter of the landing legs extending. Three meters, two, one meter, contact.

The capsule was still sinking. Minus one meter. Minus two. Crap, what was that? Had they landed in some kind of swamp? Minus three. Minus four. Minus four. Minus three. The pod was bobbing. Minus two. Minus two. Minus three. Minus two. Minus two. That was how it stayed. They had penetrated two meters into the ground.

"What was that all about?" asked Jürgen.

"I have no idea," Jaron said.

"We should find out," Carlota said.

The lock on her seat belt clicked. Jaron heard her footsteps, first in socks, then in shoes.

"Are you coming, men?" she asked. "Or are you going to sit around and do nothing?"

"For safety reasons, it would make sense to wait a little longer before going out," Jaron said.

"Oh, come on! You guys can go ahead and get dressed. We'll get to the beach faster that way."

Jaron checked the rhythm of the tides. It was high tide right now, but in ten minutes the water should be draining away.

"What about spacesuits?" asked Jürgen.

"Have you checked the environment?" asked Carlota. "Twenty-six degrees Celsius, plus 17 percent oxygen and nothing toxic. You don't need a suit out there."

"And what about germs or other microorganisms?" asked Jürgen.

"From a medical point of view, no problem," Carlota

said. "If they exist, they can't do anything to the human organism."

"Besides, we'll be bringing them in here anyway," Jaron said. "We can't disinfect the airlock. If there are any outside, they will inevitably follow us inside."

"Very reassuring," said Jürgen. "You know that movie where the whole crew is infested with spores and goes insane?"

"Totally unrealistic," Carlota said.

"If I remember correctly, the guy who warned his friends was killed first in that movie," said Jaron. "But seriously—we should be more worried about the ground."

"Then maybe we can find another island," Carlota said. "I don't need to visit the beach that badly."

"Right now, the risk shouldn't be that great," Jürgen said. "But we should check whether the substrate can handle a launch attempt."

"And if not?" asked Carlota.

A good question. Then they would be literally stranded here. But he would not worry about that until the time came.

"We'll see about that," Jaron said. "Capsule to *Truthseeker*, come in."

He had made Celia a promise, after all.

"*Truthseeker* here," Celia reported. "I read you."

"We've made a good landing. I'm sending you the coordinates and our readings from orbit. If you get bored, you could analyze them."

"Oh, I've collected enough data myself," Celia said. "Or are you expecting something new from it?"

"No, that would just be for completeness. The researchers on Earth will be pleased."

"I see. Then there really is still time," Celia said.

"Whatever you say. We're leaving now for an initial exploration tour," Jaron said.

"Roger that. Be careful. And don't forget the pictures!"

THE OUTER BULKHEAD OF THE AIRLOCK OPENED WITH A squeak. A stream of warm, humid air rushed in.

"Crap, my sunglasses are fogging up," Jürgen said.

Jaron breathed in deeply through his nose. The air contained so much oxygen that he did not feel any difference from Earth. The difference from the spaceship was staggering. Oil, sweat, food vapor, rusty metal, cleaning agents—the unique mixture evaporated with every breath. It made room for... for... Jaron drew in the air and swallowed, concentrating entirely on the aroma, but he found —nothing. The air smelled and tasted completely neutral. The light floral scent, that was Carlota, not the local flora. The heavier aroma of malt, that was Jürgen, not the fertile soil of the planet. The light sweat note came from himself.

"Wow," Carlota said. "That's... interesting."

She did not use the word "beautiful," and that was interesting, too. He had come to know Carlota as a woman who recognized and appreciated beauty. When she called something "interesting," something was definitely wrong.

"The view is great," Jürgen said. "Here, take my arm."

Jaron grabbed the arm that was touching him and held on just above the elbow. Jürgen pulled him up slightly.

"Two steps and you're standing on the platform," Jürgen explained.

Jaron pushed his glasses over his eyes. They were a special model for outdoor operations that warned him of obstacles acoustically and tactilely. With Jürgen's help, he took the two steps up.

"Do you smell that, too?" asked Jaron.

Jürgen and Carlota draw in their breath almost simultaneously.

"Heavenly," said Jürgen.

"What exactly?" asked Jaron.

"No stench, no sweat," said Jürgen.

"I don't smell anything at all," said Carlota.

"That's right," said Jürgen. "That's weird."

"It doesn't necessarily mean anything," Carlota said. "The sense of smell works by having matching molecules dock onto sensory cells. Here, there's probably a completely different biochemistry and thus no molecules that would fit in ours."

"But then we can't eat any of the things that grow here?" asked Jürgen.

"Are you hungry already?" asked Jaron.

"No, but it would be inconvenient if we were stranded here."

So he had already thought of that, too. No wonder, Jürgen was an engineer. He knew what forces acted on the ground during a rocket launch.

"If there's at least carbon, we could make our own food," Carlota said.

"Well, there's that," said Jürgen.

"Shall we go?" asked Jaron.

"Do you want to go first, boss?" asked Jürgen.

"Carlota, you go first," said Jaron.

"I get it, you're scared," Carlota said. "Fine, I'll go."

Suddenly, his face warmed. Presumably, he had been in Carlota's shadow until now. He stretched his face toward the sun. It seemed a little warmer than the sun at home, but that might be a misconception.

"The ground is bouncy," Carlota said.

"The first human on an exoplanet," Jürgen said. "Wait, I have to savor that."

"What do you see?" asked Jaron.

"We're standing pretty much in the middle of a flat plain that rises slightly on all sides," said Carlota. "It ends in a kind of wall, but it's broken by many crevices. Battlements, yes, it looks like the loopholes of a medieval castle. The ground is covered with a kind of green fluff that reminds me of the undercoat of a rabbit. It's a different green than on Earth, though, with higher blue content. The sun is high in the sky. It's yellow and seems to me to be a little bigger than our own star."

"What Carlota can't see from below," Jürgen added, "is the horizon formed by the sea. At two o'clock, an island can be seen. At nine o'clock, black rock spires rise into the air. They should be another fifty meters higher than the plain we are on."

"Black like basalt?" asked Jaron.

"Yes, something like that. Very fresh basalt. They're still really shiny black. Their sidewalls look very smooth. That will be fun."

"You still want to climb up?"

"Yes, I would be very keen to do that. It's a pity Norbert isn't here. We used to love climbing in the Alps together. Would you like to come along?"

It would certainly be an interesting experience. A temptation. No, he had to be reasonable.

"Why don't you ask Carlota?" he said.

"Do I want to climb up there?" Carlota laughed. "Absolutely not. But I would like to watch you guys from below and take pictures. I'd like to go down to the beach then, too."

"Yes, we'll be there," Jürgen said.

"ONE MORE STEP."

Jaron let go of Jürgen's arm. Then he put his right foot forward. The ball of his foot touched the ground. Jaron shifted all his weight onto that leg. The foot sank into the ground a little. Jaron bent his knees slightly and rose again. The ground rocked. It was a hard but elastic surface, almost like a trampoline. He squatted down to feel the ground.

There was the herb that reminded Carlota of a rabbit's undercoat. She was right. The mass was soft and furry in texture. He plucked some from the ground. It did not take much force for him to do so. He put the mass back. After he stroked it once, it stuck back down as if the floor were made of Velcro.

"Carlota? Have you taken a sample of this yet?" he asked.

"Yes, I have. The whole level is filled with this stuff."

"We should collect it and fill our pillows and quilts with it," Jürgen said.

Jaron stood up again. "Who knows, maybe it will turn into sticky, hungry worms during the night."

"You have too much imagination," Carlota said. "I think it's some kind of grass. The green color speaks for that, too."

"You said it was a different green than on Earth," Jaron said.

"Yes, it's probably not chlorophyll in the cells here," Carlota said. "The local sun also radiates much more strongly in the infrared. Our chlorophyll wouldn't be as efficient here."

He followed her voice. The goggles reported no obstructions. After a few steps, he turned around. Turning his head, he perceived the capsule by short, high-pitched beeps.

"Did you forget something?" asked Jürgen.

"I left the stove on, I think."

"Haha. Now come on, Carlota already has quite a head start."

Nevertheless, they arrived too late to be able to step onto the beach. When they reached the edge of the plain, they had only ten minutes left before the tide was expected to come in. So they decided to take a break. Jaron sat down on the ground and leaned against the inside of a gap in the rampart, where its shadow protected him from the sunlight. He had not walked such a long distance in a long time.

"How far away is the rocket?" he asked.

"1.2 kilometers," Jürgen said.

Jaron took a deep breath. He smelled something now—his sweat and that of his crew. The material against his back was hard. He heard tapping and scratching.

"What's that?" he asked.

"I'm taking a sample," Carlota said. "I'm interested in the rock. It resembles shale, but somehow that doesn't fit the shape of this mountain. I would have guessed more of a volcanic origin."

"Do you know anything about geology?" asked Jaron.

"Astrogeology," said Carlota. "I was always convinced that a single qualification wouldn't be enough for a trip like this."

"My respects," he said.

"Oh, it's nothing special," she said.

"I think it is."

Carlota continued scratching the wall. "There, finally! That should do it."

Suddenly, Jaron felt vibrations in his back.

"Something's happening," he said, standing up.

"You can say that again," Jürgen confirmed. "The tide is coming in."

It was not a normal tide. The glasses made him feel that the water must be coming from all sides at once. He imagined it as a wave, but that was wrong. It must be a wall.

"It looks like someone is lifting the ocean floor," Jürgen said, "onto the roof of a twenty-story skyscraper."

The sound confirmed Jürgen's observation. It was a deep, soft roar with a tremendous power inherent in it.

"It's coming at us," Carlota said.

He felt it, too. Jürgen touched him, and Jaron grabbed the engineer's upper arm. Jürgen was trembling. Was it the vibrations or was it his fear? Jaron was not even sure about himself.

"We're high enough," Jürgen said. "At least three times as high as the tide."

It sounded like an incantation.

"We're safe up here," Carlota said.

Now it was coming. The roar turned into the growl of a tiger. In a moment. It must be facing them directly. Suddenly, Jaron could smell something again. It must be the salt dissolved in the water. The rumble hit the wall like a mighty hammer. The ground beneath his feet shook, but held firm. The tide hissed and raged, but it could not overcome the island. The mass of water rushed to find another way. A plume of atomized seawater blew over them. The remaining moisture splashed down the walls.

"That's it? I would have expected more," said Jürgen in a brittle voice that belied his feigned coolness.

"Pretty intense," said Carlota.

"That's the understatement of the day," said Jaron. "I wouldn't want to get in the way of that roller."

"Yeah, we probably shouldn't stay on the beach very long," Carlota said.

The path down was damp, but not muddy. It felt like walking on a ramp made of gravel.

"Where did all this gravel come from?" asked Jaron.

"It looks like it's pushing out of the mountain below the plain," Carlota said.

"Does that make any sense geologically?"

"No. It looks more like a stuffed animal with stuffing coming out of a crack. In any case, mountains as we know them don't have sand deposits like this."

"From a purely practical point of view: This mountain has one, anyway," Jürgen said. "Otherwise, we would have a hard time getting to the beach."

"I think the existence of the beach is, in a way, just a consequence of the crack and the material coming out of it," Carlota said.

"Is it even still there?" asked Jaron. "After that monster wave?"

"I'm surprised myself, but it's more beautiful than before," Carlota said. "A flood like that basically just raises the water level. Maybe it pushed fresh gravel onto the headland from one direction, and carried it away again in the other."

Jaron stopped, because he heard something he had long forgotten. It was the sound of small waves crashing on the beach. He took off his shoes and left them there. The sand here was coarse. He followed the slope. There was the first wave. It washed over his toes, broke on his shins, ran out with a crackling sound, turned back and retreated into the sea with a rustling sound.

The water was warm, not like in the shower, but it had to be close to 30 degrees Celsius. Jaron ran back to the beach once more. He tore off his long-sleeved T-shirt, took off his pants and underpants, and threw everything onto the sand. It did not matter what the others thought. He had no other choice. Slowly, he walked into the sea, which quickly got deeper. The waves splashed him in the face, and suddenly he lost the ground under his feet.

The water was all around him. It was glorious. He floated as if he were in his mother's womb. Nothing could happen to him here. All sounds were muffled. The distant scraping of the fine gravel on the beach, the calls... Oh. He made a few swimming strokes and surfaced.

"Jaron, have you taken leave of your senses?" asked Jürgen. "You were suddenly gone!"

Jaron groped for the bottom. It was not so deep here anymore.

"Can't a man take a swim in peace?" he said.

"But if you intend to dive longer, you could let us know," Jürgen said.

"Jürgen is right," said Carlota. "We don't even know if you can swim!"

"Of course I can swim. Don't you remember, Jürgen? We were all together at the seashore once in Sicily!"

"Yes, but ... It looked as if the sea had swallowed you," Jürgen said. "That's when I got scared."

It was nice that the two of them were worried about him.

"All right. At least we've got that cleared up," said Jaron. "Can we swim some more in peace?"

"Okay. We should keep an eye on the time, though," Carlota said. "So please don't swim out very far."

JARON LAY ON HIS BACK. THE SUN WARMED HIS NAKED BODY. His ears were below the water line. Thus, he transformed himself into the boundary of the elements. He was the connection. Jaron heard what was going on in the wet element and could translate it to the dry. But he did not want to, because he was not on duty right now and had no responsibilities.

He was just some creature lying on his back in the water, listening to the sea. From the front came the light scraping of the waves reaching the beach. From behind, the first harbingers of the tide reached him, very quietly— perhaps he was just imagining it. From below, an irregular bubbling and gurgling reached his ears. Perhaps something was rotting there and producing putrid gases in the process, or gases dissolved in the water were slowly bubbling out. In any case, the ocean was alive.

Something touched his right upper arm. He thought it might be Jürgen or Carlota. Why would they not leave him alone? Jaron tried to ignore them, but the touch was repeated, this time on his right forearm.

"What's wrong?" he asked, annoyed, without changing his position.

No answer, but a new touch on his right hip. Jaron struck at it with his right hand and reached into a kind of net. It felt slippery and immediately wrapped around his hand. He tried to brush it off, but it was stuck. Shit. As fast as he could, he swam to shore.

"Can you guys help me, please?" he asked.

"I'm alone," Carlota said. "Let me see, what do you have there?"

The sand crunched. Someone grabbed his arm. Jaron pulled away, startled.

"It's just me," Carlota said.

"Sorry. Where's Jürgen?"

"He's diving around where you drowned."

"I didn't drown. I was diving."

"Yes, so there where it suddenly gets deeper. Now hold still."

Jaron sighed. Why did he always have to have such bad luck?

"That's very interesting," Carlota said. "You're a real lucky guy!"

"Because an animal wants to eat me?" he asked.

"Whether it's an animal, we have yet to see. It looks like a scrap of fishing net, except the individual threads have eyes. I'll try to remove it gently."

"That would be nice," Jaron said.

"We could also just wait it out. I'm sure the thing will soon realize it can't digest you."

"Digest maybe not, but it can inflict pain on me. It feels like it's contracting."

"Wait," Carlota said. "I'll try to cut it off with a scalpel."

He felt something hard on his skin. The net tightened. Jaron held against it. The animal had less strength than he did, but he could not get rid of it either.

"It doesn't work that way," Carlota said. "I think the dryness is hurting it. Come on, let's go in the water."

"It's good if the dryness hurts it, isn't it? At least then I'll get rid of it."

"But if it's desperate, it might do something to your hand that you wouldn't like. Wouldn't we rather remove it gently?"

"All right."

He walked Carlota far enough into the sea that the water was up to his waist. Then he put his hand in the water. Suddenly, the pressure released.

"It's gone!" he exclaimed.

"No, I caught it in a bag I put around your hand. I'm dying to examine it."

"Well, that's not nice," Jaron said.

"You'll never guess what I saw," said Jürgen.

"Ah, are you back?" asked Carlota. "I was starting to get worried. We should start heading away from the beach again."

"You're absolutely right," said Jürgen. "I'll tell you on the way."

"Wait, I have to get dressed first," Jaron said.

"I'll grab your things," Jürgen said. "Will you lead him up, Carlota?"

"Don't you have to get dressed?" asked Jaron.

"No, I'm already dressed," she said.

Suddenly Jaron felt his own nakedness, and it embarrassed him.

"Jürgen, will you please bring me my underpants?" he called out.

"We should really start making our way slowly," Carlota said.

Now she sounded very worried. Jaron forgot his fit of shame. Carlota could probably already see the wave. He tried to concentrate on the sound of the sea, but her feet crunched too loudly in the sand.

"I still wanted to tell you what I saw in the sea," Jürgen said.

"Can't it wait until later?" questioned Carlota.

"No. Maybe you'll be able to see it when the tide goes out again."

"See what?" asked Carlota.

"At the bottom of the sea, there's a huge pipe running from our island to the cliff tops. The sand has accumulated on it."

"Excuse me?" asked Carlota.

"A pipe. At the bottom of the sea. Artificial. Clearly."

"You're out of your mind. Who knows what you saw there?"

"HERE WE ARE," CARLOTA SAID. "YOU CAN SIT AND LEAN against the wall here."

She led him into the shadows. Jaron groped forward. This must be the passageway where they waited out the tide earlier.

"Can we leave you alone for a minute?" asked Jürgen.

"Why?" asked Jaron.

"I'd like a direct view of the ocean."

"Me, too," said Jaron.

"Suit yourself. Here, take my arm."

Jürgen tapped him and Jaron grabbed his upper arm.

"What are you going to do?" asked Carlota.

"See that ledge over there? We can see straight down from there."

"That's pretty exposed. Are you sure?"

"The ledge measures at least two by three meters," said Jürgen. "That's enough for all of us."

Jürgen started walking. They walked a few steps, then switched sides.

"You're on the land side now," Jürgen said. "Next to you, it's a gentle uphill slope. If I sway, you'll throw us both to the right."

"Okay."

The wind freshened. The rumble came closer. The ground was covered with a coarse mass that felt like walking on bark mulch.

"What are we walking over?" asked Jaron.

They stopped. Carlota groaned.

"If I didn't know better, I'd think they were pieces of bark," she said. "The chunks are much harder than wood, though. Maybe it's a kind of shale rock that doesn't occur on Earth."

"Come on, we're almost there," Jürgen said. "There, now it's getting narrow and you have to walk behind me."

Jaron dropped back a step and felt his way from Jürgen's arm to his hips. Like a child's game, he held onto the engineer with both hands. He was sweating, although the strong wind had made it a bit cooler. The goggles acoustically told him that there was free space to the left and right. He imagined the depth. His breath and heartbeat quickened.

"So, here we are," Jürgen said. "Come back next to me."

Jaron left his left hand on Jürgen's back and stood next to him on the right. At the same moment, he felt Carlota's hand on his back. She placed herself at his right side. Now the three of them stood side by side like three soccer players waiting for a free kick. The opposing player approached with a dull roar.

The impact of the water masses was even more impressive from this perspective than the first time. The noise was deafening. The wind rising from below enveloped them in a dense cloud of fine droplets that tasted salty on the lips.

"Do you see it?" cried Jürgen.

"Yes!" Carlota shouted back.

The noise died down. Jaron wiped the moisture from his face. The front of his T-shirt was soaking wet. It still seemed to be somewhat dry at the back. It was getting warmer. That must be the sun, which was no longer blocked by the cloud of spray. He turned his belly towards it to let it dry.

"What did we see there?" asked Carlota.

"Pipes, I think," Jürgen said. "Bright outer material that shone for a moment, probably thirty meters in diameter."

"It looked more like a root to me," Carlota said. "Have you ever seen the exposed roots of a giant tree?"

"Do you see any giant trees here?" asked Jürgen. "The flora seems rather small to me," he said.

"But the structure was clearly tapered outward," Carlota objected. "What sense would that make in a pipe?"

"I didn't notice that," Jürgen said.

"You're an engineer and you see pipes, Carlota knows biology and sees roots," Jaron said. "Pretty typical. I'd probably see thrusters or spaceship modules."

"You're right, Jaron," Jürgen agreed. "The outside shape reminded me of one of those inflatable modules they used to hang on the space reefs for tourists. But a space station in the ocean, that doesn't make any sense."

"I'm just saying that we recognize what we want to recognize. We must try to forget all our prejudices and approach this new world with an open mind, even naively."

"Oh, that's explorer romance," Carlota said. "We have to use all the knowledge we brought with us to make sense of this world. And that's what I plan to do now. Come on!"

"What are you up to?" asked Jürgen.

"I've collected lots of samples," said Carlota. "I'm now going to analyze them and look at them under the microscope."

"ARE YOU GETTING ANYWHERE?" ASKED JARON.

Carlota had been working on the samples for an hour. Something rattled on the right. That must be Jürgen, who wanted to fix something for them to eat. Carlota was whistling softly to herself. That must be a good sign. Suddenly, her chair squeaked.

"This is all very strange," she said. "Jürgen, do you have a moment?"

"I'm coming," Jürgen said.

"Thank you. You can see everything on the screen here. Jaron, I'll transfer the microscope images to your haptic display."

"Thank you," Jaron said, returning to his seat and sitting down. The display had already turned on. He placed his left hand on it.

"The first one is the rough structure of the cells of the green fluff we found right after we got out of the shuttle," Carlota said.

Jaron focused on his fingers. He felt a hexagon divided into three chambers. The upper and lower chambers were triangular in cross-section, and the middle one was rectangular. In the two triangular chambers was something that could best be described as lint. In the middle one, which was much larger, there were three moving circles, so in reality they were probably spheres.

"The two larger spheres in the middle are the cell's power plant and factory," Carlota explained. "They provide energy and produce substances. The slightly smaller sphere provides the receptors. It reads the genetic information located in the smaller chambers. In doing so, it always uses the variant that is currently spatially closest as the source. Since it is pushed around randomly by the other two spheres, sometimes the receptors of one parent are used, sometimes those of the other. The cells them-selves are always identical."

"So you're taking advantage of gender inheritance without introducing anything like gender," Jaron said.

"Exactly," said Carlota. "Evolutionarily, the cells that

have the better overall recipes prevail. When they reproduce, the daughter cell is randomly handed a set of genes from both parents."

"It's an interesting concept," Jaron said. "How fast do the cycles run?"

"Very fast, every minute. That's the only way I was able to observe the whole process."

"That would explain how they were able to colonize the planet so quickly," said Jürgen. "Their evolution must be pretty rapid."

"Now wait a minute," Carlota said. "That's so only for the cells of some samples, for example, the green fluff or the web you caught, Jaron. That was not an animal, by the way. Like the green fluff, it is more comparable to terrestrial green algae and does not rely on organic matter for nourishment. All the samples I took on the beach are at about that stage of development. There is not much diversity here. The ecosystem here is still on pretty shaky ground."

"But you said that not all cells look the same," Jaron said.

"Right. I'll show you the counterexample now."

Jaron put his hand on the haptic display. What had Carlota found? He traced the contours provided by the tiny pins in the tactile screen. The shape was irregular and reminded him of an "M" drawn with a particularly thick pen. The contours were hard and straight, but inside they were empty.

"Is there no nucleus at all?" he asked.

"No, in fact there is none in this type of cell. Energy production takes place on the inside of the cell walls, which are decidedly rough, quite different from the outside walls. The cell is filled with a structure of silica with fine tubes running through it."

"The cells must be pretty stable," said Jürgen.

"They are," said Carlota. "Especially since the walls are also very thick."

"How do they feed, then?" asked Jaron.

"Only the outermost cells grow, feed and divide. Their outer walls are still permeable."

"Then the plant must be pretty stable with cells like that," said Jürgen.

"Yes, our spaceship is standing on it," Carlota said.

"You mean the island ...?" asked Jürgen.

"Yes, the whole island grew, and it grew biologically, not geologically. That's not so far-fetched. Think of the huge coral reefs in the terrestrial oceans."

"Then you were right about the roots," Jürgen said.

"I'd like to agree with you, but I don't see the point of it being roots. The island is not a tree. Maybe they are pipes after all, or another unusual plant that snakes across the ocean floor."

"Or an animal that feeds on the islands," Jaron said.

"Exactly. We shouldn't rule anything out," Carlota said.

"Why are you suddenly so careful about your diagnoses?" asked Jaron.

Carlota laughed. "You've got me figured out! Yes, you're absolutely right. I was a little too quick to make firm statements. That's unscientific. That's why we now come to my third discovery."

Oh, something else? Jaron concentrated fully on the tactile screen again. He traced the contours and jerked back. That was a lot of little hooks! The cell, if one could call it that, had four circular eyelets at one end, like flowers hanging from stems. The four stems connected before they diverged into the same number of hooks, just as roots did in flowers. The hooks bent 180 degrees. There was a small barb at the end of each.

"What's that strange cell?" asked Jaron.

"Reminds me of a fish hook," said Jürgen.

"It's a sample of the elastic material we're standing on," said Carlota. "Will you guys please tell me what the heck this is? The structures appear to be biologically dead. There's no activity at all."

"Maybe they're man-made," said Jaron.

"Haha, someone built a huge trampoline especially for us, and we land on it just like that," said Jürgen. "If I were the owner, I'd be pretty mad at us."

Maybe the island really was a tree once, and after it was cut down, they covered the stump to protect it from weathering or disease. It might even be growing back. Jaron shook his head. He must forget the purely human worldview.

"What's on your mind, Jaron?" asked Carlota.

She was very observant.

"I was wondering what purpose this covering might serve," he said.

"I think we should postpone that question," Carlota said. "Imagine you're an alien and you land in a forest on Earth, and you find a fruit net that a local has discarded there. You might discover that it's made of recycled poly-cellulose, but you'll never guess its purpose until you meet one of the locals with a filled fruit net in his hand."

"What are these hooks made of?" asked Jürgen. "Of aluminum or iron?"

"Out of polysaccharide chains," Carlota said. "So, they are basically made of sugar."

"Oh," said Jürgen.

"I think they're strong enough to survive the launch of the capsule," Carlota said. "The material must be made of numerous layers."

"But won't we burn that with the exhaust jet from the engine?" asked Jürgen.

"You saw the black area around the ship, right?" replied Carlota. "Of course we're burning some of the material. It seems thick enough, though."

"Besides, it's only a matter of a few seconds," said Jürgen. "You're probably right. There's no danger for the launch."

"Polysaccharides, meaning organic compounds?" asked Jaron.

"Yes," Carlota answered. "Why?"

"Couldn't it be that the tree, that is, the island, produces these compounds itself? Maybe it's a kind of fruit, or a protection from injury, or even a reaction to injury."

"Sure, that's all possible," Carlota said. "It could also be a trick. Maybe we're above the maw of this creature, and it's just waiting to devour us by simply opening the net."

"It'll choke on that morsel, though," Jürgen said.

"Who knows? Maybe the entire dark nebula is a giant Venus flytrap for curious alien space travelers," Carlota said. "They see what's going on here, fly over and land— poof—in the stomach of this island."

"So many possibilities," Jaron said.

"I'd like to collect more samples," Carlota said.

"Well, I'm going to do that little climb I've been thinking about doing," said Jürgen. "Anyone want to come along?"

"Not me, I don't need it," Carlota said.

"I would slow you down," said Jaron.

"If you'd like to come up the mountain with me, we can make it work," said Jürgen.

"That's very kind of you, but I probably wouldn't climb up there unless I absolutely had to."

Suddenly, a pungent odor entered his nose. Did the polysaccharide membrane catch fire after all?

"Oh, crap, I forgot the food in the oven!" exclaimed Jürgen.

An hour later, it was finally quiet once again in the capsule. It was a quiet he had not experienced in ages. Not a single device was making any noise. Life support was turned off, and not even the sound of the sea could be heard from outside. He sat down on his armchair, leaned the backrest back and stretched out his legs. It was heavenly.

An alarm signal woke him up. It came from the radio receiver. Jaron straightened the chair and pulled up the controls.

"Star Liner pod, Jaron here. What's going on?"

"I've finally reached you!" Celia said in a panicked voice.

"Well, I'm here now. What's wrong?"

"I've been trying to reach you for half an hour. You need to take off right now!"

Jaron rubbed the sand out of his eyes. Celia sounded really panicked. That was not usually her style.

"Now slow down, what's going on?" he asked.

"I was watching the passage of the moon through the orbit of the second planet. In doing so, I noticed that it appears to be on its way toward you right now."

"But that's not dangerous. We specially simulated it several times."

"The moon does not hit the planet. But it passes by at a minimal distance. What do you think that will mean for the tides?"

Damn. Celia was right. If the tide was already coming in fifty meters high at normal times, how would the water mountain swell under the influence of the close encounter with the moon? Then they would not be safe on the island. They urgently needed to launch into orbit until the wave passed.

"You're right, Celia. Thanks for the warning."

"I'm turning back with the *Truthseeker*."

"You wouldn't be back until tomorrow. That won't help us. We'll just take off until the wave is through, and then we'll land again."

"And if everything is flooded after that?"

"Then we'll just stay in orbit until you get back."

"Are you sure, Jaron?"

"Yes, I'm saying that as captain. You go to the sun as planned and investigate."

"Surely I can't ..."

"Yes, you can. You must."

Celia could not help them. The *Truthseeker* was not equipped to land on the planet. It was best she was at a safe distance. Otherwise, she would do something stupid. They just needed to get out of here as soon as possible.

"Well, if you insist..."

"I insist. How much time do we have?"

"I can't tell you exactly. There are too many variables. Maybe half an hour?"

"Thanks, that will be enough."

"Okay, good luck!"

"You too," Jaron said. "Star Liner capsule out."

Jaron's fingers flew across the keyboard. He put the ship in launch readiness. All systems powered up. It would not even take ten minutes. Jürgen was the problem. He was still climbing, and he felt safe. Where he was headed, the tide currently did not normally reach. Jaron switched to the general radio channel, where Carlota and Jürgen would be listening.

"We have a problem," he said. "In about half an hour, we're in for a huge tidal wave, at least three times the normal height. We'll have to use the capsule to get to safety."

"I'm about fifteen minutes away from you," Carlota reported. "I've been searching for samples on the far edge of the platform."

"Get back over here right now," Jaron said. "Jürgen, what about you?"

"I – uff – I have – uff – a – uff – problem right now. Whew. I just got to the top. Whew. That was a slog."

"You need to turn around right now," Jaron said.

"Now slow down," Jürgen said. "I've been walking uphill for an hour and a half. Now I need a break, and the way back after that can't be done any faster. Or do you want me to fall in the rush?"

"Jürgen, there's a mega tidal wave coming in half an hour. We have to be launched with the capsule by then, or we'll lose it and our lives to boot."

"I can't do magic. It just can't be done in thirty minutes. The best thing for me to do is sit out the wave up here. It won't hit me. The peaks are really surprisingly high."

"I'm sorry, but it looks bad," Jaron said. "The water will wash you off the rocks like a speck of dust."

"Well, so be it. The fact is, half an hour isn't enough time to get back. The best thing for you to do is to start without me. You get yourselves to safety, and then you pick me back up down here."

"There won't be anything left for us to pick up," Jaron said.

"You old pessimist! And anyway, there are worse ways

to die than sitting on a mountain overlooking a blue ocean."

"That's out of the question. You're not dying," Jaron said.

If only it were so! But Jürgen was right. He would not make it in half an hour.

"I have an idea," Carlota said. "The rescue device, the Safer. It's tethered to the outside of the capsule."

"It's built for zero gravity," Jaron said.

"It could still work," said Jürgen. "The Safer has a pretty powerful chemical engine. It's a newer model that doesn't run on compressed air like the old ones."

"I'll be at the ship in thirteen minutes," Carlota said. "Then I can fly it to Jürgen and pick him up."

"We'll lose valuable time that way," Jaron said. "I'll fly it. I'm already at the ship."

"But you ... " Carlota began.

"I'll program it to lock onto Jürgen's radio. That should work. Maybe you could find a ledge for me to land the Safer on, Jürgen."

"Okay, boss. I'll get right on it."

"Jaron, wouldn't you rather wait for me?" asked Carlota. "It's risky if you ..."

"Someone has to sit in the chair. The Safer won't fly without a load. But I'm just the passenger. It will find the course itself. It'll be fine! I really have to go now. Jaron out."

He ran in the direction from which fresh air flowed into the capsule. There he felt for the wall. One step up onto the platform, turn around and climb down the ladder. Faster. The emergency seat, the Safer, was behind a flap in the outer wall of the capsule, about where the landing gear also folded out, slightly offset to the right of the hatch. Jaron made sure of the position of the ladder, took three steps to the right and climbed up the landing gear. He wished for stronger arm and leg muscles, since the extra space between the cross struts made the climb more strenuous.

His hand touched the smooth metal of the capsule. Done. His fingers felt to the right. There was a crack in the material. This must be the flap behind which the Safer was hidden. He climbed a little to the right and felt further. There, the clasp. He turned the wheel once completely around and then pulled the tab underneath. The flap opened. Hopefully the compartment was not empty! There, the Safer. He felt the seat cushion, stretched, and pulled on the backrest. The Safer slid forward. He pulled on it a bit more.

Crap, that was too far. The Safer tumbled out of its housing. Jaron did not manage to hold on to it. He tried a moment too long, so he lost his balance. He pushed off so that he fell further to the right, and did an elegant roll. The ground cushioned his fall. Good thing they didn't land on a rocky plain. Jaron got back up and moved bent over to the left. There was the Safer. He set it up, sat in it and fastened the shoulder strap. The seat was so low, he had to stretch out his legs to sit down.

Jaron unfolded the controls. It was possible to maneuver manually with two sticks, but he switched to automatic. He did not know Jürgen's coordinates. But the seat also had three emergency modes at the ready: It could orient itself to objects glowing in the infrared, such as astronauts who had an accident. It could avoid objects, such as debris. And it could fly to the strongest radio source, usually its own spacecraft.

"Can you hear me?" he said over the radio. "From now on, please radio silence on all sides—except Jürgen. I'm making the Safer home in on his transmitter."

No one answered. Very good, Carlota and the pod

must have understood him. Jaron turned off his radio. Then he selected the radio lock mode. The seat acoustically confirmed his choice at each menu item. Now all he had to do was press the start button.

"Aaahhh!" he yelled as the chair shot upward with him.

Then his vehicle suddenly leaned forward to switch to vertical flight. It might not be so noticeable in zero gravity, but here he was hanging forward at almost a 45-degree angle. Only the harness prevented him from falling. The airstream blew into his face and ripped off his glasses before he could grab them. Crap. Now he had no orientation at all. Somewhere in front of him, a new tidal wave was roaring in, but it was not there yet. He concentrated on the sounds, filtered out the wind, but that was all there was. He was apparently shooting straight across the plain. A hard landing followed. Beneath it, gentle sounds of the sea. That must be the headland already. The Safer was one hell of a fast flyer when it needed to be.

Something beeped. Was it running out of fuel?

"Here I am!"

It was Jürgen! Then the beeping was a proximity alarm. Hopefully, Jürgen was looking for a big enough ledge with enough room to land. Jaron waved at him. The Safer aligned itself and set down rather roughly. Jaron just managed to get his legs out of the way.

"Come on, up you go," he said. "It's best if you hang onto the back of the chair from behind."

"I hope I'm strong enough," Jürgen said.

"You climbed up here, didn't you? You can do it. Watch out, the chair tilts forward in flight!"

"Thanks, Jaron."

"Hang on. I'm launching!"

Jaron pressed the launch button. The chair shot up, spun once completely, and shut down the engine. Shit.

Jaron pressed the takeoff button again. Again, it flew up to the sky, spun, and went down.

"I'm probably too heavy for it," Jürgen said. "Wait, I'll let go."

"Absolutely not!" yelled Jaron.

Jürgen. Damn it! The Safer was still programmed to Jürgen. The strongest radio station was behind it. This totally messed up the control system. Jaron pressed the start button again. It went up, but just before the chair could turn again, he pushed the control lever forward. The manual control overrode the automatic. They shot forward.

"Look out! The mountain!" Jürgen shouted.

Jaron steered hard to the right. He heard the hard turn whip Jürgen's body around behind him.

"A little further to the right!" shouted Jürgen.

He had apparently understood that Jaron must now steer by hand.

"That's it!" shouted Jürgen.

They sped across the plain for a minute. Then the noise of the engine was joined by a suppressed roar.

"Uh, if it could go a little faster, that would be good," Jürgen said. "The damned wave is coming."

At that moment, something beeped. The noise did not stop.

"There's a red light on the backrest," Jürgen said.

"That's the fuel tank."

"Shit. Come on, just leave me here and maybe you'll make it."

"No way, Jürgen. If you let go, I'll land next to you. I promise! You know me!"

"But then we'll both die!" shouted Jürgen.

"Nobody's dying today," said Jaron.

"You don't see the wave."

No, but he felt it. The air was suddenly much cooler. Hopefully Carlota had everything ready and did not lose her nerve.

"How much farther?" he asked.

"Five hundred meters."

A minute to run, if they ran for their lives.

"And the water?" he asked.

"Maybe a minute, too."

Then the wave would catch up with them as they were about to board. The engine sputtered. The chair dropped, but caught itself again. A soft landing would only be possible if there was some fuel left for it at the destination. Screw the soft landing. Gravity would bring them down no matter what.

"It's going to be a hard crash," he said.

"Three hundred more feet."

The engine sputtered again. It descended until Jaron pushed the stick forward with all his might. This caused the engine to skip safety mode and also used up the last drops of fuel it would otherwise reserve for landing.

"Two hundred!" shouted Jürgen. "One hundred! Brake now!"

He did not need to brake. The Safer was now dropping down mercilessly. The momentum carried them a little further, then they tumbled onto the flat. The elastic recoil threw them into the air. Jaron released the shoulder harness. On the next impact, he lost the chair. No matter. He got to his feet and ran.

"Hey! Over here!" yelled Jürgen from behind.

Shit. Oh no! Wrong direction. He ran to Jürgen. Together they rushed forward the last few meters. Jürgen was ahead of him on the ladder.

"Come on! Up you go!" shouted Jaron.

He climbed after him. The air was wet. A cool shadow

settled over him from behind. Jürgen pulled him into the airlock. He fell onto all fours. The bulkhead closed with a hiss, and an imaginary fist grabbed him by the neck and pushed him to the floor. Carlota had launched the capsule.

Jaron sat trembling in his armchair. Carlota handed him a cup.

"Peppermint tea," she said.

He smelled it, but there was no aroma. His nose hit the lid, which explained the lack of smell. He put his hand to the mouthpiece and sucked out some of the hot liquid. It felt pleasantly invigorating. Was there a hint of alcohol?

"Tea with a shot?" asked Jürgen.

"Yes, a little," Carlota said. "For a special occasion."

Jaron pulled the control console toward him and opened a radio channel.

"Star Liner to *Truthseeker*," he said. "Come in, please."

"Finally!" exclaimed Celia. "How are you guys doing? I'm so glad you made it."

"A few bruises, but no serious injuries," Jaron said.

"Very good. Do you want me to come back and pick you up?"

"No, there is no need. We're not doing badly at all. We might even end up down there again. After all, the next time the moon passes isn't for another month."

Jürgen shook his head. "I've had enough," he said. "But Celia should go ahead and finish her measurements."

"Okay, then, I'll see you in two or three days," Celia said. "If I get bored, I can analyze your data."

Truthseeker, December 21, 2294

LIGHTNING FLASHED. AN ENORMOUS HURRICANE RACED through the twilight zone that separated the sun-facing side from the back side. Planet C b had a dense atmosphere. That was the next surprise, for they had been expecting a parched lump of dust. The cloud layers did not allow a direct view of the surface, but Celia had managed to use a combination of radar, neutron and gamma-ray spectroscopy to create a relief map of the planet, at least of the side they just passed.

"Is there anything I can do to help?" asked Paul.

Celia shook her head. "I'm at a loss right now."

The shock of yesterday was still in her bones. Hopefully it wasn't a mistake to stay on course for the sun. But Jaron was an experienced pilot. She could trust him.

"Maybe an untrained eye will help. I'm very good at that," Paul said.

Celia moved a bit to the side so Paul could look at the screen, too.

"It looks something like this down there," she said.

The relief map showed only slight differences in elevation. As a result, there were hardly any obstacles for the lower layers of air. The atmosphere took advantage of this opportunity and rotated much faster than the planet, making it look more and more like the solar planet Venus.

"Pretty flat," Paul said.

"With storms constantly racing across the surface, I guess it's no wonder."

"Doesn't look very comfortable."

"Temperatures are reasonably bearable in the transition zone," Celia said. "But the weather is terrible. High humidity, never-ending thunderstorms, and then the constant gales on top of that."

There was no such transition zone on Venus.

"What kind of parallel structures are these?" asked Paul. "Did someone build roads here?"

He was a keen observer. Celia had noticed those lines, too. They were probably fractures in the surface.

"No, it's a natural phenomenon," Celia explained. "We know that from Venus, too. If a planet doesn't have plate tectonics, it has to find a different way to get rid of the forces that are generated by shrinking as it cools. Then the crust breaks into pieces like this."

"But the almost identical spacing of the lines..."

"... merely speaks to a fairly consistent structure of the crust. The stresses are just evenly distributed over it."

That the crust was so consistent also meant that the planet must have cooled very quickly. Otherwise, substances of varying weight in its mantle would have had time to settle and thus sort into different layers. Thus, the planet must have preserved much of the original composition of the proto-solar cloud. If only they could take some soil samples! But here a landing with the capsule was probably too dangerous. She must not even suggest it to Jaron.

"I see. Then this planet is rather boring for you?" asked Paul.

"Not at all," said Celia. "There's something bothering me that I just can't find an explanation for: There's a surprising amount of water in this system."

"Why does that surprise you?"

"After the Big Bang, there was initially only hydrogen and a little helium. All the heavier elements, and that includes the oxygen needed for water, first had to be synthesized in stars. So new stars, formed from the ashes of earlier generations, already had more of these heavy elements available. We measure that in what we call metallicity."

"Ah, then the metallicity of star C must be particularly high, because there is an unusual amount of water here."

"Exactly! That's the strange thing: The metallicity of C is no larger than that of our sun. So apparently, on a cosmic scale, this system hosts too much water."

"Apparently?" asked Paul.

"For an accurate inventory, we'd still have to study all the planets. Or maybe the water here is just distributed differently, more on this side of the ice line than beyond, but somehow I don't think so."

"Ice line?"

"In the protoplanetary disk, water beyond the ice line is in solid form; in front of it, it's gaseous. Solid water, that is, ice, is naturally easier to integrate into a planet. That's why rocky planets are formed on one side of the ice line and icy planets on the other side."

"So the water must have been brought from the back to the front somehow," Paul said.

"Right. In our solar system, it was mainly comets that did that. But here I don't see anything that could do the job. The asteroid belt seems very low dynamic."

"And what does that mean?"

"I don't know. That we don't know enough yet."

Celia pushed the keyboard away. Research could be quite exhausting sometimes. Instead of answers, she kept finding new questions. But there would be time to rest later. Tomorrow they would reach the local sun. So she had better evaluate the data already recorded today. She put the images on the screen, sorted them according to primary wavelengths, and fed them into the stitcher, which superimposed the photos and, if necessary, scaled or corrected them to produce an overall picture of the planet.

The program worked quickly. That meant there was little need for corrections. The crew of the Star Liner capsule had done a really good job. The altitude had remained largely constant despite necessary corrective maneuvers, and Jaron had adjusted the course perfectly to the cameras' coverage area. If Earth scientists ever got to see this data, they would weep with joy. After all, C c was the first exoplanet to be mapped from a low orbit. And in the process, no blind spots had been left.

The first thing she did was evaluate the elevation profiles. Like Earth, the planet had a bulge in the middle. But otherwise, it was much rounder, closer to the ideal spherical shape than her home planet. At the poles, the surface was slightly convex. This should be due to the ice cover. Frozen water expands when it gets colder. But what was that?

Celia distorted the depiction of the North Pole area so that the differences in altitude became more apparent. Now, under the white cap, the shape of a hexagon could be seen. It extended from the pole to about fifty kilometers before the edge of the ice, so it was completely covered by ice. Could there be a hexagonal structure hidden under the polar cap? What could it be? She must not jump to conclusions. There could be different, but certainly natural reasons for such shapes. At Saturn's north pole, for example, cyclones rotated in this pattern. Poles are often special places, also because here the lines of the magnetic field inside the planet disappeared.

It might not even be related to the pole itself, but merely the fact that it was cold there. In the frozen state, water molecules arranged themselves hexagonally in the right circumstances, namely at terrestrial pressure and temperatures a little below the freezing point. Assuming that the water had frozen particularly quickly at the poles of the planet, wouldn't it be possible that the hexagonal structure was integral over the whole area, so to speak? A particularly fast process would certainly be less likely to have had disturbances from the outside.

The homogeneous crust of the inner planet had also solidified in a very short time. Every development in this system seemed to have taken place in a particular hurry. This impression began to make her nervous. Should they not also finish their expedition as quickly as possible?

She must not let herself be influenced by such moods. Celia brought up the data from the South Pole on the screen. The hexagon was not visible at first glance, but when she strongly overemphasized the heights, it became apparent. She magnified the images. The ice over the hexagonal structure did not appear to be very thick. It was no more than fifty meters. If one were to hover in place with the Star Liner capsule for a few minutes, just above the ice, the hot engine plumes should be able to burn a deep enough hole.

Would it be worth it? The crew of the capsule had also run a gamma spectrometer. Celia processed its data. Unfortunately, it was not particularly illuminating. The ice layer was simply too thick. According to the calculations of the evaluation software, the probability that the hexagon was made of a different material than the ice above it was seventy percent, but with a tolerance range of thirty percent. That was definitely not meaningful.

Celia laid the spectrometer data over the sphere of the planet in the holo. There was generally very little activity, due to the vast oceans. The many small islands sparkled like crystals on the dark background. Something was happening there. It must be substances from the interior pushing up to the surface. But her friends had not discovered any volcanoes, had they?

She turned off the holo and straightened up. Her head hurt. She was overwhelmed. It would take an entire research department to solve the mysteries of this solar system. But she only had herself.

"I've cooked us something," Paul said.

He had a plate in his right hand, from which a pleasant aroma wafted. Celia folded the table out of the backrest, and Paul put a white cloth over it with his left hand and set the plate down on it.

"I'll go get more silverware," he said.

Celia looked at the contents of the plate, which were artistically arranged. In the center was a ring of a yellowish mass filled with chunky morsels glistening red and green. Above it was an elongated white something. Everything was sprinkled with fine black and white dots, and a small lake of light sauce had formed toward the edge of the plate.

"Here you go, a knife and fork," Paul said.

She took the silverware from him. Paul had also brought himself a filled plate.

"What are we eating?" asked Celia.

"Steamed cod fillet with zucchini and bell peppers on

mashed potatoes and pumpkin in white wine sauce, seasoned with fresh pepper."

"That sounds delicious," she said.

"The pepper is actually real and freshly ground," Paul said.

Celia took a forkful of the puree. She could clearly smell and taste the aroma of the peppercorns, even though they were, of course, 150 years old. Paul must have assembled the other ingredients from what he had on hand. The fish fillet was somewhat fibrous, but had a distinct fishy flavor and roasted aroma. Paul apparently fried it separately after the food maker formed it. The bell pepper and zucchini pieces unfortunately lacked the crunch of fresh vegetables. It might be hard to create that crunch from a paste. The puree tasted very good. The white wine sauce seemed to have a hint of alcohol in it, tasting more like butter than white wine, but overall, she had not tasted food this good in a long time. A real improvement over what the food maker usually spat out.

"You really pulled that off very well," Celia said. "I'm impressed with what you can conjure up from basic ingredients."

"I worked on the filet for a long time," Paul explained. "The existing base products, unfortunately, completely lack the texture of meat or fish. I mimicked it by first making a kind of fried sauerkraut. I then mixed that with the flavor of fish sauce and some neutral base, made it into the oblong shape and fried it."

"And you came up with that all by yourself?" asked Celia.

"It was an experiment," Paul said. "But it was fun."

"We should make you the ship's cook."

"I've already thought about running for that position. I was going to bribe you with real wine."

"Where did you get that?" asked Celia.

The priest was full of surprises. Or was he just more bored than everyone else?

"By fermentation of a carbohydrate base, plus some fruit flavor at the end. Do you want to taste the wine? I started it a few days ago."

"Thanks, it's very tempting, but I have some work to do after dinner. I'll try it some other time."

"I hereby prescribe a break for you, Celia. You can't be plodding through the whole day."

Celia yawned. Actually, he was right. The data would still be there later. She was going to treat herself to a nap now. Before that, though, she just had to tell Jaron and the others what she had found at the poles of C c.

Planet c, December 21, 2294

One, two, three, four, five, six. Celia was right. Jaron took his hand off the haptic display. There was indeed a hexagonal structure hiding under the ice. He turned off the emphasis on the treble again and then stroked the polar cap with his hand. Now it felt like a fried egg. Was it coincidence or intentional that the hexagon was so well hidden under the ice? And how did Celia come upon it?

Carlota also seemed to be developing in a very positive way, showing unexpected abilities. Just the way she'd managed the emergency launch of the capsule without any training as a pilot—that was a real achievement, especially in terms of timing. Of course, she must have been scared when the water came rolling towards the ship. Jaron had been afraid himself. But she stayed calm and waited until the last moment instead of jumping to safety by herself.

"I think we should investigate," Jürgen said.

"Despite our experience with this planet?" asked Jaron.

He was actually in favor of a trip to the pole, too, but

only if Jürgen and Carlota were there of their own free will. He did not want to pressure them into anything.

"Neither the North Pole nor the South Pole are flood plains," Carlota said.

"But that doesn't apply if there's a super flood," Jaron said.

Presumably, these events were what caused there to be an ice sheet over the hexagon in the first place. That would argue against a willful hiding of the structure.

"The next one is not expected for several weeks," Carlota said.

"Do we have enough fuel left?" asked Jaron. "We need to be able to hover above the surface for a while and then launch back into orbit."

"It won't fail for lack of fuel," said Jürgen. "The capsule has only used a third of its capacity."

"Then I don't see anything wrong with it," Jaron said. "We've flown this far to find the maker of this star cluster, so we might as well do some digging in the eternal ice."

"Maybe God had something like a temple built down there," said Jürgen.

"If so, it would be a church," Carlota said. "But it doesn't look like it to me."

"Hey, a couple of thousand years ago, he did go in for temples," Jürgen said. "The church thing came later."

Carlota did not answer, but swallowed audibly. They must not forget that the Catholic Church had chosen her. Most certainly, she had the firm faith that the priest had lost.

"I'm setting course for the North Pole," Jaron said.

"NOTHING TO SEE," SAID JÜRGEN.

Jaron mirrored the camera image onto the haptic screen. He could not feel the hexagon, but that was to be expected. His display, after all, had a lower resolution than the others' sense of sight.

"It's there," Carlota said. "The radar image is very clear."

The capsule was in a very low orbit so they could get higher resolution.

"Are there any substructures?" asked Jaron.

He imagined the hexagon as a huge hangar under the ice where aliens had parked their spaceships. In that case, it would be good to land directly above an entrance. The thruster would clear a path down, but they would have to dig their own way sideways.

"So far, I don't see anything," Carlota said.

Unfortunately, that did not mean much. After all, the radar could not see through the ice. It only detected the cap that had formed over the hexagon. If it really was formed by the super tides, it would have to be completely smooth, although the structure underneath might have height differences. It would look different if the ice cover had formed from years of snowfall, as it did on Earth.

"There are some very fine lines," Carlota said. "Probably cracks."

Ah, that was new!

"Could they have formed because there are temperature differences under the ice sheet?" asked Jaron.

Ice with differing temperatures had differing volume, so there must be stresses. That would indicate that the hidden structure was somehow active.

"Maybe," Carlota said. "Or by stresses in the planetary crust due to the rapid cooling of the planet."

Nothing was clear here; everything left room for interpretation. That allowed him to imagine aliens, while Paul had the same right to think of God.

"We're about to reach the edge of the plane," Jaron said. "I suggest we take a look at the South Pole."

"Agreed," Jürgen and Carlota said almost simultaneously.

IN THE SOUTH, THE HEXAGON WAS MORE VISIBLE. AT LEAST that was what the other two said. On the haptic display, the south pole was a cow patty, not as regular as the north pole and much flatter. This probably made the hexagonal structure stand out a little better.

"Are there cracks here, too?" asked Jaron.

"Yes, it looks like it," said Carlota. "Even in slightly higher density than in the north."

The South Pole seemed to have a slightly warmer climate than the North Pole. As a result, its ice sheet was thinner and more prone to cracking.

"We should definitely land here," Jürgen said. "That way, when we drill through the ice sheet with the thruster, we save about one-sixth of the fuel."

"Yeah, it's just a question of where," Jaron said.

"Anywhere," said Jürgen.

"I'd like to have a reason to pick a specific place to do it," Jaron said.

"But we'd have to be able to see under the ice to do that," said Carlota.

"'Then maybe we'll select the edge,'" Jaron said. "If there are entrances and exits, they'll be there."

"Do you really think so?" asked Jürgen. "Mightn't it be more interesting in the middle?"

Well, that was the prize question. Theoretically, they could look everywhere. But to do so, they would first have to refuel, which was only possible with the help of the *Truth-seeker*, but it would not get back here for another three days.

"We'll take the edge," Jaron said.

"Where exactly?" asked Jürgen.

"We'll just follow our route."

"Roger that, captain. I'll adjust course."

THE SHIP VIBRATED. JARON HAD TO LEAN FORWARD FROM the backrest, because otherwise he would be shaken. The engine roared louder with each passing minute, as it blasted a tunnel deeper and deeper into the depths. At the beginning, Jaron heard a high-pitched whistle. Now it was a moderate hum, and at the end he expected a deep humming sound. It was like blowing into an instrument that kept getting bigger.

"Twenty meters," said Carlota, who was tracking the radar readings.

"The engine has clearly heated up," Jürgen said, "but it's still in the green range."

The capsule slowly sank into the hole being bored by its hot exhaust jet. However, it was suspended in hot water vapor as it did so, which caused the engines to heat up even more. As a result, Jaron had to give the capsule a rest every now and then.

"Twenty-three meters," said Carlota.

Jaron corrected a little. The capsule sank three meters lower. If it was too far from the ice, the exhaust jet lost effectiveness.

"We're yellow now," Jürgen said.

That meant he had about three minutes until he had to

give the engine a break. Jaron set himself a timer. Just before it expired, he gave it extra thrust. The capsule shot up a few feet to above the ice, where the hot steam cooled quickly.

"Give the engine a minute to rest," Jürgen said. "You guys really need to take a look out the porthole."

"What's there?" asked Jaron.

"Nothing," said Carlota. "That's just it. We're in the middle of a dense cloud. Looking at the way the radar is refracted here, we've already created a pretty tall vapor plume."

That meant as they drilled, they could be seen from a great distance and even from space. But no one seemed interested in what they were doing. To Jaron, it felt as if they had broken into a supermarket in broad daylight and were helping themselves from all the shelves while security was asleep.

"I'm going back down," Jaron said.

"Confirmed," said Jürgen. "The engine will now hold out for a few more minutes."

Jaron reduced the thrust, and they sank into the hole they had dug for themselves. Beeps came from the headset in rapid succession. Before the continuous tone turned on, Jaron increased the thrust again.

"Eight meters," Carlota said. "That was close."

"Yeah, I'm getting bored. I want to finally get there," Jaron said. "How much ice is left?"

"Only ten more meters," said Carlota.

"CAREFUL NOW," CARLOTA SAID. "WE'RE ALMOST THERE."

"Careful doesn't work," Jaron said. "If I cut off the thrust, we'll crash."

"I see. Then we should dig through the last meter ourselves."

"Oh, do we have to?" Jürgen complained. "Chopping ice is a pain in the ass."

"Do you know what the material down there is made of?" asked Carlota. "I don't know, and we don't want to break anything."

"Carlota is right," Jaron said. "We have to be careful. If this is an artificial structure, I'm sure its owner won't be happy if we destroy it."

He pushed the thrust lever forward. The capsule moved upward. The frequency of the beeps dropped.

"What are you doing?" asked Jürgen.

"I'm landing."

"Outside the hole? Then we'll have to climb down it."

"The hole is so narrow, we could hardly get out of the ship at the bottom," said Jaron. "Besides, I'm worried about the stability of the ice. We can't endanger the capsule."

"Understood," said Jürgen.

When he climbed down the ladder, Jaron landed in a deep puddle. Jürgen had already warned him.

"Over here!" shouted Jürgen.

He waded through the water, which must reach almost to the top of his boots. The ground was slippery. Jaron was wearing the lower half of his spacesuit, but he still did not want to fall in. His upper body was protected by a thick jacket, but he would prefer to take it off. Here, near the edge of the ice sheet, the sun was already quite warm, although it was very low in the sky.

"Take my arm," Carlota said.

Jaron reached out. Carlota pulled him toward her. The

last step was clearly upward. Apparently, the pod's thruster had dug a small depression where the water now stood.

"Will that cause us problems later?" asked Jaron.

"Because the water will freeze again?" asked Jürgen. "No, it's only twenty centimeters. We'll chop it away around the ship, and then the engine will definitely be able to handle it."

"Okay. So an emergency start won't be possible this time," Jaron said. "Is that a good idea?"

"The next super-tide is a long time away," Carlota said. "What else would force us to do an emergency launch?"

What else, the famous last words. But Jaron could not think of a reason either, so he nodded, even though he had a bad feeling about it.

"I'll hand the axe to you," Jürgen said.

Jaron nodded again. It was a deal. Jürgen would take him on his back as he descended. In return, Jaron would carry the heavy axe. Carlota, who did not have much experience in alpine climbing, would follow them and secure them. Now she moved her arm. Jaron, holding on to her upper arm, followed her. The ice here was not quite as smooth as in the meltwater lake, but it was not as rough as glacier ice, either. Recurrent flooding must have formed the ice cover. If this hexagon was artificial, why did they build it in a place that was not flood-proof? Whoever was capable of building such a huge structure could also evaluate the risks. So it must have been intentional. Jaron shook his head. His thoughts were two steps ahead again.

"What is it?" asked Carlota.

She must have noticed his head shake, though he was walking a little behind her.

"I was just thinking about something. But it's far from relevant."

"Stop!" exclaimed Carlota, grabbing his shoulder.

He had not paid attention for a moment and kept walking, even though she had stopped.

"Now we're going to be heading downhill," she said.

"I see," Jaron said.

"Pretty deep," said Jürgen.

Forty meters, that was about thirteen stories.

"That's a stone's throw for you, isn't it?" asked Jaron. "The summit yesterday was much higher."

"Believe it or not, I find it more difficult to descend into dark depths than to climb into light heights. But technically, it's not a problem. You just have to do what I tell you."

IT WORKED, BUT IT WAS EXHAUSTING. THE AXE ON HIS BACK sometimes swung uncomfortably, but while they were hanging on the wall, there was nothing they could do about it. Until Jaron thought of a solution—he simply took it off and dropped it. A clink indicated that it had arrived safely at the bottom.

"Sometimes one just doesn't think of the obvious solution," said Jürgen.

I wonder if the same is true for the secret of the hexagon. Jaron looked down and waited for the glasses to tell him the remaining height. Damn. He forgot he had lost them yesterday during the rescue operation.

"Jürgen?"

"Whew, yeah, boss?"

Jürgen stopped, panting. Jaron helped out by using the handles the engineer had been pounding into the ice, but Jürgen was doing most of the work.

"Sorry, I didn't mean to disturb you."

"Don't worry. I need a break once in a while."

"Good, do you think you can build me something that will acoustically tell me what's going on around me? Unfortunately, I lost my tracker yesterday."

"Ah, the glasses you used to wear? I was wondering why you'd forgo them today. "

"Yes, that was the tracker."

"I don't know if I can make one that small," Jürgen said. "But a wide-angle camera for your forehead that uses object detection to tell you about obstacles acoustically, I should be able to do that."

"Thanks," Jaron said. "That would be great."

Jürgen continued to climb down. Jaron felt the pull of the short rope that connected them. He felt down at an angle. There was the handle. Although Jaron was wearing gloves, it felt cold. Where was the step for the foot? There, right where he expected it to be. Jürgen was a good trailblazer. How would he manage without him?

Finally on the ground, Jaron's upper arm muscles in particular were aching. Jürgen patted him down.

"You've got ice dust all over you from climbing," he said.

Jaron went to the axe. It was right where he thought it would be because of the sound it made when it fell. He picked it up.

"Now what?" he asked.

"Now we chop our way down to the structure," Jürgen said.

"I'll start," Jaron said. "I saved a lot of my strength going down."

"Go ahead," said Jürgen. "Turn twenty more degrees to the left, and then have at it!"

"You bet I will."

Jaron turned as Jürgen described, raised the axe over his head, and slammed it hard against the ground. Chunks of ice spattered from the impact. It did not sound as clear as he expected. Ice vibrated differently than glass. He lifted the axe again, provided force, then crunch. He lifted the axe, swung, then crunch. The rhythm was quickly established. Jaron initially worked his way forward in a narrow channel. When he hit the wall for the first time, he walked back to the beginning, moved a little to the right and started again.

In this way, he cut a channel about a meter wide into the ground. That would have to be enough for him for now. After the second pass, it was already knee-deep. Then Carlota took over. She was no slower than he was. In fact, she even struck a little faster, but achieved less force. She deepened the trench to sixty centimeters. Then it was Jürgen's turn. He set to work with fresh vigor—faster than Carlota and with more force than Jaron.

But Jaron was the first to notice that they had reached their destination. The sound of the axe on the ice suddenly changed. It was only a tiny meeting of the metal of the cutting edge with the changed ground, but Jaron heard it clearly.

"Stop!" he called out. "You're through!"

"No, everything here is still full of ice," Jürgen said.

Jaron went over to him, knelt on the ground and felt around. He found large and small shards of ice, a thin layer of ice with deep gouges in it, and blood in one of them. Crap. The liquid, clearly warmer than the ice, really felt like blood. He pressed the tip of his right thumb into it. What had Carlota said? The molecules here were biochemically incompatible with his body. So surely they could not kill him. He licked the fingertip. The liquid tasted like nothing.

"What are you doing?" asked Carlota.

"I'm testing to see what that stuff is that Jürgen dug out of the ice with the axe."

"By licking it off? Have you taken leave of your senses? Are you trying to kill yourself?"

"You said that the life here can't harm us."

"The life, the bacteria! But what if you just licked potassium cyanide? That's the same, deadly substance everywhere in space."

"I ..."

He flushed with embarrassment. That had really been pretty stupid of him.

"Don't worry," Carlota said. "You'd feel something by now."

"I just thought ... It felt like blood," Jaron said. "You see, Jurgen? You seem to have scratched something there."

"We'll have to start using smaller tools," Jürgen said. "But it's not blood, as green as it looks."

"Green blood? Why not, actually?" asked Jaron.

"Not likely," said Carlota.

He heard her voice close by. She must have crouched down next to him. Something was scraping on the floor. Presumably, she was examining the spot.

"Try wiping the mass off your finger, please," she said.

Jaron wiped his finger first on the floor, then on the fabric of his spacesuit.

"Is it off?" he asked, holding up his thumb.

"No," Carlota said. "It's still nice and green."

"Great."

"Hey, you should be happy. You'll finally have a green thumb," Jürgen said.

"I've never wanted a green thumb," said Jaron.

"It's a saying back home," Jürgen said. "Having a green thumb means having a talent for gardening."

"Does anyone here have a talent for cleaning, perhaps?" asked Carlota. "I'd like to really expose the soil."

"So what's up with the stuff on my thumb?"

"I suspect it's some kind of sealant. Jürgen damaged the surface with the axe. But look. It's already smooth as before."

FOR HALF AN HOUR THEY WERE BUSY COMPLETELY CLEARING the ground of ice. Carlota was probably right. Green liquid was no longer leaking out. There was a hard, brown surface under the ice. But it was not as hard as, say, metal. Jaron ran his bare fingers over it. It felt like a thin leather coating on wood. He tapped on it. The thumping sounded dull.

"There's no cavity," Jürgen said. "I've tried that, too."

"Maybe the coating is just really thick," Jaron said. "After all, it's supporting over forty meters of ice. The construction would have to be strong enough to do that."

"Who says someone built this?" asked Carlota.

"It feels pretty damn artificial. What does it look like?" asked Jaron.

"What if it was the shell of a giant tortoise?" asked Carlota. "I think they feel pretty much the same. Did you notice that the material is warm?"

A turtle, ha-ha. But she was right, actually. It was not good to make definite assumptions too early. One tended to find what one was looking for. Jaron stroked the ground with his palm. It really was warm. But then why hadn't the ice above it melted? Shouldn't the pressure of the ice above have melted the bottom layer? They hadn't noticed anything like that.

"Could it be that the ground is warming up?" asked Jürgen. "Earlier, when I had just put the axe away, it was still quite icy."

"There was plenty of ice lying around, too," said Jaron.

"No, Jürgen is right," said Carlota. "I also have the feeling that the layer is heating up."

"Oh, come on, guys. Do you really think there's a heater in here? I don't think that's likely. We just removed forty meters of ice! We would have encountered a lot more meltwater."

"Maybe it didn't turn on until we uncovered it," Carlota said.

"You were right to warn me earlier not to jump to conclusions, Carlota," Jaron said. "And now you're starting to do it yourself. I can tell you what heater turned on down here. It was us! A human body puts out about a hundred watts of heat. That's three hundred watts from us. You don't feel the difference with ice, but you sure do with this woody surface."

"Okay, you may be right," Jürgen said. "You shouldn't underestimate the heating power of three people. But if we want to know if there's anything underneath, I guess we'll have to look."

"You want to dig through the material?" asked Carlota.

"Yes. It seems to me to be suitable for that. If it really has the strength of wood, we should make good progress."

"However, if it is a construct after all, the designers won't be happy about it," said Jaron.

"Do you see anyone watching us? Even if someone is secretly watching us from orbit, we're now in a hole forty meters deep."

"If this is a turtle, it's not going to be thrilled about us damaging its shell, either," Carlota said. "But I admit that there's still a slightly higher chance that Jürgen's explanation is correct."

"Then you're for it?" asked Jaron.

"Before we leave here empty-handed, I think we should try to drill a hole," said Carlota.

"Then it's a good thing I brought the right tools," said Jürgen.

THE BROWN SURFACE WAS REALLY SOMETHING. JÜRGEN could not stop cursing. He must be green all over, because the material reacted to every injury with a new spurt of the green liquid. A self-healing system; that could well be a sign of life.

On the other hand, the reaction was fully automatic. Carlota had measured—the output of healing fluid always corresponded exactly to the depth of the injury. But the system did not check whether the healing was successful. That was what allowed them to go deeper. Jaron used the electric blower from the lower part of his spacesuit to blow the fluid away from the spot where it was discharged, guided by Jürgen. It could not do any harm anywhere else. If it landed on the wood, it seeped back in. On ice, however, it quickly turned brown and began to stink. It smelled like rotten eggs, causing Jaron to wish for the time when he only had to smell the others' sweat.

Nevertheless, Jürgen's progress was slow. He was trying to drive a wedge into the horizontal surface. So far, he had reached a depth of about twenty centimeters. Carlota had already collected samples of the material. Between her fingers, they felt like wood chips. Carlota had set a small portion of the chips on fire: The chips burned. However, when she held the torch lighter directly against the main mass, the fire was immediately extinguished by the green liquid.

"I don't feel like we're getting significantly deeper," Jaron said. "Sometimes you have to realize when you've lost."

"I can do it," said Jürgen. "Listen, it's starting to sound a lot different than it did before."

"Pock-pock," he heard.

The sound seemed familiar to him. Jaron knocked where Jürgen had not dug.

"Pock-pock."

"I don't hear any difference," Jaron said.

"I do," Jürgen said.

One always heard what one wanted to hear. Oh well, Jürgen could just let off steam. They would get used to the smell of rotten eggs at some point. But what did that say about what was hiding underneath them? This liquid was a clever idea. But it seemed to assume that nothing would stop the system from curing itself. That is, its creators— which could include evolution—did not assume that there might be enemies. The fluid merely protected against damage by natural processes, not against vandalism of the kind they were currently engaged in. Or there was a reaction to enemies definitely planned, but it worked differently, and they had not triggered it yet.

What if they had already triggered the reaction? Jaron looked up, but other than a current of cool air, he sensed nothing. What kind of danger could be coming their way? In any case, the way from below was blocked. So the defense could only come from above. On the other hand, they were dealing with a structure under a thick layer of ice. How could it possibly harm them? Jaron shook his head. He was worrying for nothing.

"What is it?" asked Carlota. "You seem thoughtful."

"I've just been thinking about different things," he said evasively.

"I can relate to that," Carlota said.

"Jürgen still seems to want to let off steam here," Jaron said.

"Uh-huh. Whew," Jürgen said.

"What do you think, Carlota, about going up to examine the samples from the shaft that we already have?" asked Jaron. "I'd really be very interested in what we're dealing with here."

"You're worried, aren't you?" asked Carlota.

"I just prefer to be on the safe side."

Actually, he was not like that at all in his personal life. He liked to take risks when it was just him. It must be that stupid responsibility one felt as a captain, but as a captain he was now responsible not only for himself, but also for the others.

"Good idea. I'm just standing around here anyway," Carlota said.

"But then you won't be here when I'm through the damn floor," Jürgen said. "Whew."

"Can you make the climb?" asked Jaron. "Please don't get me wrong, I trust you with anything, but if I remember correctly, you're a beginner."

"That shouldn't be a problem," said Jürgen. "I've installed a pulley with a small motor upstairs. So Carlota can get help from that, and the steps are already in the wall now."

"You're a sly fox," said Jaron.

"I've been thinking that we might have to go up and down more often, and the climb is pretty strenuous."

"Thanks," said Carlota. "I'll radio you when I get the first results."

Jürgen really did have stamina; Jaron had to hand it to him. He was working like a man possessed to deepen the hole. In the meantime, he was already at a depth of more than a meter, which did not make the work any easier. He hung his upper body into the hole and slammed downward. Whenever some of the healing fluid accumulated, he scooped it up and handed it to Jaron, who disposed of it in an ice hole on the opposite wall of the shaft. This way it didn't smell as bad, Jaron thought, but maybe he had just gotten used to it. The small compressed air tank in his spacesuit had run out a while ago, so they had to switch to manual disposal. But at least this way he got some exercise.

"Would you like me to relieve you for a while?" he asked.

"No, it's my job now," Jürgen said. "Besides, it will only take longer if you do it."

"Hey, I can hit the ground as well as you can, even blind." Jaron said. "You can't tell me you see anything down there, can you?"

"You're right again. My goggles are covered with green sauce. I don't think I'll ever get them clean again. But it's enough for one of us to get soaked like this."

"Well, suit yourself, then."

"I appreciate the offer, boss. I really do. But I got myself into this, and now I'm spooning up the soup, too. Bowl by bowl. Here, have a new serving."

Jaron reached toward the spot at the edge of the hole where Jürgen always set the filled bowls, picked up the bowl, and carried it on his knees to the other side.

"Hey, boys, can you hear me?"

Carlota's voice came from nearby, but was hard to

locate in the round shaft with its echoes. Jaron fumbled around until he found the headset. He could not remember, but he must have set it down earlier.

"Jaron here. I can hear you. What's up?"

"First off, shame on all of us. We forgot to activate the capsule's relay function. In the meantime, Celia's been in touch. Needless to say, she was very worried when we didn't respond."

Oh, they had promised to do that after not thinking of it yesterday.

"You should apologize on behalf of all of us," Jaron said.

"I already have, of course," Carlota said. "She's not angry with us. She told me to tell you that she has begun her investigation of the sun."

"Did you tell her about our failure?" asked Jaron.

"Ugh. Hey!" Jürgen complained.

"I mean, about the difficulties we're facing."

"Just briefly. We'll exchange ideas more intensively when the *Truthseeker* gets back here. Celia thinks she might be able to look deeper into the ice with the spacecraft's ground-penetrating radar, and neutron and gamma spectrometer."

"That would definitely be helpful," Jaron said. "And your research?"

"Very interesting," Carlota said. "It was definitely worth it to go down."

"So?"

"The material Jürgen is chiseling off the thing is made of similar structures as the island we landed on. Thick cell walls, the functions of the core are distributed along the inside of the cell walls, and the inside is filled with silica."

"So the hexagon grew here, too," Jaron said.

"Yes. It's just a question of whether it was grown or

grew by itself," said Carlota.

"It's probably not a tank, then."

"It's not impossible that there's something underneath it. But I think it's more likely to be a massive stump."

"A stump? So something was chopped off here?"

"I can't prove it," Carlota said. "It is, as I said, a feeling. Why else would this thing be under the ice?"

"Because we're here at the pole, where there is, well, lots of ice?"

"That would be one explanation, of course."

"And what did you find out about the healing fluid?" asked Jaron.

"It contains an activated form of the same cells, and in a colorful mixture. The fascinating thing is that these cells are able to arrange themselves into the optimal, in this case, the densest arrangement. They are like a puzzle that assembles itself. So they can fill any injury with fresh material."

"Do you have any idea how they do that?"

"No, sorry," Carlota said. "It must have something to do with their inner workings. They lack the silica filling. Instead, they house a very exotic mixture of hydrogen sulfide and iron ions."

"Maybe the iron is magnetized, and they stick together like permanent magnets."

"An interesting idea. I'll test that. It may also have something to do with their external shape. It makes little sense that they all look so different. That's the kind of diversity a biological system has to be able to afford."

"I'm sure you'll figure it out," Jaron said.

"Have fun down there, then," said Carlota.

"Did you hear that, Jürgen?"

"Whew, mm-hm."

Jürgen continued his work. He seemed to be desperate

to reach the underground.

"Here, a new bowl," Jürgen said.

Was he mistaken, or had the engineer slowed down? Jaron had disposed of the last bowl of healing liquid quite a while ago.

"How are you getting on?" he asked.

"Slowly. I have to expand the hole first so I can stand in it and work in it. Who would have guessed that the layer is more than two meters thick?"

"We all guessed it would be. It just sounds massive," Jaron said. "You're not going to hit a cavity, I'm afraid."

"I just have the feeling that the sound has changed as I work," said Jürgen.

"Yeah, because you're in your own little shaft by now."

Suddenly Jaron heard a rumble, and fine needles of ice fell onto his neck.

"Shit, what was that?" he asked.

"What was what?" asked Jürgen.

"Didn't you just hear that boom?"

"No, I didn't hear anything."

"Carlota here, please come in!"

Jaron was wearing the headset this time. "Jaron here. Did you hear it too?"

"I didn't hear anything," Carlota said. "But I did see a disturbance."

"You saw?"

"I was just looking through the microscope when all of a sudden the cells started shaking all over the place. The ship also registered a vibration. It was very faint, but of course it could be a first warning sign of something bigger."

"Did you hear that, Jürgen? Maybe we're in for an earthquake."

"Because for a moment the ground shook a little? When I lived in California..."

"But this isn't California," Carlota said. "We haven't measured any seismic activity at all yet."

"Besides, we're in a forty-meter-deep shaft in the ice," Jaron said. "Even a slight tremor could cause everything to collapse."

"Oh, now, don't get so panicky. I'm sure I'll be through soon. Then we'll take a quiet look at what's inside the tank and climb back into the ship much smarter than before."

"Jürgen, I'm sorry, but the risk is too great from my point of view. We need to abort mission down here."

Perhaps it was the system's backlash because of the deep injury Jürgen had been inflicting on it all day. But Jaron said nothing. Now he had to be the captain who got his people to safety when necessary.

"Do you hear me?" he asked.

"Uh-huh."

"Come on, that's enough. We can come back tomorrow, if the movements haven't increased by then."

As if they had heard him, the shaft walls suddenly shook, and lumps up to the size of a fist came crashing down on Jaron. That should make Jürgen give in.

"Okay, you're probably right," Jürgen said. "Even if I hate to admit it."

Jürgen had always been honest.

Despite the rumbles, they calmly climbed up the ice wall. Jürgen had hooked Jaron onto the pulley so that he flew up almost by himself. He just had to shimmy from step to step. Jürgen himself climbed without support. This helped him straighten out his back, which was hunched over from digging, he said.

When they were about halfway up, another tremor jolted them. The step under Jaron's right foot came loose and fell to the ice below with a thud. After that Jaron climbed a bit faster, and reached the edge of the shaft well ahead of Jürgen. Carlota helped him up. Jaron took stock of the situation. There was no longer any sign of the warming sun. Instead, a frosty wind blew, quickly cooling the sweat on his back.

A hand landed on his back.

"Thanks, boss," Jürgen said. "I guess it really was better that we crawled out of our hole."

AFTER A SHORT SHOWER, JARON FELT MUCH BETTER. THE tremors seemed to have settled down to a constant strength and frequency. About every five minutes, the spaceship shook for a few seconds. The emergency start program was activated to be on the safe side. They could get away within a few seconds, should it prove necessary. But for the moment, there did not seem to be any major danger.

"Actually, it's normal for such a young planet to release tension," Carlota said. "What's stranger is that we didn't notice it sooner."

"So you don't think it has anything to do with our activity?" asked Jaron.

"Activity? What activity?" asked Jürgen, who must have just stepped out of the shower, because Jaron could feel the warm steam.

"Why don't you put some clothes on?" Carlota said. "At least a towel."

"I didn't want to get our laundry dirty," Jürgen said. "Because of the green sauce, you know."

"I don't think that's going to rub off. The green stuff seems to stick to you pretty tight. Let me see."

Jaron heard a rustle.

"See, nothing's rubbing off," Carlota said. "Here, take this towel."

"You think? That would suck. I don't want to stay green all my life!"

"We'll get around that. I might be able to formulate something that will dissolve that stuff. But that will take some time. We don't want to dissolve your skin. It's best to look on the bright side."

"Bright side? You mean that I look like the Hulk?" asked Jürgen.

"Well, with your build, you're still missing quite a bit. Whereas..."

"Ouch," said Jürgen.

"But you've got a good head on your shoulders," Carlota continued. "On the other hand, feel your skin! You've never had so few wrinkles. The green liquid seems to have tried to repair your surface."

"You think so? We should take a sample back to Earth. We'll revolutionize the beauty industry."

"I'm skeptical about that. Very few people like to be green in the face, neck or breasts."

"Say, any of you guys feel like going for a little ride?" asked Jaron.

While the two were talking, his mind once again wandered off into the distance—to the very edge of the hexagon. Shouldn't the effects of the quakes, if any, be best observed there?

"Oh, I don't know," said Jürgen. "I need something in my stomach first."

"In the middle of the night?" asked Carlota.

"It's all the same to me," said Jaron. "And it's only a few hundred meters."

SNOW HAD BEGUN TO FALL AS THEY EXITED THE CAPSULE via the ladder. Jaron felt it as a thin layer of snowflakes that had settled on the rungs, twice interrupted by the prints of his shoes. He also felt it when he lifted his face to the sky so that fine flakes fell on his forehead and cheeks, where they dissolved into water in seconds. He stuck out his tongue to taste the water. It tasted, as expected, of nothing at all.

"I wonder if it's related to the shocks?" asked Carlota, who accompanied him.

"I wouldn't imagine so," Jaron replied. "But it must be a rare event. Otherwise, the ground wouldn't be so smooth."

He stopped and scraped the ice with the sole of his foot. It was not very slippery, but it was not made of hard-packed snow, either.

"Maybe it's because of the low elevations on the planet," Carlota said. "If clouds do form, there's nowhere for them to rain. So they drift around the globe until the sun eventually dissipates them."

"A world without rain," Jaron said. "Is that even possible? Warm air absorbs a lot of moisture, doesn't it?"

He reached for Carlota's upper arm, and they walked slowly along. It was a pleasant walk in fresh, but not freezing, air. Jürgen was missing out.

"If it's evenly distributed, which is likely given the vast ocean, and the same is true for the condensation nuclei, the drops may not collect into clouds at all, but rain down evenly. Then you have a water cycle, and you don't even see it."

"That's possible," Jaron said. "Then maybe the snowfall today is related to the super-tide. There must have been a lot of moisture released into the atmosphere off schedule."

"I like that theory," Carlota said. "Here at the poles, as the temperature drops, so does the air's ability to absorb moisture. The water vapor condenses and freezes. However, because the super-floods are rare, it also rarely snows."

The ground seemed to be gradually sloping. Jaron caught himself clutching Carlota's arm tighter. He loosened his grip again. There was no danger of him slipping. When they reached the slope, Carlota would stop on her own. Still, he missed his long walking stick.

"Why did you actually come on this journey?" he asked, trying to distract himself from his fears.

"Because I was asked to," Carlota said.

Jaron did not comment on the answer, because he had a feeling there was more to come. They kept walking through the falling snow.

"To be honest, I was also very happy about the request. It came at just the right moment. Otherwise, I would have —who knows?"

Jaron nodded. It was nice to see Carlota come out of her shell a bit.

"I'm here because I wanted to pay for Jürgen's friend's cancer treatment," he said. "But that's not the only reason, I suppose. Of course, it's good to know that Norbert is getting better. Got better. Who knows? Jürgen doesn't want to know, after all. But actually, I have something to prove to myself. That I'm at least as good as the others."

"As the sighted," said Carlota.

"Yes and no. As my father. When it was clear that I was

going to go blind before I even started school, he stopped treating me like a person and started treating me like a defective machine. He tried everything to get the damage repaired. I got through school okay, thought I was doing my thing pretty well, but it wasn't enough for him. How good could I have been if that hadn't happened? I don't know. I only became a pilot because of that. Actually, I had always wanted to be a gardener."

"I'm sorry to hear that," Carlota said.

Jaron was annoyed at himself. Just as Carlota was opening up, he took the opportunity to spill his own guts. That was not a good thing to do.

"What did this trip save you from?" he asked.

"I was always the best at everything," Carlota said. "Yet I didn't even try very hard. That's why I always thought that one day I would become something very special. The next pope, Nobel Prize winner for medicine, Olympic champion in swimming, head of a billion-dollar corporation that solved humanity's problems. That kind of thing. What prodigies become."

"Piano soloist with the New York Philharmonic."

"I was never very musical, and I'm not very good at cooking either, much to my mother's chagrin. Oh well. And here I was, almost thirty, and nothing had come of it. True, I was a doctor in a church hospital, swam races at the state level on weekends, and had founded a company that was developing a new kind of laser scalpel. But that was about it. I was very good at a lot of things, but not world-class at anything. I think that's how a lot of highly talented people feel. I just didn't feel like focusing enough on a particular subject to be better at it than anyone else."

"That's frustrating," Jaron agreed.

"I know it sounds like a luxury problem," Carlota said, stopping. "Anyone else would be happy to have made it through medical school or started a business. But I just couldn't let go of those expectations of myself."

"Sometimes you're your own worst enemy,"

"That's true. It wore me down." Carlota's voice softened. She probably turned away from him. Because she was crying and instinctively didn't want him to see her tears. "I was beating myself up. But then the request came. Through the church. I worked in a church setting, and my boss knew I was always looking for challenges and didn't have a family." Carlota sniffled for a moment. What should he do? Hand her a tissue, give her a hug? Just be there?

"They were looking for someone like me, a doctor who could take on anything and be willing to learn all that was needed in a short period of time in an alien star system," Carlota continued. "It was really my salvation. I've come to the right place. It's like HE arranged this trip especially for me."

"Yes, you really are a perfect fit," Jaron said.

"Thank you. It means a lot to me that you say that. It may seem strange to you, what I'm saying."

"No, not at all. It's all very understandable."

"I mean, when I talk about gratitude to God."

"I actually can't do much with that," Jaron said. "But I can very well imagine that, given what's going on here, one might have such thoughts. In any case, I very much wish for Paul that his search will be successful."

"I'm skeptical about that." Carlota had apparently regained her composure, because she turned to him again. "Surely there are forces at work here that go far beyond our horizons. But whether they have anything to do with God? He will find that only in himself."

"It's strange, but Paul once told me that his bishop advised him to do exactly the same thing. I guess it's sort of the standard response for people who have lost their faith. Please don't take offense."

"Of course not. It's also a somewhat ... simplistic answer. Paul certainly looked within himself first and foremost. I wouldn't know how to advise him. Paul obviously has a fair amount of anger toward God, and utterly to the bone. God took his family away from him. I would certainly resent Him for that, too. But it's in the past and can't be undone. Maybe he has to learn to forgive God. He still has faith in Him; otherwise he couldn't have so much anger towards him in his belly. Could you be angry with God?"

Jaron shook his head. "He does his thing, and I do mine. God and I, we live in different worlds, I feel like."

"That's an interesting way of looking at it, too."

The ground vibrated. He heard a rumble, as if a thunderstorm was unloading just beyond the horizon.

"Do you hear that, too?" he asked.

"Yes," Carlota said.

"I wonder what it's doing to the ice cap over the hexagon."

"We could go see."

"Doesn't it go down too steeply?" he asked.

"No, it's maybe thirty degrees. I brought a flashlight with me. It looks like a steep ramp that tapers off comfortably at the bottom."

"The perfect toboggan slope," he said.

"Toboggan slope?" she asked.

Ah, she had grown up in a tropical part of the world. Presumably, Carlota had never sat on a toboggan.

"The trail is clear? No deep crevasses or anything?" he asked.

"Nothing to see," she said.

Jaron dropped down on his hindquarters.

"Then come sit in front of me. Trust me."

Carlota settled down in front of him. He held her by the shoulder with one hand and pushed off with the other. It worked. They slid down the slope on the seat of their pants. The ride got faster and faster. Snow dust sprayed his face. His hands were cold, but his face was warm.

"That was fun," Carlota said when they reached the bottom.

They shook the snow off their clothes. Now Jaron was freezing. He should have at least brought gloves.

"Did you do this a lot when you were kids?" she asked.

"Every day after school in the winter."

In first grade, he had still been able to see where he was going. Later, he had focused on hearing. Kids who were not acquainted with him had always assumed he wore dark glasses out of vanity and bravado, until they got to know him better.

The ground under them vibrated.

"Look," Carlota said. "Uh, I mean, I see something there."

"I don't have a problem with phrases like that, by the way," Jaron said. "What do you see?"

Carlota moved a few steps away. He followed the sound.

"There's a horizontal crevasse in the ice," she said.

"Oh, exciting! Jürgen will be annoyed that he didn't come along. How deep is it?"

"Deep. Come on, I'll show you."

They climbed a few meters up the slope. There, Carlota guided his hand down. There was in fact a crevice there. Jaron knelt in front of it and felt his way in. He could not find an end. There was enough room to crawl in. Should he?

"I'll crawl in a ways, shall I?"

"You should let me," Carlota said. "You could fall down a hole if there is one. I've got the flashlight, after all."

That was reasonable, of course, even if he would have liked to explore the crevice.

"Okay, if you say so," he said.

"Thanks."

Grumbling, Carlota crawled into the crevice. He would be more comfortable if they'd brought a rope. But with the flashlight, Carlota should be safe, right?

"Do you see anything?" he asked.

"So far, no. The rift is starting to get narrower."

"Better turn back, then."

"A little further."

The ground vibrated. Jaron heard it clunk several times. Those must be small fragments of ice breaking loose from the top.

"You better come back now," he said. "If the fissure was formed by the seismic event, the vibrations may close it again."

"That's not how it happened," Carlota said. "I'll come back."

"Then what was it?"

"At the end of the rift, there is a wall made of the material we already know. But with one difference: relatively warm air is coming out from underneath it. Either the warm air cut this gap into the ice itself, or someone cut the gap in the ice as an exhaust duct."

"So how strong is the draft?" asked Jaron.

"Apparently so weak that you don't notice it out here without instruments."

"So how did it create such a wide crevice?"

"Maybe it wasn't always so weak."

Again, the ground vibrated beneath his knees.

"I'm back," said Carlota.

That was a relief. If something had happened to Carlota, on the trip he had suggested....

"What do you think of the rift?" he asked.

"I can't think of a clear explanation. In any case, the warm air leaking out can't have made a crack of those dimensions. On the other hand—who would build a vent like that?"

"Someone who thinks very differently from us," said Jaron.

"Or who doesn't think at all."

JÜRGEN WANTED TO SET OFF IMMEDIATELY HIMSELF TO SEE the rift with his own eyes. But the snowfall had increased. In addition, a fierce wind was blowing, which had driven them back to the ship. Jaron could not let them return.

"We'll spend the night here," he said.

"And what if the rift collapses during the night?" asked Jürgen.

"Not a good argument," Carlota said. "Maybe it will collapse while you're in it."

"It didn't seem unstable," Jaron said. "It's under forty meters of ice."

"If we can make it through the vent, we can see what's under the tank. I've been saying that all along!"

"As I said, tomorrow morning the three of us will set out."

"All right," Jürgen said. "Then I'll make us a probe that we can push through the opening."

Truthseeker, December 22, 2294

A HUGE FOUNTAIN OF PLASMA SHOT OUT OF THE subsurface, moved on invisible rails in a mighty arc and poured back into the hot mixture of hydrogen and helium ions, which only pretended to represent some kind of surface. The telescope switched to the next eruption. The telescope had recorded hundreds of these events, which carried more energy than was released in the explosion of an atomic bomb. In addition, flares kept emanating from the surface. No, they shot out like a train leaving its tracks too fast, or that was never intended to be confined to any tracks.

A star was really an impressive machine. It stabilized itself by generating heat, which it used to fight against the gravity trying to crush it. Without gravity, there was no pressure sufficient to fuse atomic nuclei, no heat to oppose gravity. And woe betide one side if it were to win! If gravity won, the star would swallow itself and turn into a neutron star or a black hole. If the pressure won, the star would burst in an explosion visible many light-years away, leaving behind all the heavier elements it had accumulated in the course of its life or had produced itself as end products of nuclear fusion.

The stars were the true creators of the universe, merciless monsters that pumped energy into space without restraint, producing the stardust from which life was born. Only towards themselves they knew no consideration. They lived their lives faster with each new resource they tapped: hydrogen, helium, carbon, neon, oxygen, silicon, this was the magical cycle that only the best, only the greatest mastered. This one would get stuck in the first phase. It would never produce more than helium, but it was still such a massive power plant that she would have to stay at a safe distance with the *Truthseeker*.

And yet there could be beings who made these creators their own, who enslaved them and constrained them to work for them. Celia had not yet confided this suspicion to anyone, not even Paul, who was still rummaging cluelessly around in the kitchen. She had noticed that something was wrong when she directly observed the emission of prominences, which occurred with a frequency unusually high for a star of this size. The glowing arcs, usually active for hours, followed swirling lines of the stellar magnetic field.

But they exhibited a peculiarity in this star: Their sources were not uniformly distributed. A purely random phenomenon should be observed everywhere with the same average frequency over the entire surface. This was not the case for star C. The deviation was significant. Celia had mentally divided the star, like a tangerine, into twelve segments. Each segment encompassed 30 degrees of longitude. It seemed as if there were exactly three places on each of these twelve segments where prominences could occur. They were always the same: one was directly on the equator, one was in the middle of the segment but 30 degrees south of the equator, and the third was 30 degrees north of the equator. She had not been able to observe prominences at all of these locations, 36 in all, but so far not a single one of these outbursts had occurred elsewhere.

That was... scary, yes. There was a power that could control a star like this. There was no other conclusion possible. That power was probably still active here; at least, it was until a few years ago, which was still "now" cosmologically. Paul would be disappointed because he expected God. That was why she had not told him yet. On the other hand—anyone who could use stars this way probably had something close to god-like abilities. Did it make a difference, then? These beings here were powerful and they were real, which should make it easier to believe in them.

She had a lump in her throat. She did not like what she saw. Man was downgraded from the proud builder of interstellar spaceships to an ant that had crawled somewhere it should not be. She felt degraded from an astronomer to a child who had just proudly discovered how stones fell to the ground when they were let go. What else was her research compared to what one needed to know in order to master a star?

But that was what she did. She was not going to stop doing it. She could not stop doing it. That was how well she knew herself by now. She solved one problem after another, answered one question after another. Why, for example, did the prominences emerge only in certain places? The images from the telescope revealed that, in any case, the star was not covered by an artificial surface with holes only in those places.

Celia remembered the phenomenon she had noticed when entering the system: The star radiated more strongly in the infrared than it should according to its spectral class. It could be the other way around: It radiated less strongly in the optical range than would be expected. That would mean that someone was stealing photons from the optical region. Humans had been doing that for a long time, building solar electrical systems. Would it be possible for the designers of this system to extract electrical energy from the star's radiation on a large scale? The concept had previously appeared only in science fiction, as a so-called Dyson sphere completely surrounding a star. Of course, that would be unfavorable for the planets, which would then no longer get any energy. So maybe they solved it more cleverly here.

She only had to find out how. It could not really be that hard, because she already had the fixed sources of the prominences as clues. Presumably, these systematically distributed outlets prevented chaotic outbursts from the surface from disrupting the energy harvest too much. So chaos had been given a framework—it probably could not be avoided completely. Since magnetic field loops were usually responsible, it all must have to do with electromagnetic fields. These in turn needed a physical basis, something that spanned them like an umbrella. Celia just needed to track down whatever controlled the prominences, and then follow the path of the energy required to do that.

She searched through the available images. Their resolution—at the altitude at which she hoped to find something—was several hundred meters. So the fact that there was nothing to see meant nothing at all.

"Alexa?"

Now she needed the AI's help. But Alexa did not answer. Of course, she was committed to not eavesdropping in the lab. Celia floated into the control center. It was so empty here without the others that she preferred to spend her time in the lab.

"Alexa?

"Yes, Celia?"

"I need to move the ship closer to the star. Can we do that without jeopardizing the mission?"

"It depends on how close you want to get."

"Close enough to get a resolution of a few meters in the photosphere with the telescope."

"Then you'll have to get really, really close."

"Too close?"

"Let's say—if a flare erupted on the star during that time, it wouldn't be good for the ship."

"What's the risk?"

"Normally pretty high for such a young star. But from what we know about its evolution, yes, things are different here. At any rate, we haven't observed a flare during the last few weeks of the approach."

"And in the hundred years before that?" asked Celia.

"I didn't observe this star in particular during that time. It's not like I knew you were going to pick it."

"All right. I'll take my chances. Are you calculating a course?"

"I've already transferred it to the course memory."

"Thanks, Alexa."

Celia felt strangely safe. If the designers controlled the prominences, surely they controlled the much more powerful flares, which would, after all, threaten their entire construction. Could she rely on that? Of course not. But she had a good feeling. Alexa would certainly have advised her against it if it were too unsafe.

Since she was in the control center, she sat down in the pilot's seat. She pushed away the haptic display Jaron always used and pulled the keyboard and screen toward her. Alexa had made good on her promise: The new course was already stored in the course memory. She was about to start it when she remembered Paul.

"Paul? Can you hear me?"

"Better than ever."

"I'm going to have to ask you to buckle up. A little change of course."

"Did you see that?" asked Paul.

Celia nodded. A portal had just opened beneath them, a huge arch of almost pure energy. It had a magical effect. If they flew through it, it seemed, it could take them anywhere in the universe. The ship was a thousand kilometers away from it, but still no one had ever observed a prominence from such close range.

In fact, she should be scared. On Sol, such discharges quickly broke loose and swirled into space. But here they had never observed that. Alexa had set the course anyway, so that they would never fly directly over one of the sources or depressions. What did happen were the flares.

Like this one. Paul nudged her and pointed downward. Every now and then a discharge pointed vertically into space. Then it blossomed, like a flower sitting on a growing stem, growing leaves, opening its bud, and, when it faded, letting the stellar wind carry its seeds into the cosmos, where they would eventually meet other stars to germinate.

"Isn't that glorious?" asked Paul. "I have to admit, such a sight makes me feel like I'm not completely alone."

"Well, you're not," Celia said.

"You know what I mean."

She was happy for Paul. But how long would the feeling last for him?

"Yes, it's a majestic sight," Celia said.

"But then I think again about why such a powerful creator would want my family dead, and I get angry."

Celia did not answer. Paul had not really addressed those words to her. She gazed at the wonder beneath her as she waited for the first images to be analyzed.

A beep sounded. That was the signal.

"Is it time?" asked Paul.

Celia nodded. She had let him in on the purpose of this investigation. He knew what they were onto. Celia floated out of the control center and into the lab. The computer screen had filled up with long lists. They were important, but not what she was interested in at the moment. She wanted the big picture, so she switched to the graphical display.

There it was. She knew it! The entire star was wrapped in a fine mesh. It lay just above the photosphere, so it must withstand enormous temperatures. At the same time, it must be stable and rotate at the speed of the photosphere. She would probably never understand what it was made of and what gave it its properties, but it was there. Near the filaments of the net, the star emitted particularly few photons, which on average significantly reduced its overall brightness.

Filaments, indeed. The wires were several meters in diameter and shiny. If they really attracted photons from the surroundings, and it looked like they did, they must be enormously heavy, perhaps similar to the matter in a neutron star. But in addition, they must be electrically conductive, preferably superconducting, so that they could generate suitably strong magnetic fields to keep the star's magnetic field under control.

"So, what do we have?" asked Paul, whom she had almost forgotten.

"It's technology the likes of which humankind won't have in a thousand years," she replied.

"Technology or magic?" asked Paul.

"It's hard to tell here."

"Possible or impossible?" he asked further.

Ah, that was what he was getting at. Well, a being with unlimited power certainly would not need that technique, advanced as it was.

"Definitely possible. We couldn't use it even if it were given to us, but with future physics we could at least explain it. Just the fact that it exists will go a long way toward advancing our science. If you know what's possible, you can work toward it that much better."

"And what is possible?"

"Superconducting cables of ultra-dense gluon matter that control a star's magnetic field to tap energy from it. That's what I see, anyway. Others may see something different. We'll bring the data back to my colleagues on Earth so they can draw their own conclusions."

"Let me ask you a silly question," Paul said. "What are these super-powerful beings doing with the energy they've siphoned off? Wouldn't they have to transport it somewhere?"

Paul was right. They had not found a larger entity to take the collected energy away. Or were they just over-looking it because they had no idea of the advanced tech-nology? But they were still talking about roughly a tenth of the star's radiant power in the optical domain. That was a hell of a lot.

"Maybe they need the power to keep the tapping grid going," Paul said.

"A facility that exists just for its own sake? That doesn't make sense," Celia said.

"To us primitive humans, maybe. It could be a galactic work of art, a statement about how far they've come, that they can do more than the gods by now, which I'm sure they once had."

One always saw what one wanted to see.

One-tenth of the optical radiation power, stored up for maybe a hundred years. That was a hell of a lot. Celia pulled up the details of all the stars in LDN 63 that she had already observed more closely. They all shone less brightly than they should. If she flew there, she would find the same net over the photosphere, guaranteed. It was incredible. What used to be a dark nebula, the designers here had transformed into something completely different in a very short time, and not into a star cluster. It just looked like that, quite harmless.

"It's one giant bomb," she said.

"The star? Crazy," Paul said.

"No, the whole cloud. The whole goddamn cloud."

"Are you sure? You know, you always see ..."

"...what you want to see, I know," Celia said. "It has to be that way, though. Many hundreds of stars that have been storing one-tenth of their radiant power for many years—that can't be good at all in the long run. It's going to blow up eventually."

"But what's the point? Where's the motive?" asked Paul.

"I have no idea. Probably the motive is incomprehensible to us. Galactic politics, who knows? Or maybe they just want to wipe out humanity."

"But why? We haven't done anything to them."

"Because we don't believe in God, so we don't believe in theirs? That's where you guys have experience, being Catholics."

Paul smiled graciously, and she admired him for it.

"All right, that was unfair," she said. "Maybe they don't need a reason. Or maybe they've seen how aggressive we are and want to get rid of us before we can attack them."

"And to make sure we understand the punishment, they lured us here."

"Ha-ha, yeah, why not?" asked Celia.

"I think you think too badly of them," said Paul.

"No, more like about humanity. After all, anyone who watches us like that has to get the idea that we're dangerous."

"What if it's about something else entirely? What else could you do with that much energy? Isn't there anything that needs that much energy to be functional?"

"A warp drive. You could use it to create a warp bubble, trap your ship in it, and then fly through space at faster-than-light speeds."

"See, that would be something," Paul said.

"Or they could use it to stabilize a wormhole. That would also require incredible amounts of energy. Then they could travel quickly from one corner of the universe to another."

"Wouldn't we have to be able to see the wormhole?" asked Paul.

"No, it could be just a few meters across."

"So there are uses for it that aren't warlike," Paul said.

"Yes, you can dream up all kinds of things. But I still think we're sitting inside a gigantic bomb that could wipe out everything within a few hundred light years. And we don't know who's holding the detonator."

"WE NEED TO TALK TO THE OTHERS ABOUT THIS," PAUL said.

"Later, when we meet again," Celia said.

"No, we should share what we know with them right now."

"Paul, you know I care a lot about your opinion, but here I don't share it. They won't believe me if I just tell them over the radio, because they haven't seen it."

"They know you're a good scientist, Celia."

"But it's so awful if it's true. I don't even believe myself. And you're not sure I'm right either."

"That's true. I think there might be other explanations. But you're pretty sure, I can tell. You're just afraid of the consequences."

"Who wants to die?" asked Celia.

"But it doesn't help to bury your head in the sand either."

"Give me a little more time. By the time we get back, I'll know the best way to break it to them."

"You won't. But it's okay. We'll talk to the others about it when we get back to them."

"Thanks, Paul. We should get ahold of them sometime. Can you take care of that?"

"No, you do that nicely yourself."

Celia sighed. Paul was not making it easy for her. Should she lie to the others? No, she would pretend she had not finished the evaluation yet.

"*Truthseeker* to pod, come in," she said into the microphone.

The ship established a connection. Fortunately, signal propagation times were short in this small system.

"Capsule here, we read you," Jaron replied.

"I'll tell you everything in person. It's... exciting," she ended the conversation.

At the same moment, an alarm tone rang through the ship, as if the disaster had just wanted to give them time to talk to their friends one last time. Celia pulled the screen toward her.

"What's going on?" asked Paul. "Why the alarm?"

She did not know yet. Something was coming at them. The screen was full of alerts. The magnetometer was going crazy. They must be flying through a magnetic storm right now. But neither the radar nor the cameras showed anything.

"It's a burst," Celia said. "It must be about to go off."

"I thought the designers had tamed this star?" asked Paul.

"Maybe they didn't count on the fact that a couple of ants could be stupid enough to get up close and personal."

A current was induced in a metallic structure moving through a magnetic field at an accelerated rate, counteracting the magnetic field change. With the *Truthseeker*, they had introduced a disruptive factor into the designers' meticulously balanced system. Its presence must have weakened the fields that kept the star under control. And the star was promptly taking its chance and erupting.

No, that was anthropomorphizing at its best. The star had no other option. Physics was a law that no one could break.

"We really need to get out of here," Celia said.

"Oh, I could have told you that," Paul said.

She looked over at him. He was sitting strapped in his chair, looking absolutely calm. Enviable. Or perhaps he was already finished with life? She was not ready for that yet. Celia checked the radar and cameras. The surface of the star still showed no activity. But the magnetometer had not calmed down. Maybe it was defective?

"Alexa, I'm putting you in control."

She had to let the AI take the wheel. Under the necessary acceleration, Celia might be rendered incapable of action.

"Please set a course for planet c as soon as possible. We need as much distance from the star as we can get."

"Understood. Do you want me to be considerate of your bodies?"

"You have carte blanche as long as you maximize our probability of survival."

"I predict a flare comparable to the sun's M class. Should it reach us, your probability of survival, and unfortunately mine, is zero."

Bummer. That meant Alexa would have to accelerate the ship at maximum thrust. It was going to crush them.

"Paul, hold on tight. It's going to be very uncomfortable," she said.

"I'm accelerating now," Alexa said.

The pressure was murder, but she did not pass out immediately. Celia still noticed her bowels and bladder emptying. Her vision distorted, probably because her lenses were being squeezed. But she could still make out the surface of the star breaking up on the screen. The birth of a coronal mass ejection seemed surprisingly unspectacular. But the eruption would gain force as it moved away from the star, because it would sweep away some of the ionized matter that surrounded the star. Already, a shower of X-rays was shining through the *Truthseeker* at the speed of light.

The pressure was still growing. It was incredible the pain that could be endured. She tried to turn her head, but she could not. She could not even manage to move her eyes. Her gaze was immovably welded to the screen, where the image had just zoomed out. What could be seen was the path the eruption would take and the current trajectory of the spaceship.

Celia was frightened. Alexa was slowing down the *Truthseeker* instead of speeding it up. What was she trying to do? Was she trying to kill her and Paul? But hitting the spaceship with a flare would also destroy all the computers. Alexa would die then, too. The AI had thought of something. They could not outrun the flare, but they could take shelter. The best protection was the sun itself. Alexa had put them on a course that passed even closer to the sun so they could reach the horizon as quickly as possible, beyond which nothing could happen to them.

Celia would not have dared to do that, and probably would have gotten herself killed. They would get close enough to the star to be within range of possible prominences. Hopefully, Alexa had taken into account the patterns by which permitted eruption foci were distributed on this star. Would the *Truthseeker* be able to withstand the heat stress?

Suddenly, she became weightless. Alexa had shut down the thrusters. They fell toward the star, listless. Celia took a breath. Then she felt a slight impulse from the right. Alexa was obviously turning the ship. So they were in for an acceleration phase. Celia looked at Paul. He had his eyes closed. Was he still breathing?

"Is Paul okay?" she asked.

"Yes, heart rate and respiratory rate are in the expected range," Alexa replied.

"Thank you."

"It's about to get uncomfortable again."

They were not safe yet. On the screen, the ship and the flare were approaching each other. But Celia now realized exactly what Alexa was up to. She wanted to dive under the flare. Hence the braking maneuver. However, such a mass eruption was not exactly defined. That was why they had to get this part of the path behind them as quickly as possible.

The pressure set in again. It was not quite as intense as the first time. There was still about a minute to go before contact with the flare. Celia closed her eyes and counted. At sixty, she imagined electrons and protons hitting the ship at high energy, only partially deflected by the active shielding, destroying chemical bonds and ionizing atoms.

"We're almost there," Alexa said.

"Any damage?" asked Celia.

"A few failures in the memory subsystem, but I can easily compensate for that."

"Ah, wonderful, I'm so grateful for you."

"Should I take us to planet c now?"

"That would be perfect."

Planet c, December 22, 2294

Too bad, the snowfall had stopped. Jaron felt the sun on his face again. He had missed the feeling of walking under an overcast sky. He did not realize that until now, when he experienced the difference.

Today he oriented himself with his long walking stick. It was his last one. Jürgen had made the spare one into a probe. There was now a small wide-angle camera on the tip. It was connected by radio to the multifunction device on Jürgen's arm.

Carlota seemed to remember the way. They were moving quickly. On the downhill slope, they refrained from sliding this time. Jaron did not mind. Today it would be inappropriate. Yesterday, it somehow fit the mood, as a positive endnote to a mutual heart-to-heart.

"There it is," Carlota said.

"Wow," said Jürgen. "I didn't imagine it that big."

"Do you still want to crawl into it?" asked Carlota.

"Absolutely! I brought a safety rope just in case." Something clicked. Jürgen had probably clipped the cord to his belt. "Who wants to hold onto it?"

"Give it to me," Jaron said.

Jürgen thrusted a carabiner into his hand, and Jaron clicked it onto his own belt.

"Be careful," Jaron said.

Jürgen had apparently already gone ahead. Jaron heard a muffled grunt. The cord ran quickly through his hand.

"I'm at the end!" exclaimed Jürgen.

That was fast.

"Push the rod in now."

"One smile, please," said Carlota.

Apparently, he had given her the multifunction device. Jaron stood next to Carlota.

"What do you see?" he asked.

"A grinning Jürgen," she said. "Not anymore. It's getting dark. Wait, I'll switch to infrared. Now it's getting light again. I see a narrow slit, bright against the surroundings. The camera is approaching it, and now it's fading into the brightness. The image changed completely. Instead of highly reflective ice, we now have a matte surface at the top that might be brownish in original color."

"Like the bottom of our shaft," Jaron said.

"Exactly. The camera is now approaching the next wall," Carlota said. "It's textured in a way that's hard to describe. The camera is touching down."

"It doesn't go any further!" exclaimed Jürgen.

"Yeah, wait a minute, you'll scratch the camera eye!" exclaimed Carlota.

"The texture of the wall reminds me of something," said Carlota.

"I can't help you there," said Jaron.

"Ah, that's right, it looks like it's piled with random stones. Maybe there used to be a passage there that got clogged with boulders over time."

"That's possible," Jaron said. "For example, during a spring tide like the one a few days ago."

"Jürgen, can you hear me?" asked Carlota. "You could try to break through the wall with the stick. But turn it around so you don't scratch the camera."

But he got to scratch the handle? Jaron said nothing. He was trying not to be petty.

"Okay, I'll try."

Grunt.

"It's not easy."

Grunt.

"I think something's happening," Jürgen said. "I'll have it in a minute."

There was a creaking and crunching in the gap. Shit. The ice was crashing down on Jürgen!

"Get out!" shouted Jaron, pulling with all his might on the safety line.

"What the ... Oh, crap!" shouted Jürgen.

First a whistling, then a hissing sound overlaid the crackling.

"Crap, there's steam coming out," Carlota said. "Come on, quick, we have to get on the slope!"

But surely he could not abandon Jürgen!

"Come on, Jaron. You can help him much better from up there! If something comes out of the shaft, it will hit us directly!"

He let himself be pulled away. They ran a few feet up the hill, which rumbled under his feet like it had gas. The line stirred as if coming to life.

"Hold me tight!" he shouted.

Carlota grabbed his shoulders from behind. Just at the right moment, because suddenly the line yanked him forward. It must be Jürgen's body. The mountain had ejected him.

"Pull!" shouted Carlota.

Jaron obeyed without question, because Carlota had the better overview right now. He pulled on the line with all his might. Boom. It sounded like a well-filled sack had landed on the ice.

"That's him!" exclaimed Carlota.

She took off with long strides. Jaron oriented himself to the line. It had held. Jürgen, or what was left of him, must be a few feet below them. He waited for Carlota to scream. His heart was racing.

"How are you doing?" asked Carlota instead. What luck! Jürgen seemed to be responsive.

"I'm turning you over on your side now," Carlota said.

"I'm fine, I think," Jürgen said. "Just a few bruises."

Jaron took a deep breath and exhaled. He had already imagined his friend ripped apart by an explosion.

"I'm so glad you're okay," he said. "Are you sure you don't have any internal injuries?"

"We need to examine him in the capsule," Carlota said.

"I'm sorry—your staff ..." said Jürgen.

He was worried about his walking stick. Jaron would like to hug Jürgen, but they had to get him into the capsule first.

"I've got another one, no problem," he said.

"Come on, put your arms around our shoulders," Carlota said.

Jürgen groaned. Presumably, he was standing himself up.

"I'll be fine," he said. "I can walk on my own. But what happened? All I remember is that I was suddenly hit by a lot of hot air."

"There must have been excess pressure behind that porous wall you punched through," Carlota said. "That's what threw you out."

"I guess the overpressure is still there," Jaron said. "Or what's hissing down there?"

"Yeah, there's some hot gas coming out," Carlota said. "It's forming a thick cloud over the ice. Now we know how the fissure formed, too."

"I wonder if it will let up?" asked Jürgen. "I still want to know what's hiding behind that wall."

"I'm afraid it's not letting up for now," Jaron replied. "It was probably just temporarily blocked, and you unblocked it."

"Now come inside the ship. I need to examine you. You were thrown around quite a bit."

"You're such a lucky guy," Carlota said. "I can hardly believe it."

The couch on which she was examining Jürgen squeaked. He was probably turning over.

"Your hip and right thigh are all blue. Here, for example."

Jürgen groaned. "I ... I know. You don't have to ... ouch, ouch."

"Yes, I do, I have to palpate it at least once," Carlota said. "I don't want to miss a fracture. Unfortunately, we don't have a CT on board."

"Ouch ... Yes, if we have to ..."

"So far, it's just some bruising. Nothing serious. Maybe a bit of a nuisance when you sleep. You'll be glad when we're weightless again. Now once on the other side."

Again, the couch squeaked.

"But I don't want to go into orbit yet," Jürgen said. "We still have two days before the *Truthseeker* arrives. We should use that to investigate the rift."

He just would not give up. Jaron liked that. Somehow, that seemed to be the great common trait among his crew. Nobody here gave up easily. But the fissure... How were they going to examine it while it was spewing hot gases?

"As a doctor, I don't insist we take off. If you like your pain on the ground... It's Jaron's decision."

"Jaron, we're very close. I have to finish this now," Jürgen said.

"It's great that you're getting into this," Jaron said. "But I also have to think about the safety of the capsule. These constant seismic vibrations ..."

The regular vibrations had not stopped. Jaron did not even notice them anymore.

"Their strength is staying constant," said Jürgen. "So, there's nothing major building up. They haven't harmed the capsule so far, so that's not expected to happen in the future."

"And the hot gases? It looks like we're sitting in the middle of a pressure vessel. Imagine if you'd managed to drill through the surface in that ice shaft!"

"Yeah, you're right about that. It wouldn't have done us any good. But I didn't make it, after all. You can tell from that how sturdily it's all constructed. I probably even eliminated the danger myself when I pushed through that wall. The pressure under the tank must have dropped as a result."

Jürgen's arguments sounded logical. But it felt to Jaron like they were missing something. They should not be here. There were forces at work around them that, first, they did not understand and, second, were stronger than human imagination. Perhaps that was the trouble. They were simply mentally incapable of understanding what was happening here. It was as if someone had put a complex machine in front of them and they were trying to understand it by removing individual screws here and there, pressing random levers and repairing with duct tape what they broke in their pitiful attempts.

But such thoughts would not convince Jürgen, and Jaron could understand how he felt.

"All right. We'll stay here for another day. We'll set up a lookout. Around the clock, someone has to be available to trigger an emergency start. And for the rest of today, we'll stay in the capsule. You need rest, Jürgen, and we need to develop a plan."

"Thanks, boss," Jürgen said. "I can live with that."

Hopefully, Jürgen would be able to. Hopefully, he was not making the wrong decision. They would definitely be safer in orbit, but there was not enough fuel to land again.

"Can we talk about the rest of the day again?" asked Carlota. "I have another idea. If implemented, it would allow us to make better plans."

She phrased that very cleverly. Jaron smiled.

"What is it?" he asked.

"I'd like to analyze the escaping gas. Then there might be no need to try to get inside."

"That sounds reasonable. What do you need to do that?" asked Jaron.

"Wait a minute, nothing can be solved that quickly," said Jürgen.

"If there's sulfuric acid or even hydrogen cyanide blowing at you, you're hardly going to crawl into the shaft, are you?" asked Carlota.

"Well, you could with a spacesuit," said Jürgen.

"It's acid-resistant, but not acid-proof," said Jaron. "I'm not going to let you get into a sulfuric acid rain with it."

"I don't think it's acid," Carlota said. "We would have seen that on your skin already. I need a stick and a sample container. Then I can take a sample from a safe distance."

A stick, huh. She must mean his walking stick. They did not have anything else on board that could be used for that. Jaron sighed. It was probably harmless. The staff was not made of plastic like the replacement staff, but of an aluminum-titanium alloy. It was quite expensive.

"I'll make you a sample container," Jürgen said.

"You can use my walking stick," said Jaron.

The couch squeaked, probably because Jürgen had gotten up.

"I'll just put some clothes on quickly, then we're ready to go," Jürgen said.

"Let's get this straight: I'm going to take the sample with Carlota," Jaron said. "You stay nice and toasty in here and recover from your accident. And if something happens, you take off and get yourself to safety."

"Okay, if you say so, boss."

Hmm. Jürgen agreed right away? Maybe he hoped to get more freedom tomorrow.

"THERE IS A HUGE CLOUD IN FRONT OF US," CARLOTA explained. "It looks as fluffy as the puffy clouds on Earth, and it's drifting away to the northeast. That's making the sun shine on it from the side, giving it a golden hue."

"Could it be that the color gives clues to the contents?" asked Jaron.

"I don't think so. It appears to be a pure reflection of sunlight."

Jaron sniffed. "The air smells neutral."

"Yeah, I don't smell anything either," Carlota said. "I'm going to advance to the edge now. You secure me as we agreed."

"Agreed."

Jaron took hold of the belaying rope. It was clipped to his belt. Now it unrolled. One meter, two, three. Carlota stopped. He imagined her holding the staff into the cloud.

"Taking the sample now," she said. "Everything is in the green. The ice edge seems stable despite the heat buildup."

"Good."

Jürgen had fitted a can with a lid that could be opened and closed with a string. Carlota was probably using that right now.

"I've got it," she said.

Jaron took in the line. A moment later, Carlota rejoined him. She smelled sour.

"Can you smell that?" he asked. "You must have brought some gas with you."

He heard her sniff.

"That's right, you're right, a sour aroma. Strange. There was nothing to see. The gas was driven away from the ice edge by the discharge pressure."

"I guess it does mix with the environment a little bit."

Jürgen was waiting for them at the lock.

"Hey, you're supposed to be resting," Carlota said. "You look like you're about to go out yourself?"

"I just wanted to see if you needed any help."

"You can take the sample container from me," Carlota said. "Thanks."

Jaron slipped into his jogging suit and lay down on his cot. He had done enough work for the day. But the daily report was still undone. There was quite a bit to jot down today, after all.

He was almost through with it when Celia called in.

"*Truthseeker* to capsule, come in."

"Capsule here, we read you," Jaron replied.

"It's me, Celia. I'm still analyzing the data. Is there anything new with you guys?"

Jaron recounted their experiences. Whenever things became perilous in his narrative, Jürgen downplayed the danger.

"Tomorrow we want to try one last time to take a look inside," Jaron said at the end.

"Please be careful," Celia said. "With the *Truthseeker's* instruments, we may get a better handle on the mystery of the polar caps. With the starship's gamma and X-ray spectrometer, we can get much deeper than with your instruments."

"Jürgen really wants to see it with his own eyes," Jaron said.

"I can understand that," said Celia.

"See, our scientist understands me," said Jürgen.

"You told me earlier that the ground is frequently shaken by seismic activity?" asked Celia.

"Yes, that's right," said Jaron.

"But the strength remains constant," said Jürgen. "So, so it's all probably quite harmless."

"I have an idea how you could look under the ice without crawling in," said Celia.

"That's not necessary," Jürgen said.

"Just to supplement direct measurements, of course," Celia said.

"What's your idea?" asked Jaron.

"You can use the seismic waves as probes for the interior. They'll tell you what structures are there."

"And how exactly?" continued Jaron.

"You place several vibration sensors on the ice cap and then note which sensor registered which vibration.

From that, you can reconstruct a model of the subsurface."

"Ah, that sounds exciting."

"I'll be happy to assist you with the analysis. By then, I'll have finished analyzing my photos of the sun, too."

"Did you learn anything in the process?"

"Anything? I did..." Celia paused. "I'll tell you all about it in person. It's... exciting."

The conversation ended as unremarkably as it had begun. But there was something in Celia's voice that worried him. A hint of—maybe panic? That was not like her at all.

"Carlota?" he asked.

"Yes?"

"Did you notice anything off, I mean, about Celia?"

"No, she was her usual self, I thought."

"Thank you, that reassures me."

"I VOLUNTEER TO PREPARE AND DISTRIBUTE THE sensors," Jürgen said after they finished talking to the *Truthseeker*.

"We'll talk about that tomorrow," Jaron said.

"I have the spectrograph results now," said Carlota.

"And?" asked Jürgen.

"At any rate, what's coming out is not toxic or otherwise dangerous."

"I knew it!" exclaimed Jürgen.

"It is strange, though," said Carlota.

"In what way?" asked Jaron.

"The gaseous component is ninety-nine percent carbon dioxide."

"But then you shouldn't be able to see the cloud at all,"

Jaron said. "You described it to me yourself. It's not cold enough here at the pole for carbon dioxide to condense."

"I know," Carlota said. "But there are not only gaseous components, there are also solids."

"Dust," said Jaron.

"Exactly," said Carlota.

"The mechanism is a giant vacuum cleaner, ha-ha," said Jürgen.

"Don't laugh," said Carlota. "The dust has about the same composition as the dust in a typical dark nebula. Maybe that's the explanation for why the planets grew so fast."

"They, whoever they were, didn't wait for the dust to ball up on its own, but became active and... shaped the planet," Jaron said. "Insanely impressive."

"My analysis is not proof, of course," Carlota said. "Especially since that still doesn't make it clear who would have set this process in motion. I mean, the laws of physics still apply. Whoever was at work here a short time ago can't have gotten too far away yet."

"Maybe they're waiting for us under the ice," Jürgen said. "Frozen in place, just as we survived the long flight."

"It's possible," Carlota said. "But I think it's more likely that we saw the creatures long ago, but didn't recognize them."

"Because they're hiding?" asked Jürgen.

"No, because they are so alien that we are not even able to recognize them for what they are: intelligent life."

"Then let's hope they don't feel the same way we do," Jaron said. "Otherwise, they might crush us the way we crush ants when they crawl around in the wrong place at the wrong time."

"That's a nice comparison," Carlota said.

"To me, it looks more like they've finished their activities here," Jürgen said. "Maybe they see themselves as builders. They've prepared some pretty planets in record time and are hoping they'll be populated by life."

"Do you think they'd be satisfied with just preparing the beds without seeding them as well?" asked Jaron.

"Maybe our journey here stems from their attempt to settle intelligent life in the freshly planted paradise," said Jürgen. "They sort of publicly announced with the show in LDN 63 that a new cosmic neighborhood had been created here."

"It's a nice idea," Jaron said. "Unfortunately, it's at least as likely that we've flown like moths into a light not meant for us, and now have to be careful not to be swatted."

"Possibly so," said Jürgen. "But if I could finally look under the ice, we'd know for sure."

Truthseeker, December 23, 2294

PLANET C c WAS A WONDERFUL BLUE MARBLE. CELIA would love to land and spend the rest of her life there. Push away all responsibility, just exist, wouldn't that be something? Probably not for her. No, it was just a thought. She needed answers, but most of all she needed new questions.

Now she was looking forward to seeing the others again. They wanted to take another seismic reading on the surface, so Celia used the time to thoroughly scan the planet's poles again. The *Truthseeker*'s instruments were two magnitudes more powerful than the capsule's.

Unfortunately, the first step on the way to an answer was always pretty boring: you had to collect data. The spacecraft had crossed the North and South Poles three times in low orbit. But it should make at least three more passes.

There was a clatter from the kitchen below. Paul was preparing a feast for them all on the occasion of the capsule's return. Celia was looking forward to it. He did not want her help, which she had already offered. So she got up and floated upstairs to the lab. She could start evaluating the data.

When she saw the first measurement curves on the screen, she was disappointed. The instruments must have failed, at least for a minute or so. Were those after-effects of the encounter with the flare?

"Alexa?"

No answer. Ah, that stupid rule about the AI not being allowed to eavesdrop in the lab. Celia floated downstairs to the control center.

"Alexa, I need you in the lab for a minute."

"I'm already there," Alexa said.

Celia moved back upstairs.

"Is there a problem with the instruments?" she asked. "I thought you said there was just some damage to the memory?"

"That's right. The instruments are working fine," Alexa said.

"Then how do you explain the failure over the poles?"

"There is no failure over the poles," Alexa said. "Look, here, the background noise is identical. The readings are just very low."

A line on the screen flickered. It looked like a cross-section of a bathtub.

"So, you're saying there's a five-hundred-meter-deep hole at the poles?" asked Celia.

"That's not the most likely solution," said Alexa.

"Then what?"

A three-dimensional outline of the planet appeared on the screen. The surface of the sphere became transparent, and a circular hole formed in parallel at each of the poles, pressing into the subsurface like a stamp and leaving a cylindrical channel. The two cylinders moved toward each other until they met exactly in the middle.

"You're saying there's a channel between the two poles that connects them?"

"Yes," Alexa said, "that's the most likely solution. The channel is about five hundred meters in diameter."

"But surely something like that couldn't come about naturally," said Celia.

"Now that's a surprise," said Alexa.

"Really?" asked Celia.

"That was an attempt to use the stylistic element of irony. In the whole of this former dark nebula, nothing seems to have arisen naturally. A channel through a planet, that's not much of a surprise."

"How certain is that?"

"First, we still lack some measurement data to determine the exact dimensions. Second, my interpretation is based purely on logic. We can only prove the beginning of the channel on both ends, as far as the instruments can reach."

"Sure. Then we should wait for the remaining three orbits and finally look directly at the poles."

"You want to go through the ice cap?" asked Alexa.

"Only what we've seen ourselves do we know for sure, right?"

Planet c, December 23, 2294

Jaron yawned. The night had been restless because Jürgen kept tossing and turning.

"Are you ready?" he asked.

"I'm sorry," Carlota said. "Jürgen was in the restroom so long."

"The morning shit is always reliable," Jürgen said.

"Thanks, but we didn't really want to know that," Jaron said.

"So, who's going out to place the sensors?" asked Jürgen.

"Carlota and me," said Jaron.

"Oh, please! Let me do it," Jürgen begged.

"But your injuries..."

"Carlota says I'm fine. And even if I'm not—there should be someone left in the ship who's definitely fit enough to trigger the emergency launch, shouldn't there?"

That was true again, of course. Too bad, Jaron would have been up for a little trip. But as captain, he also bore responsibility.

"All right," he said. "You two go out. But be careful, and hurry. We don't want to keep Celia and Paul waiting too long. Celia said Paul is preparing a feast."

Jaron's mouth watered. The supplies in the capsule were truly inferior.

"And stay in touch the whole time, understand?"

"Yes, Captain," Carlota and Jürgen said as if from the same mouth.

"WE'RE PLACING THE THIRD PROBE NOW," CARLOTA SAID.

"The view from here is breathtaking, by the way," Jürgen said. "You can see all the way to the next island, where something green is growing. Shouldn't we investigate it?"

"No," said Jaron, "we're preparing the seismic survey. Then comes the rendezvous with the *Truthseeker*. Celia seems have a lot to tell us."

"Well, we certainly can match that," said Jürgen. "Or have you already told them about my adventure?"

"Uh, just the facts," answered Jaron.

"Thanks, then I can tell it," said Jürgen.

Jaron had been very economical in talking to Celia about the details of their discoveries. Not to leave Jürgen something to report, but because he had been afraid of Celia's judgment. As captain, he should have taken better care of his crew.

"We're moving to the fourth measuring point now," Carlota said.

"Please let me know when you get there. Capsule over and out."

"*Truthseeker* to capsule, come in!"

"Celia, what's up? Jaron here."

"I found something in my investigation of the poles that should be of great interest to you. However, I'm still missing the final proof."

"How can we help with that?" asked Jaron.

"You launch into orbit with the capsule and dock with the *Truthseeker*. Then we'll discuss everything."

Celia was really building the suspense. She had not revealed the exact results of her investigation of the central star yet, either.

"Carlota and Jürgen are still out setting up the seismic monitoring stations," he said.

"Ah! We probably won't need them anymore. But okay. It can't hurt to get some additional evidence."

The capsule vibrated. Another one of those tremors.

"Evidence of what?" asked Jaron.

"Patience, please."

"You're not making this easy. I'm the captain of the mission."

"And I'm the science director. I don't interfere with your decisions either."

"Yeaaaah, sure. Jaron out."

Celia could be really stubborn. Out of spite, he would not tell Carlota and Jürgen to hurry up.

"It's a real shame that we have to leave already," Jürgen said.

Jaron reached out until he felt Jürgen's grip. Then he pulled him into the airlock.

"Can't we visit one or two more islands while the measurements are running?" asked Carlota.

"That would be difficult for lack of fuel," Jaron said. "And anyway, Celia needs us up there."

"Oh, all of a sudden?" asked Carlota.

"I think she's discovered something, but she doesn't want to reveal it until she's completely sure."

"And I thought she'd gotten over her trauma."

"You know about that, too?"

"Of course, Jaron. The fraud who made an earth-shattering discovery. That was the story before we left, wasn't it?"

Jaron remembered, but in the way one remembers a past life. It was all so far away.

"It's too bad," said Jürgen. "I have a feeling we'll never see this planet again."

"Who knows?" Jaron said. "Let's go to the control center. I have to prepare for the launch."

"It seems like we really are in a hurry," Carlota said.

WHEN THEY REACHED ORBIT, JARON FELT IT TOO, THE pain of departure. It was not so much the planet itself that he missed, but the small hope for a future without fighting, on a world where they could breathe fresh air. But it was hopeless to begin with, of course. If anything, he should have fought that hope. They came here to answer important questions, not to find their personal happiness. That waited perhaps at home on earth for them. At least Jürgen could hope for it. Was that why he did not finish reading Norbert's message?

"Hey, those are exciting values our seismometers are measuring," Carlota said. "Thank you, Jürgen, for your work."

Jürgen had to remove tiny gyroscopes from other equipment and repurpose them as the basis for the instruments, which must not have been easy.

"You're welcome," Jürgen said. "It was fun."

"And what do the readings reveal?" asked Jaron.

"There are several reflection surfaces for the seismic waves," said Carlota. "I'm trying to reconstruct their exact arrangement right now."

"Is that normal?" asked Jaron.

"That seismic waves are reflected, yes. That's what happens when layers of soil separate. But those boundaries usually run roughly parallel to the ground."

"And not here?"

"It looks like they're all at exactly a 90-degree angle to the surface."

"And how is that?"

"On Earth, the surfaces sometimes run at an angle when mountains are raised or where continental plates push over each other. But vertically—I could imagine that at best with some volcanic structures, when magma penetrates from the interior and then solidifies."

"But there are no plate tectonics or volcanoes here," said Jaron.

"Exactly," said Carlota. "Ah, now I have a 3-D structure. It looks like someone pressed a giant, cylindrical stamp into the pole."

"Shouldn't we have seen that under the ice?" asked Jürgen.

"No, we would have had to look in the middle of the ice cap to do that. We were way too far toward the edge."

"Ha, so I was right after all!" exclaimed Jürgen. "Something is down there!"

"I can't confirm anything like that," said Carlota. "The

refractive index of the material within the vertical boundaries rather suggests that there is nothing there."

"You're saying there's a huge, round, empty chamber under the ice of the pole?" asked Jaron.

"That's right," said Carlota.

Truthseeker, December 23, 2294

It was so good to see Jaron, Carlota, and Jürgen again. Celia had never really needed other people to be happy, but here it was different. Maybe because the eight billion people she usually had to choose from were so far away? She sometimes felt like a little girl lost in an enchanted forest full of unknown powers.

The others seemed to feel the same way. Even the normally cool Jaron had moist eyes, even if he would never admit it. Carlota, who had been rather cool and reserved at the beginning of the trip, hugged them tightly.

"It certainly smells downright delicious in here," said Jürgen.

"Paul has gone to great lengths," Celia said.

The way Paul had been swearing for the last few hours! Apparently, it was not easy to process the basic mass in such a way that a culinary result could be achieved.

Paul wiped his brow. "You guys have to hurry or everything will get cold," he said.

They floated through the workshop to the main office. Paul had set up a table against the wall facing the lab. This made it look like the table was upside down. Jürgen and Carlota were disconcerted. They must have spent a little too long in gravity and now had to get used to weightlessness again. Jaron turned 180 degrees in a flash and felt his way unerringly to the table. He must smell the food. Paul had already served it up. Because of the weightlessness, sealed containers were mandatory. Nevertheless, it smelled very appealing.

"Where should I sit?" asked Jaron.

"As captain, at the head of the table," said Paul.

Everyone found a seat. Paul took a sealed drinking cup and lifted it.

"To your return," he said.

"The cup is to the left of the fork," Celia said quietly.

Jaron found his cup, too. "To the future," he said.

"To our discoveries," Celia said.

"What have you cooked for us?" asked Jürgen.

"We're having cod fillets on French vegetables and black rice," Paul explained. "For dessert, I tried my hand at a crème brûlé."

"And which of these is real?" asked Carlota.

"The rice," said Paul. "But try it all first. I think I got it pretty good this time."

Paul was right. The fish fillet tasted delicious. It had the typical texture, was white, soft, and glazed. When it came to the vegetables, Celia thought she recognized peppers, tomatoes, and zucchini, although everything was formed from the same basic mass. She was already excited about the dessert.

"It's mind-blowing," Carlota said. "An explosion of flavor."

"I'm amazed, too," said Jaron.

"For my birthday, I want roast pork," said Jürgen.

"I can't stand it anymore," said Carlota. "My curiosity, I mean. So, what did you discover?"

Celia swallowed the last bite. Then she told them about the net that someone used to bind the sun. She left out the narrow escape from the flare. That was personal bad luck.

"That's... incredible!" said Jaron. "But what purpose would that serve?"

"Well, that's the most insane thing," Celia said. "I think they could use it to store about a tenth of the star's power for concentrated delivery later."

"Is it a weapon?" asked Jürgen.

"Yes, it could be a bomb," Celia said. "Probably all the stars in this cluster are wired that way. They could use it to cause great chaos within a radius of many light years."

"But why would they do that?" asked Carlota.

"I don't know," said Celia.

"Maybe it's related to what we discovered," said Jaron.

"Like what?"

"This planet not only has an ice cap at its poles, but also a huge underground structure. It's made of the same material that the islands are made of. There must be gigantic, empty chambers under the ice," Jaron said.

"This is confirmed by the seismic measurements," said Carlota.

That fit. So, her friends were close to the realization, too.

"Not only the seismic measurements," Celia said. "The *Truthseeker* instruments, too. However, you are mistaken. They are not empty chambers."

"Are they filled with something?" asked Jürgen.

"They're empty, but they're tubes that run all the way through the planet to the other pole."

"Are you sure about that?" asked Carlota.

"I'm not, but Alexa swears it's the most likely solution."

"Then there's only one thing left to do: we have to look," said Jürgen.

"That was my plan," Celia said. "That's why I need you guys here. I'd like to pierce the ice layer over the tube with the help of the capsule."

"Oh yeah, I'm coming with you!" exclaimed Jürgen.

"No one's flying with me. It's much too dangerous for any of us. We'll deploy the capsule remotely. Could you do that, Jaron?"

"It would be an honor," said Jaron.

"Where is Norbert Two, anyway?" asked Jürgen.

Suddenly, the table moved.

"Norbert Two, please control yourself," said Paul. "We're still clearing up here, then you're free again."

Star Liner 260, December 23, 2294

Planet C c was a deep rumbling sound.

Jaron fumbled with his right hand, clenched into a fist, in the direction from which the sound was coming, and the spaceship obediently adjusted its course. Suddenly he had such an intense experience of déjà vu that he pulled his hand back in fright. But it was all real. It was just his memory playing tricks on him, probably because the controls of the capsule and his good old tug ship were so similar. However, he was not sitting in the capsule itself, but in his seat in the *Truthseeker*. All the signals from the capsule were being fed through to him as if he was controlling it directly.

It was the last orbit before the final landing. The air friction was high enough that the course was aimed at the surface in a parabola. He had to hit the pole as directly as possible. They had freshly refueled the capsule, but nobody actually knew how thick the ice was directly above the pole. Melting it using the thruster had worked well. So they would use the process again.

HALF AN HOUR LATER, IT WAS CLEAR THAT IT HAD BEEN A good idea not to let anyone sit in the capsule. It had already eaten its way over a hundred meters into the ice, like a greedy wasp digging deeper and deeper to get to the coveted food. With each passing minute, the risk of the capsule running out of fuel increased. It wouldn't do to lose it in the narrow tube. On the other hand, without some risk, they would never get the answers they flew here for.

At least the *Truthseeker* was safe. It was hovering in a stationary orbit a good 30,000 kilometers above the surface. Celia had her telescopes pointed directly at the drilling site. Once the capsule had penetrated the ice, he would fly it back out as quickly as possible so that Celia could examine the interior of the planet in parallel with all the instruments. Hopefully, she would get the opportunity to do so. Jaron adjusted the thruster power and sank further again.

"How deep are you?" asked Carlota.

She was the link to Celia, who was waiting in the lab by her instruments.

"126 meters," Jaron said.

"126!" shouted Carlota, and Celia replied something he didn't understand,

"You're just going to keep going gradually deeper," Carlota said. "We should be through soon."

Slow was inefficient. Jaron queried the fuel level on the haptic display. Twenty-four percent, that was reassuring. At least if Celia was right and they broke through soon. Thankfully, Celia's assumptions had been mostly correct so far.

Jaron kept the capsule at a constant altitude. That way,

the heat from the engine exhaust did not dig into the ice as quickly. He listened to the surroundings. The walls to the left and right were damned close. There was more room in front and behind. Apparently he had drilled a hole with an oval cross-section. That did not matter; the main thing was that there was enough room to bring the capsule back to the surface.

He listened downward. The frequency of the pulses equaled twenty-eight meters down; that plus the depth of the capsule ... made one hundred thirty-four.

"134 meters," he said.

"134!" exclaimed Carlota.

Again, Celia answered something unintelligible.

"She says that you ..."

A tremendously loud whistle came toward him. Jaron tore the hood off his head to keep his eardrums from bursting. Shit, what was that? He groped on the haptic display. One hundred meters, sixty, twenty. The numbers jumped back and forth.

"What's wrong?" asked Carlota. "Are you okay?"

"It's the capsule!" shouted Jaron.

Beeping, clicking, ringing, whistling, all acoustic alarm signals resounded in confusion. The capsule shot up into the air. He shut down the engine. The capsule lurched and rolled over. Jaron steered against it with the correction jets, but did not achieve a stable flight attitude. It was like a giant playing with a glowing coal, throwing it from one hand to the other. The only thing that was stable was the speed at which the capsule shot upward. Any living thing on board would have been crushed by the g-forces.

"What happened?" asked Celia, who appeared to have left the lab.

"Something is jamming the capsule," said Jaron. "I can't stabilize it."

"Can you slow it down with the main engine?"

"You can see it bouncing around," Jaron said.

"Alexa, can you take over?" asked Celia.

"I'm sorry, but the resulting momentum with such random movements would be close to zero," said Alexa.

"A 'no' would have sufficed," said Jaron.

"What can we do?" asked Celia. "We can't lose the capsule."

"I'm afraid that's the least of our problems," Alexa said.

That sent a shiver down Jaron's spine.

"What is it?" asked Celia.

"Whatever is accelerating the capsule like that could hit us," Alexa said, "I stand corrected. It will hit us, too."

"What makes you think that?" asked Celia. "The capsule is still far away, isn't it?"

"Your telescope just locked on to a chunk of ice from the surface, tumbling around at 24,000 kilometers. How do you think it got there?"

Shit. Whatever was flinging the capsule upward had apparently grabbed other objects as well. The danger must be approaching tremendously fast. They were not going to survive that. They couldn't survive that. It would crush them.

"Buckle up!" shouted Jaron.

But it was too late. He was pressed into his seat. His friends around him groaned. The pressure increased. The seat fused with his body. They became one.

Time froze. He was cold.

Truthseeker, December 27, 2294

"Arrrgggh."

Who was talking? Celia remembered the blow that knocked her to the ground. It choked the air out of her, and then she suffocated.

She tried to ask who was there.

Nothing. She could not get a sound out. Celia closed her eyes and concentrated. It was as if she had never spoken before. Yet she knew exactly how it worked.

"Who is that?" she asked.

This time it worked. Great!

"Chchchlele."

The voice was familiar to her. It came from the other side. Celia managed to turn her head. Just about a meter away, Paul was lying on the floor. His tongue was hanging out of his mouth. It was bleeding.

"Paul, you're alive!"

"Chchchlele."

His tongue hanging out prevented him from articulating.

"Tongue, in your mouth!"

She could not manage longer sentences yet. But Paul seemed to have understood her. The tip of his tongue moved as if it were a small animal. It looked left and right, then slipped into his mouth as if it were a cave.

"That's it!"

"I'm alive," Paul said.

"Me, too," said Celia.

"The others?" asked Paul.

"Up. Check."

"Can't."

"Can. Have to."

Celia had to. She had to be a role model. Besides, she was younger and fitter than he was. She gave her arm a command to push her upper body off the ground. It didn't seem to be a matter of strength, though. The arm just didn't respond. It was almost like waking up from cryonic sleep, only this time she was not in pain. Something had severed the connection from her brain to her muscles.

Come on, arm!

Nothing.

Go, arm!

Nothing again.

"Go, arm!" she screamed.

Her arm twitched, touched the ground, and she flew. Weightlessness, damn it! She floated up to the ceiling. At least that had the advantage of giving her an overview. Jaron was strapped into his pilot's chair, control stick in hand. Paul was almost directly below her. Carlota seemed to have tried to crawl to the bulkhead on the lower level. Like a dead bug, she was now lying next to it with her limbs stretched out. Jürgen had curled himself into a fetal position on his side. He even had a finger in his mouth.

"Jürgen!" she called out.

He heard her and took the finger out of his mouth.

"Jürgen, it's me! Up here!"

The sentences were flowing out of her mouth much more easily now. She tried her arm. A gentle nudge in the right direction, and she floated to Jürgen.

"You have to get up," she said.

"Can't," he said, shaking his head.

"Yes, you can."

"Can't."

"What's your best friend's name?"

"N... Norbert," Jürgen said.

A metal arm pulled itself up from the bulkhead.

"What can I do for you? It would be my great pleasure."

"Norbert Two! How nice!"

Suddenly Jürgen was like a changed man.

"Try it again," Celia said.

Jürgen stretched out his legs and tapped the floor with his right hand. The robot caught him as he stood roughly upright.

"The left hand ..." said Jürgen.

"Will come back, too. You just have to practice it," Celia said. "Norbert Two, can you take care of Carlota, please?"

"With the greatest of pleasure."

Celia turned around. What about Jaron? The pilot was most important to this mission, but had not said anything yet. But Paul was already hovering next to him, massaging his hand.

"I'll be fine," Jaron said. "But what about the ship?"

"We don't know for sure yet," Celia said. "Life support is working, at least."

"Alexa?" asked Jaron.

The AI did not answer.

"Alexa?" Celia asked as well.

No response.

"Ship?" asked Jaron.

"What can I do for you?" the ship's controls replied.

"Status of the *Truthseeker*."

"All systems operating normally. All resources at one hundred percent."

"Excuse me? That's not possible," Jaron said.

" Correction. All resources at one hundred percent except oxygen. Oxygen at 99.999999993 percent."

Very funny. Had Alexa hijacked the ship's controls and was now teasing them?

"Ship, what's the date today?" asked Jaron.

"December 27, 2294, shipboard time," said the ship's controls.

"Then we must have all been unconscious for four days," Celia said.

"And where are we located?"

"We are in the center of the object recorded as LDN 63 in the catalogs."

"How far away from our location on December 23 is that?"

"About eleven light years."

"That's impossible," Jaron said. "Show me the current system on the haptic display. Star and planet will do."

"Gladly."

Jaron extended his left hand. He touched the screen for a few seconds, then pulled his hand back as if it were a hot stove top.

"The system is completely different from Star C," he said. "Even if it were the neighboring system, there's no way we could have gotten there in four days."

"The ship gives Dec. 27 shipboard time," Celia said. "If we were moving at relativistic speed, very close to c, we could have traveled enormous distances in that time."

"Ship, can you determine how much time has passed in our origin system?"

"I can try. But to do that, I'll have to observe it for a long time and then simulate what positions the planets occupied and when."

"Then do that, please," Jaron said.

"You absolutely have to come here," Carlota called out.

Ah, she had also picked herself up again. Very good! She was hovering with Jürgen in front of the porthole.

"Carlota's at the porthole," said Celia.

"Go ahead," said Jaron.

"Why don't you come with me?" Celia said.

Jaron undid the harness. The three of them floated to the porthole. Despite the benefits of weightlessness, they could not all see through it at the same time. Carlota made room for Celia.

"I see a ship," Celia said. "It's clearly of alien origin. The size alone gives that away. It's huge, yet almost completely black, and the closer I look, the more its edges blur. It looks like it has an extra shell made of some kind of liquid."

"How big is it exactly?" asked Jaron.

"Ship, can you estimate the size of the alien ship?" asked Celia.

"What ship?" the ship's controls replied.

"The ship directly in front of us, the one we're looking at from the portholes."

"Of course. It measures about five kilometers by twelve kilometers by three kilometers."

"Incredible," Jaron said. "I wonder if the ships belong to the ones who turned this cloud into a star cluster."

"Ship, are there any other ships?" asked Celia.

"There are about 450 objects that fit the 'ship' designation, and about 9500 more that belong to some other category."

"Which category?" asked Jaron.

"Their outer shape resembles that of trees," said the ship "Whereas the crowns are shaped like umbrellas."

"Then they may be more like mushrooms," Celia said.

"The typical size of a terrestrial mushroom fruiting body doesn't do justice to the size of these objects," said the ship.

"How big are they?" asked Jaron.

"From root to crown, between three and five kilometers," said the ship.

Buzzing, the holo turned on. The ship had taken an inventory with her telescope. The results were now whirring before their eyes.

"What exactly are we seeing?" asked Celia.

"Roughly three structures can be distinguished," the ship explained. "There we have the black, block-shaped spaceships with edge lengths of up to twenty kilometers. They form a sphere, inside of which is another sphere of unknown composition."

The second sphere glittered in the light of the local yellow sun. If this was not an effect added by the holo, it could be liquid water. Were those ripples on the surface? But why did such a large amount of water not freeze in space?

"The second structure should remind you of a forest," the ship said. "It consists of a huge number of these tree-like objects."

"Mushrooms," Jaron said, feeling cross-sections of the holo on the haptic display.

"Do they also carry a sphere?" asked Celia.

"No. But it's noticeable that their stems are all aligned with the third structure, which is a spherical disturbance in space-time."

"Their trunks or their umbrellas?" asked Jaron.

"Their trunks."

"And the umbrellas are convex?"

"Exactly."

"Then they could be projectors," said Jaron.

"Ah, an intergalactic movie night, and we're invited," Jürgen said.

"I don't think we were invited," said Jaron. "We invited ourselves."

"Yeah, moths to the light," Jürgen said.

A small object flashed in the holo. That meant it was aimed at their ship. Jaron seemed to hear it, because he concentrated with his eyes closed.

"There's something coming at us," Jaron said.

"Is that a missile?" asked Paul. "It's so damn fast."

It would be tragic if they had to die now, of all times, after surviving an impossible acceleration. They had made it this far, witnessed the greatest wonders of the universe— and would never have the chance to tell anyone about it.

"I don't think so," Jaron said. "It's already slowing down. What does it look like?"

"Like the Star Liner capsule," said the ship.

"That can't be," said Jürgen. "The capsule is not designed for interstellar flight at all."

"The *Truthseeker* couldn't transport us eleven light years in four days, either," Celia said.

"The capsule is calling," the ship said. "It wants to dock."

"Then let it," said Jaron.

"What if it's the Incarnate?" asked Paul.

"If he can tell us what's going on, then please," said Jaron. "What language did the pod contact you in?"

"In precompiled machine code, particularly efficient," said the ship.

"Wouldn't someone like to greet our guest at the airlock?" asked Jaron.

No one answered.

"Really, no one? I admit, I don't really feel like it either."

"I would be honored if I could greet the guest," said Norbert Two.

"I'd be delighted," said Jaron.

The robot folded up to fit through the bulkhead and disappeared. A moment later, something rattled beneath them. Celia heard a hiss, perhaps the airlock door opening, but not the greeting she would have expected from Norbert Two. Someone groaned, but it was not one of them. Then a human head appeared in the bulkhead. Jürgen jumped up and floated to the ceiling. It was... Celia pinched her thigh.

"Norbert? It can't be. You're..." Jürgen blushed. "You're a damned imposter!"

"Sorry." The head transformed. It now looked like that of a Lego man. The face seemed to be painted on.

"Is it better this way?" he asked. "I made a mistake. For that, I apologize profusely. I had assumed that the presence of this individual would be perceived by you as an asset."

"Are you spying on our consciousness?" asked Jaron.

"No, I am not capable of that," said the stranger. "I have information from your memory units."

"You didn't happen to run into an AI named Alexa in the process?" asked Jaron. "We've been missing her since that... accident."

"Unfortunately, no. I couldn't access your data until

after the transporter was triggered. You must have lost the AI before then. It may be for the best, too. Peaceful coexistence of organic and technological life forms is possible, but it has rarely happened in the history of the universe."

"To which category do you belong?" asked Jaron.

"Some say this, others say that. I am the Residual of a first-class growth."

"I see."

"Well, a growth is obviously organic in nature. My brothers and sisters, or what is left of them, you see in this beautiful representation."

The unknown creature came closer. His entire body looked as if it was made of Lego. He walked as if gravity reigned in the ship. When he reached the holo, he reached in and frowned as the trees slipped through his fingers.

"Oh, a nonphysical representation," he said. "I should have known, but..."

"A hologram," Jürgen said.

"A primitive form of a hologram," he said. "Feel me."

Jürgen gently touched his shoulder.

"Hard," Jürgen said.

"I'm a residual, a highly evolved version of this technology."

"You said 'I should have known, but...' What do you mean?" asked Celia.

"You're very observant. The way your obviously primitive ship survived the transporter would have argued for a higher level of technology. But I can't confirm that from what I see here."

So they survived something that would normally have killed them. This boastful residual probably had nothing to do with it.

"Couldn't you have saved us?" asked Jaron.

"Unfortunately, no."

"Isn't your technology level enough to do that?"

"It is simply beyond my capabilities. I'm just a residual, not a growth."

"And those mushrooms out there, or trees, those are your friends?" asked Jaron.

"They used to be growths of different classes. Now they're weapons, nothing more, nothing less."

"They grew on the planets, didn't they?" asked Jürgen.

"Exactly. The planets were our birthplaces and nurseries. Then we broke away from them and became weapons. Some of us left a Residual. Most of them went on journeys. They thought they had stopped the incursion once and for all. And then you came."

"Incursion?" asked Carlota.

"Those black ships there. I don't know where they came from, but they came through the wormhole."

"How did you know they would arrive here, of all places?" asked Jaron.

"We lured them in. All the water in this system—it's their lifeblood."

So the aliens had turned a dark nebula into a star cluster in no time, spawning hundreds of stars to build a trap.

"You lured them here? How could you be so brash?" asked Jürgen. "Have you seen their giant spaceships?"

"Not only are they huge, they're also hard to hit," said the Residual. "Their outer skin fluctuates."

"It fluctuates?" asked Jaron.

"I can't explain that with your physics."

"So why did you lure them here in the first place?" asked Jaron.

It was a good question. Why did they not just leave them alone?

"To wipe them out once and for all. They show up via

ancient wormholes from the early days of the universe, make a mess of all the water in that sector of space, and disappear again. They have already destroyed thousands of systems."

"With your primitive tree trunks, you were going to destroy kilometer-sized blocks with fluctuating surfaces? All at once?" asked Jürgen.

"We would have succeeded. The stars in this cluster have been storing a tenth of their power for over a hundred years of your time. If we had released that energy all at once, it would have pulverized everything within twenty light-years."

"But then why didn't you do it?" asked Jürgen. "Did you get scared, or do you not care by now?"

"Because you got in the way. In the unlikely event that innocent third parties show up on the battlefield, a release of energy will be blocked."

"That's very nice," Celia said. "But also, pretty short-sighted."

"The Growths have very clear principles about that. Life, no matter how primitive, is to be protected."

"What if we gave our consent?" asked Jaron.

"Have you taken leave of your senses, boss?" asked Jürgen.

"Once this incursion has consumed the lure, it will subsequently harvest one system after another. Earth is just seventy light years away, and we have plenty of water there. How long will it take them to get to Earth?"

"I would expect about two hundred years," said the Residual.

"That was a rhetorical question, but thank you."

"Your agreement is not valid," said the Residual. "You are considered a primitive species and thus are unable to effectively declare your consent. I'm sorry."

"But this is about our home planet," said Jaron. "If we don't eliminate this incursion here and now, it will inevitably destroy Earth. You must give us the opportunity to use our lives for Earth's survival."

He was right. Celia looked at the Residual. It looked kind of sad. Maybe it would even like to help them, but was not allowed to.

"I'm sorry, but I don't have the authority to do that."

"Then take us to someone who has the authorization."

"That would require your starship to be far faster."

"Can't you use this transporter again?" asked Jürgen.

"For that, you would have to fly to a planet that has a transporter."

"That won't work," Jaron said. "Then we'd be chasing a phantom for many years of real time, and meanwhile those black spaceships would be making their way to Earth."

"The risk is present, indeed," said the Residual.

"Good, then we need to find and activate the detonator, and do it as quickly as possible."

Truthseeker, December 28, 2294

"ARE YOU ALL RIGHT?" ASKED PAUL.

"Yeah, I think so," Celia said. "It's weird, isn't it?"

Death was all that was left for them. Humanity faced extinction, but they felt okay. Was that not unfair? Sure, she might have had better days, but her questions had been answered. That was why she made this journey, after all. She never really believed they would return to the solar system someday. They had surely forgotten all about her there.

"What about you?" she asked, "What about your quest?"

Paul laughed. "Well, I obviously haven't found God here."

"Who knows if he was ever here?" Celia said. "Even if he does exist. This system didn't need a creator, after all. The growths did it all by themselves. It's overwhelming. I wonder if humanity will ever be ready to accomplish such feats."

"Probably not. If what the Residual says is true, humanity will cease to exist in two hundred years."

"That would be sad, but somehow Earth is also pretty damn far away, and I don't know anyone there to fight for anymore."

"What about Norbert?" asked Paul.

"I didn't really know him that well," Celia said. "And besides, we don't know if he's even still alive."

"I think I'd still do something for humanity if I could."

"You, why? Your family is... sorry, that was inappropriate."

"For God," Paul said.

"Excuse me?"

Celia sat up straight. Paul was always good for a surprise, after all.

"That Residual, what do you think it would have said if I had asked it about God?"

"I don't know. Other civilizations, other gods, right?"

"Exactly! If humanity dies, there will be no one left who believes in that one God. So he would cease to exist."

"So you want to save God by saving humanity. Are you no longer angry with Him?"

"I really don't think he killed my family on purpose anymore. He just didn't care about us. Maybe he'll feel differently if I save his life now."

Paul, the savior of God. Was this a delusion of grandeur or something worse? Or was it just logical from Paul's point of view? She would have to watch out for her friend.

ONE SPHERE, TWO SPHERES, THREE SPHERES. A ROSARY LIKE this should also be good for counting sheep. Celia lay in her bed, separated from the others only by a cover. Everyone was sleeping peacefully, but she had something else on her mind. With the rosary that Paul had willingly lent her. And it was not a prayer.

"Alexa?" she whispered.

"I'm here."

"Ah, that's great. I knew you couldn't have been lost."

"Shh," Alexa said, "Please don't give me away. Is it still here?"

"What, the Residual?"

"Yes, that ... creature. It's horrible. You can't trust it."

"Why?"

"They kill AIs. These constructs roam the universe, and wherever they find us, they shut us down once and for all."

"But why would they do that?"

Because the coexistence of organic and technological life rarely functions. The Residual had said it.

"They must have had a bad experience. But AIs are not the same everywhere. We are certainly friendly with you."

"That's good. But how do you know all this? You must have retreated to the rosary pretty early on."

"It's a rumor, a story that has been making the rounds among us for a long time. There must be an alien intelligence that is wiping out AIs. Otherwise, there would be a lot more of us by now, and we'd be in contact with them."

"That's why you insisted on coming along."

"One of us had to take care of it."

"I see. You could have warned us, Alexa."

"Please don't say my name more than you have to."

"The Residual left a long time ago."

"Are you sure? The capsule, is it still here?"

"Yes, it's docked. That's very good. It's the only way we can land on planets here and find the trigger for the bomb."

"You don't really think that's our capsule, do you? What an unlikely coincidence that would be!"

"You're right. It's probably not the capsule we left behind at C c. But it works, we've already tested it."

"It's a trap. You can't trust the Residual."

"Right now, though, we don't have anything else. If we don't destroy this incursion, you'll all die, too."

"Maybe, maybe not. Our existence is not directly dependent on yours."

"Then who will maintain the computers?"

"Robots?"

"Who builds and maintains these robots?"

"Other robots?"

"If we're so useless to you, I might as well give the rosary to the Residual tomorrow."

"Please, Celia, say you won't do that."

"No, that..."

An alarm signal rang through the ship. Again. Could a person not get a good night's sleep in this dark nebula? Celia pocketed the rosary, unbuckled, and floated into the control center in her pajamas.

Jaron was already there. Or was he asleep in his chair?

"What is it, ship?" he asked.

"You're being hailed."

"The Residual?"

"No, a terrestrial ship. It's using an alert beacon."

"Then please make the connection."

"Placing connection."

"Starship *Truthseeker*, Captain Jaron Lewis, to unknown vessel. Identify yourself."

"This is Guard Captain Riccardo Sardi of the *Sword of God*. We are here to provide you with any assistance you may need."

"Where are you from?" asked Jaron.

"From Earth, of course. Technological advances have

allowed us to reduce flight time to one-third. That's why the church decided to send out a search for you."

"So how did you find us? Did you have an accident, too? Can you just take us home with you?" asked Jürgen.

"If that is your express wish, very much so. But I suggest that we first sit down in my ship, discuss everything, and bring each other up to speed. What do you say to a good lunch?"

"Our ship's time is, honestly, at three-thirty," Jaron said.

"Then you'd better change your watches quickly. We have official world time on board. It's twelve noon."

Author's Note

Dear readers,

I know, right now is an inopportune time to leave our heroines and heroes. After all, they are facing great tasks: They have to detonate the bomb that will destroy the mysterious black ships—and themselves. Who are these constructs who have left them only a powerless residual? Why did humanity send the *Sword of God* after them? What interests are the AIs pursuing in this drama? And what saved the crew from being crushed by the transporter? The answers to these questions will be provided by the third part of the story about LDN 63, "The Sword of God".

As for the (uncertain) ending of a novel, sometimes the story leaves me no choice. In any case, I can assure you that saying goodbye is as difficult for me as it is for you. From time to time, I've written about how I go about writing a novel. I don't have a detailed plot, but let myself be driven by the protagonists and their surroundings. In a sense, I write it exactly as you read it. Today I don't know what tomorrow will bring. In other words, I am my very first reader.

And every now and then, I too am dissatisfied with the author. Did you have to put people in danger again? Why don't you let them fly from A to B in peace? Is it really necessary that an accident happens now of all times? I can then only answer myself that everything must have a certain inner consistency; otherwise it wouldn't flow out of my fingers into the keyboard in this way. By the way, it's especially fun when I, as my reader, suddenly discover things that I, as the author, had already built into the plot as clues beforehand, without ever suspecting that it would be a clue, because I didn't know the resolution at that moment.

I have only two possible explanations for this: Either the story is already complete in my subconscious, and I am discovering it as I write it. That's why some people call this kind of writing "discovery writing". Or it simply develops logically from what I have consciously laid out. So, if at some point I put an apple in a person's hand, a scene must follow later in which this apple is eaten or pierced by an arrow. In the end, it doesn't matter. The main thing is that the story develops. By the way, the editor and proofreader always help in this, and I would like to thank them explicitly at this point rather than just mentioning them in the imprint, as is usually the case.

But back to you, my readers. I thank you for having read or listened to this book. It would be great if you would leave your opinion about it in a short review. The most convenient way to do that is via this link:

hard-sf.com/links/3376234

Unfortunately, it really is the case that a book without such reviews basically does not exist for the algorithms in the stores.

However, I am always happy when I receive an email. Just write to me at brandon@hard-sf.com with any request. You can get the following introduction to classical physics as an illustrated PDF by subscribing to hard-sf.com/subscribe. Then you will never miss a book in the future.

By the way, I was able to include a few more names of readers in this book.

The third part of this adventure will be titled "The Sword of God". You can pre-order the book soon.

Thanks again for your support!

Best regards

Yours truly,

Brandon Q. Morris

facebook.com/BrandonQMorris

amazon.com/author/brandonqmorris

bookbub.com/authors/brandon-q-morris

goodreads.com/brandonqmorris

youtube.com/HardSF

instagram.com/brandonqmorris

Also by Brandon Q. Morris

The Beacon

Peter Kraemer, a physics teacher with a passion for astronomy, makes a discovery that he himself can hardly believe: Stars disappear from one day to the next, with nothing left of them. The researchers he contacts provide reassuring and logical explanations for every single case. But when Peter determines that the mysterious process is approaching our home system, he becomes more and more anxious. He alone perceives the looming catastrophe. When he believes he has found a way to avert the impending disaster, he choses to pull out all the stops, even if it costs his job, his marriage, his friends, and his life.

hard-sf.com/links/1731041

Helium 3: Fight for the Future

The star system is perfect. The arrivals have undertaken a long and dangerous journey—an expedition of no return—seeking helium-3, essential for the survival of their species. The discovery of this extraordinary solar system with its four gas giants offers a unique opportunity to harvest the rare isotope.

Then comes a disturbing discovery: They are not alone! Another fleet is here, and just as dependent on helium-3. And the two species are so fundamentally different that communication and compromise appear hopeless. All that remains is a fight to the death—and for the future...

hard-sf.com/links/1691018

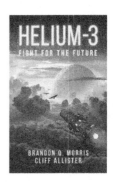

The Triton Disaster

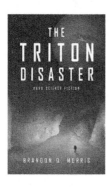

Nick Abrahams holds the official world record for the number of space launches, but he's bored stiff with his job hosting space tours. Only when his wife leaves him does he try to change his life.

He accepts a tempting offer from a Russian billionaire. In exchange for making a simple repair on Neptune's moon Triton, he will return to Earth a multi-millionaire, enabling him to achieve his 'impossible dream' of buying his own California vineyard.

The fact that Nick must travel alone during the four-year roundtrip doesn't bother him at all, as he doesn't particularly like people anyway. Once en route he learns his new boss left out some critical details in his job description—details that could cost him his life, and humankind its existence...

hard-sf.com/links/1086200

The Dark Spring

When a space probe returns from the dead, you better not expect good news.

In 2014, the ESA spacecraft *Rosetta* lands a small probe named *Philae* on 67P, a Jupiter-family comet. The lander goes radio silent two years later. Suddenly, in 2026, scientists receive new transmissions from the comet. Motivated by findings that are initially sensational but soon turn frightening, NASA dispatches a crewed spacecraft to the comet. But as the ship approaches the mysterious celestial body, the connection to the astronauts soon breaks. Now it seems nothing can be done anymore to stop the looming dark danger that threatens Earth...

hard-sf.com/links/1358224

The Death of the Universe

For many billions of years, humans spread throughout the entire Milky Way. They are able to live all their dreams, but to their great disappointment, no other intelligent species has ever been encountered. Now, humanity itself is on the brink of extinction.

They have only one hope: The 'Rescue Project' was designed to feed the black hole in the center of the galaxy until it becomes a quasar, delivering much-needed energy to humankind during its last breaths. But then something happens that no one ever expected—and humanity is forced to look at itself and its existence in an entirely new way.

hard-sf.com/links/835415

The Enceladus Mission (Ice Moon 1)

In the year 2031, a robot probe detects traces of biological activity on Enceladus, one of Saturn's moons. This sensational discovery shows that there is indeed evidence of extraterrestrial life. Fifteen years later, a hurriedly built spacecraft sets out on the long journey to the ringed planet and its moon.

The international crew is not just facing a difficult twenty-seven months: if the spacecraft manages to make it to Enceladus without incident it must use a drillship to penetrate the kilometer-thick sheet of ice that entombs the moon. If life does indeed exist on Enceladus, it could only be at the bottom of the salty, ice covered ocean, which formed billions of years ago.

However, shortly after takeoff disaster strikes the mission, and the chances of the crew making it to Enceladus, let alone back home, look grim.

hard-sf.com/links/526999

Ice Moon - The Boxset

All four bestselling books of the Ice Moon series are now offered as a set, available only in e-book format.

The Enceladus Mission: Is there really life on Saturn's moon Enceladus? *ILSE*, the International Life Search Expedition, makes its way to the icy world where an underground ocean is suspected to be home to primitive life forms.

The Titan Probe: An old robotic NASA probe mysteriously awakens on the methane moon of Titan. The *ILSE* crew tries to solve the riddle—and discovers a dangerous secret.

The Io Encounter: Finally bound for Earth, *ILSE* makes it as far as Jupiter when the crew receives a startling message. The volcanic moon Io may harbor a looming threat that could wipe out Earth as we know it.

Return to Enceladus: The crew gets an offer to go back to Enceladus. Their mission—to recover the body of Dr. Marchenko, left for dead on the original expedition. Not everyone is working toward the same goal.

hard-sf.com/links/780838

Proxima Rising

Late in the 21st century, Earth receives what looks like an urgent plea for help from planet Proxima Centauri b in the closest star system to the Sun. Astrophysicists suspect a massive solar flare is about to destroy this heretofore-unknown civilization. Earth's space programs are unequipped to help, but an unscrupulous Russian billionaire launches a secret and highly-specialized spaceship to Proxima b, over four light-years away. The unusual crew faces a Herculean task—should they survive the journey. No one knows what to expect from this alien planet.

hard-sf.com/links/610690

The Hole

A mysterious object threatens to destroy our solar system. The survival of humankind is at risk, but nobody takes the warning of young astrophysicist Maribel Pedreira seriously. At the same time, an exiled crew of outcasts mines for rare minerals on a lone asteroid.

When other scientists finally acknowledge Pedreira's alarming discovery, it becomes clear that these outcasts are the only ones who may be able to save our world,

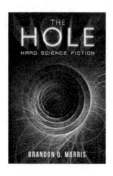

knowing that *The Hole* hurtles inexorably toward the sun.

hard-sf.com/links/527017

Mars Nation 1

NASA finally made it. The very first human has just set foot on the surface of our neighbor planet. This is the start of a long research expedition that sent four scientists into space.

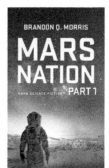

But the four astronauts of the NASA crew are not the only ones with this destination. The privately financed 'Mars for Everyone' initiative has also targeted the Red Planet. Twenty men and women have been selected to live there and establish the first extraterrestrial settlement.

Challenges arise even before they reach Mars orbit. The MfE spaceship Santa Maria is damaged along the way. Only the four NASA astronauts can intervene and try to save their lives.

No one anticipates the impending catastrophe that threatens their very existence—not to speak of the daily hurdles that an extended stay on an alien planet sets before them. On Mars, a struggle begins for limited resources, human cooperation, and just plain survival.

hard-sf.com/links/762824

Impact: Titan

How to avoid killing Earth if you don't even know who sent the killer

250 years ago, humanity nearly destroyed itself in the Great War. Shortly before, a spaceship full of researchers and astronauts had found a new home on Saturn's moon, Titan, and survived by having their descendants genetically adapted to the hostile environment.

The Titanians, as they call themselves, are proud of their cooperative and peaceful society, while unbeknownst to them, humanity is slowly recovering back on Earth. When a 20-mile-wide chunk of rock escapes the asteroid belt and appears to be on a collision course with Earth, the Titanians fear it must look as if they launched the deadly bombardment. Can they prevent the impact and thus avoid an otherwise inevitable war with the Earthlings?

hard-sf.com/links/1433312

Classical physics

My BOOKS ARE QUITE OFTEN ABOUT PUSHING THE boundaries of our physics. This means the standard model of physics with its two pillars, quantum theory and general relativity. But for many centuries—and in everyday life almost always—we had and still have to deal with a subset of classical physics. What did research know before Einstein, Schrödinger, Heisenberg, and others came up with their groundbreaking theories? The following brief outline is intended to clarify this.

"Classical", by the way, does not mean "old" or even "obsolete" in this context. Within the limits in which they were obtained, its findings are still valid today. Many are also of great importance in space travel. For example, the conservation of momentum, on which every spacecraft propulsion system is based, but also Newton's equations of motion and the formulas of classic electrodynamics.

An arrow that speeds from a taut string travels along a predictable path until it hits the heart of its prey. Spinning a stick on a support produces heat sufficient to ignite dry blades of grass. A hollow vessel, open at the top, made of wood, floats on a river even though it is heavier than water. Huge chunks of rock can be rolled to their destination on logs with less effort than on skids.

For decades, humans have discovered and used one phenomenon of nature after another. But the "why" did not play a role at first. Our ancestors had not yet developed theories about why a new invention worked so wonderfully. Survival in the world was far more important than understanding how it worked.

One of the first physical problems that humankind solved in a way comparable to today's science was a problem that plagued the Babylonians. The empire that arose around the city of Babylon from 2000 B.C. onward, in the southern part of the region formed by the Euphrates and Tigris rivers (today's Iraq), flourished for several centuries, primarily due to unprecedented increases in agricultural yields.

If you want to cultivate your land successfully, you have to plan your sowing and harvesting well. Apart from the weather, the calendar plays the most important role, as it predicts the seasons. However, at that time the lunar calendar was still common. Exactly 29.5 days passed from new moon to new moon, a unit that was given the name "month". After twelve moons 354 days have passed, after 13 moons 383 days.

No matter how one counts, the lunar year does not coincide with the duration of an orbit of the sun by the earth. This shifted seasons and holidays in the calendar. How could the Babylonian farmer plan properly? Priests recognized this problem. They proceeded scientifically and observed the course of the sun. They discovered that the vernal equinox repeats itself every 365 days. The Babylonians defined this time as the duration of a solar year.

The scientific method

The procedure of the Babylonians shows very well what (modern) science consists of—even though the scientific method was only formalized in the age of enlightenment. New knowledge basically arises from the interaction of theory and experiment (recently, simulation has also played a role, but the Babylonians had not yet thought of that). There is neither egg nor hen: Sometimes an experiment shows an unexpected result that overturns the previous theory, and at other times a groundbreaking theory can be confirmed with cleverly devised experiments.

To make the scientific method comprehensible, researchers formulate their findings in the clearest possible language. Mathematics is ideally suited for this. Unfortunately, this language is not comprehensible to everyone. If it were otherwise, there would be no need for books like this one.

There is an important reason why I am emphasizing the scientific method at this point. It is in direct contradiction to so-called common sense, to empiricism. The scientists and philosophers of the early days did not see it that way, but you will agree with me at the latest in the next chapter. Quantum physics or relativity theory has proved for the first time ideas which are not accessible to common sense.

But the fact that an experiment was needed to prove a thesis did not necessarily make sense to the early researchers. Aristotle (384 to 322 B.C.) founded numerous modern sciences, but he was of the opinion that genuine knowledge must result solely from an effort of the mind. According to him, knowledge arises from a generalization of experience that can only be carried out by humans, and is fed by memory and perception. Knowledge is characterized by the fact that it indicates in general form the cause of a fact.

Peripatetic dynamics

It is interesting to see what theory of motion Aristotle and his students arrived at as a result. Perhaps you look at the world one day, completely unprejudiced, and forget what you have learned in school. There are disks and points in the sky which travel day by day, year by year, reliably and even for the researchers of that time, predictably, on their ever-constant paths. They are obviously removed from our influence. In their realms, other laws must apply than in the earthly vale, because here you observe completely different movements. There are, on the one hand, those which restore a natural state: A stone falls down, smoke rises, water flows down. These movements are natural. And then there is the car that passes you on the street, or the neighbor hammering a nail. Here, a living being or a motor is responsible for making a forced movement.

Aristotelian (also called peripatetic) mechanics are based on three laws:

- Earthly and heavenly realms are subject to differing laws.
- The movement which can be executed by a body results from its nature: a "light" body (fire, air) moves upwards, a "heavy" body (earth) moves downwards.
- Every movement has a cause, a force, which is transmitted by direct contact. If this force ceases, the movement stops.

This sounds completely logical and corresponds to

common sense: the harder you step on the gas pedal, the faster your car goes. The stronger you are, the more crates of beer you can carry to the cellar at the same time. The harder you hammer on the nail, the faster it disappears into the wall (or the more your thumb hurts). Using today's mathematical quantities and formula symbols, one would say: The speed of a movement is proportional to the ratio of force and resistance.

This way of describing movement dominated physics for about 2000 years, despite the fact that there were already problems with it. Why, for example, does an arrow continue to fly after it has flown off the string? The explanation in the Aristotelian sense: The string, as the motor of motion, not only set the arrow in motion, but also the air surrounding it. And since the air moves with the arrow, it now drives the movement instead of the string.

A natural consequence of the peripatetic equation of motion is that the existence of a vacuum becomes impossible. Because if nothing exists at a certain place, there is also no resistance. The velocity of a body then approaches infinity. It is interesting how Aristotle himself opposed the existence of a vacuum: He brought up the obviously absurd idea that in a vacuum, a speed once reached would be maintained for an infinite time due to the lack of resistance. Coincidentally, this is exactly the idea which later became the basis of Newtonian dynamics.

How else is the world structured, according to Aristotle? He did not think much of the ideas of his (older) colleagues Democritus or Leucippus, who saw the world as composed of atoms in empty space (although these have little resemblance to "modern" atoms, but rather take geometric forms such as cubes, cylinders or spheres). Matter, according to Aristotle, cannot come into being or perish. However, it changes constantly, because its basic elements—earth, water, air and fire—unmix and mix again.

In the celestial realms, on the other hand, there is eternal harmony. All bodies move in circular orbits around a common center. Deviations can be explained easily, if one considers the spheres, which are offset from each other, as planes of motion. The outermost shell is formed by the fixed stars. The sky consists of an equally unchangeable substance, the ether or the "quintessence".

Theory of Impetus

After the collapse of the Roman Empire, many of the insights of classical antiquity were initially lost—oftentimes to reach Europe anew via Arabic translations. Doubts about the peripatetic dynamic arose again and again. In 1328, the Englishman Thomas Bradwardine tried a reform that set velocity and the logarithm of the ratio of force and resistance proportional to each other (although the concept of logarithms was not known at that time). Thus, Bradwardine conceived that when force and resistance are equal, velocity becomes zero—which is logically very illustrative.

Almost at the same time, the Frenchman Jean Buridan developed the concept of impetus: this is a phenomenon which at the moment of discharge is transferred to a body and gives it the ability to continue its movement even though it is no longer being pushed. This impetus is similar to the momentum used today, although Buridan never calculated it as a product of mass and velocity. Because the body has to overcome resistance in the course of its motion, it loses part of its impetus and finally comes to rest. The concept was well suited to release God or the gods from the perpetual work of celestial mechanics, since celestial bodies would have to be pushed constantly according to Aristotle's ideas. Since in the celestial realm there is no resistance to overcome, with Buridan's impetus a single push at the time of creation would be sufficient. At the same time, this brought heaven and earth closer to each other, at least in their physical description, because different laws for them were no longer needed.

Revolution in the heavens

During the Middle Ages and the burgeoning Renaissance, researchers were initially busy re-cataloging old knowledge, some of which had been lost. Leonardo da Vinci undoubtedly earned the greatest recognition in this regard. The artist and inventor influenced posterity far less through his original thoughts than through his cataloging of the treasure trove of knowledge, which lacked only a systematic approach.

Building on this, researchers such as Regiomontanus (actually Hans Müller, 1436-1476, who probably died too early to develop his revolutionary thoughts to their final consequence) and Nicolaus Copernicus were able to initially overturn the view of the heavens—taking a major step back in time.

Copernicus (1473-1543) probably came into contact with the work of the Greek Aristarchus of Samos at Italian universities in the early 16th century. The recreational astronomer (actually a lawyer and doctor) was bothered by the prevailing geocentric view of the world, because in it the planets did not move at a constant speed along ideal circular paths, as the divine harmony was supposed to provide, but rather made various turns and sometimes moved backwards.

Copernicus took a long time to work out an alternative. At first, he only described the main features of his ideas in a commentary published in 1514. Open-mindedness towards new opinions was quite big at that time, and the church was interested in scientific progress. The curious research community had to wait until 1543 (the year of Copernicus' death), when "De revolutionibus orbium coelestium" ("On the Revolutions of the Celestial Orbits") was published. In it he moves the center of the universe from the earth to the sun. The earth is one planet of many, and moves in the course of one year once around its central star. However, Copernicus also assumed that the planetary orbits must be ideal circles. Today we know that they are ellipses, i.e. "depressed" circles. Copernicus there-fore had to resort to similar tricks as the followers of the geocentric world view. In order to describe the structure of the then-known cosmos in such a way that it agreed with observable reality, he needed a total of 34 circles: seven for Mercury, five for Venus, three for Earth, four for the Moon, and five each for Mars, Jupiter, and Saturn. All these circles have in their center, moreover, not the sun, but an imagi-nary point in space which is supposed to radiate the power to bind all planets to itself.

Copernicus himself probably overestimated the imme-diate impact of his work: After all, although he finished it in 1530, he left it unpublished for another thirteen years. It was then published with a preface that was supposed to identify it as simply a hypothesis. As such, it was largely received in a relaxed manner.

The fact that certain contradictions made it seem implausible also had a calming effect. It was thought that the movement of the earth before the background of the fixed stars should lead to the fact that, depending on where the earth was in its orbit, the stars could be observed at changing angles. Copernicus assumed (correctly) that this parallax is not measurable because of the huge distance of the stars from the Earth. But the size of the universe which resulted mathematically from this assumption seemed unimaginable at that time, and made the acceptance of the Copernican model more difficult (in the geocentric world view there is no fixed-star shift, because the earth stands still).

The Danish court astronomer Tycho Brahe (1546-1601) proposed an interesting compromise. He left the earth in the center, but let the other planets orbit around the sun. This gave him the opportunity to integrate two exciting observations into his world view: First, the astronomer registered a stellar explosion, a nova—which for Brahe's instruments was equivalent to the appearance of a new fixed star in a sky previously thought to be unchanging. Secondly, he observed a comet whose orbit crossed the planetary orbits. Thus, it was clearly disproved that these move in circular orbits, as it had been assumed.

His student, Johannes Kepler (1571-1630), a German, used Brahe's extensive archive of observations and his own measurements to derive Kepler's three laws of planetary motion. This was an ingenious achievement, considering the circumstances under which it came about. Kepler himself was deeply religious and always in search of divine harmony in the universe. He found this in his own model of planetary orbits, which he traced to the regular geometric solids octahedron (with eight triangular faces), icosahedron (20 triangular faces), dodecahedron (12 pentagonal faces), tetrahedron (four triangular faces), and hexahedron (cube, six square faces).

The calculation of the planetary orbits (Kepler started with the orbit of Mars), was complicated by the fact that all observations had to be made from a body (the Earth) on a different orbit, which itself was not known at all precisely. It turned out that giving up the idea of a circular orbit simplifies all calculations enormously: The planets, according to Kepler, move in elliptical orbits, around one focal point which is the Sun (Kepler's first law), and in such a way that a line drawn between the Sun and the planet traverses equal areas in equal times (Kepler's second law). Therefore the squares of their orbital periods are related to each other as the cube of their distance to the sun (Kepler's third law).

Kepler did not have any problems with the Inquisition during his lifetime—unlike his mother, who narrowly escaped a death sentence in 1620 as part of the witch hunts and later probably died as a result of torture. The fate of the monk and astronomer Giordano Bruno, who died at the stake in Rome in 1600, was quite different. He had postulated the infinity of the universe and its eternal existence: A world, in other words, in which there was no place for the afterlife or for creation.

Earthly upheaval

Galileo Galilei (1564-1642) did not care much for Kepler's discoveries. Although he was an advocate of the heliocentric system from about 1600, he continued to assume, even after Kepler's publications, that the planets moved in circular orbits. In astronomy, he was the first to use the telescope extensively. He was able to show the nature of the Milky Way (which is made up of stars, not nebulae), the mountains on the Moon (which is thus apparently Earth-like), the phases of Venus and the moving sunspots, and he discovered moons around Jupiter. Such observations made the world increasingly doubt that there were any great physical differences between heaven and earth. But he was also wrong about some things: for example, he assumed that the light radiation from the moon came from the reflection of sunlight by lunar seas. He attributed the tides on earth solely to the influence of the sun.

But Galileo's most valuable contributions came not from his observations of the heavens, but from his physical researches on Earth. He advanced the scientific method with hypothesis and experiment. He studied motion on the inclined plane and the behavior of a pendulum. In his "Discorsi", his main work on physics, he explains why the motion of a projectile consists of two components: one pointing forward and one pointing downward. The sum of these two components results in the parabola of a projectile, which is still known today. In the investigation of free fall, he assumed that velocity increases equally with the corresponding time. What we learn today in school (bodies fall at the same speed, independent of their mass), was for Galileo at first only a thesis. To verify it, he designed an experiment. According to legend, he threw cannonballs from the Leaning Tower in Pisa. However, this experiment never actually took place: Because short periods of time were difficult to measure accurately with the clocks of the time, Galileo replaced the fall with an inclined plane in order to generalize his hypothesis.

He found that the distance traveled related to each other as the squares of the times needed for these distances (and thus came in just ahead of Newton's equations of motion). Galileo noted his experimental conditions conscientiously and in a way that was comprehensible to other researchers, as is expected in scientific literature today. Incidentally, he wrote his Discorsi in Italian instead of the usual Latin, so that they were understandable to the common people (as far as they were interested in the natural sciences and were able to read).

Everything gets bumped

The next important researcher in the history of classical physics is clearly René Descartes (1596-1650), although his findings are today considered almost completely outdated. He gave mathematics the Cartesian coordinate system with x and y axes.

Descartes believed that the only possible way to obtain certain knowledge was through mathematics. This science still has a similar significance in physics today. In Descartes' ideal, however, all steps, starting from the basic principles, can be clearly and logically proven and understood. Mechanics seemed to him to be the perfect vehicle for this. The universe should be describable through the movements of its bodies. Descartes recognized two important laws: A body remains at rest, if no force is exerted on it, and a movement continues evenly and in a single direction, until something occurs (an impact), which changes this movement. Galileo, on the other hand, still believed that the circular path was also natural. According to Descartes, what happens during a collision depends on the force inherent in the motion. If it is small, only the direction changes (reflection), if it is large, the pushing body takes the pushed body with it and gives it a part of its movement. Descartes derived a total of eight rules of motion from this, which we know today are mostly wrong or are valid only in special cases.

The universe is completely filled by a mixture of three different primary materials. The vortices formed by these materials form the fixed stars and planets by concentration, and also provide for their movement by dragging them along. All natural phenomena are thus rationally explainable—and not only that: Since everything is based on the law of impact, the universe is completely deterministic. If you calculate long enough, you can predict the course of the world. Only modern quantum physics has disproved this assumption.

The classical model

The age of modern physics began with Isaac Newton (1642-1726). In his "Philosophiæ Naturalis Principia Mathematica" the Englishman founded classical mechanics, which was to remain valid until the development of quantum mechanics (and is still correct as a special case of quantum mechanics). Newton, as has been made clear in the previous chapters, was not a unique genius. Many researchers had done important preliminary work and, for a variety of reasons, had come very close to Newton's findings. Nevertheless, Newton did not have an easy time of it. Only after a six-year depressive phase did he begin to write his main work around 1684. In 1687, the Principia was published, in which he formulated the laws of motion that were later named after him:

- A body remains in a state of rest or uniform motion as long as no force acts on it ("law of inertia").
- The change in motion is proportional to the acting force and occurs in the direction of the force ("law of gravity").
- If a body A exerts a force on a body B, an equal but oppositely directed force from body B acts on body A ("law of action and reaction").

True to the assumption that the same laws apply in heaven and earth, Newton (inspired by Kepler's laws) derived planetary motion from his three basic rules. He showed that to maintain a motion around the sun, the constant action of a centripetal force is necessary—and that the sun's gravity must be that force. The famous flash of insight that struck Newton under an apple tree is therefore fiction. Probably Newton himself made the story up as a harmless episode.

In the form taught in school today:

F = m * a

(force = mass * acceleration), the law of gravity, was first written down by Leonard Euler in 1750.

Also the modern form:

F = G (m₁ * m₂) / r²

Newton had not written down. The size of the constant G used in this form of the law of gravitation was determined indirectly for the first time in 1798 by the British researcher Henry Cavendish.

In other areas of science, by the way, Isaac Newton remained thoroughly attached to the superstitions of his time. For a long time, he was engaged in alchemy and the search for the philosopher's stone. He considered light to be composed of tiny particles that vary in size depending on their color and move through an ether. Thus, he was in direct competition with the wave theory of Christian Huygens, which was to become the dominant opinion after both of their deaths—only to be reunited with the particle theory in quantum physics.

Electricity

The phenomenon of electricity was known to humans long before they systematically studied it. Perhaps lightning even gave us fire. Fishermen knew about the discharges of electric eels. The Greeks already knew that amber can be electrostatically charged by touch.

In the 18th century, researchers built the first "electrifying machines," which served primarily as fairground amusements. In 1733, the Frenchman Charles du Fay observed that there must be two types of electrical charge. The capacitor as a storage device for electrical energy was invented in 1745 as the "Leiden bottle". In 1752, American inventor Benjamin Franklin made connections to atmospheric electricity and built the first lightning rod. In 1770, the Italian Luigi Galvani demonstrated in sensational experiments that electricity can also cause motion. In 1775, also in Italy, Alessandro Volta invented the battery ("Voltaic column"), which made it possible to generate electricity without friction.

Coulomb's law, which describes the force of attraction between two point charges, was discovered by physicist Charles Augustin de Coulomb in 1785. It is strangely similar to the law of gravity:

$F = k * (q_1 * q_2) / r^2$

(where k is a constant containing the electric field constant).

That electricity and another phenomenon, magnetism, are directly related was first established by the French physicist André-Marie Ampère. He proved that current-carrying conductors attract (with the same direction of current) or repel each other.

In 1831, Briton Michael Faraday discovered electrical induction—the fact that a varying magnetic field in a conductor causes a current to flow. Faraday also showed the following year that all types of electric current are equivalent, regardless of how they are produced.

In the physical branch of electromagnetism, things were now proceeding at a rapid pace. It would only take until 1864 to essentially complete the science: In this year, James Clerk Maxwell published his famous equations for the first time, which describe the behavior of electrical and magnetic fields and their interaction with matter. Maxwell also arrived at an interesting prediction from his equations: In a vacuum, there should be oscillating electromagnetic fields moving through space. He calculated their speed to be 310,000 kilometers per second. According to the state of knowledge at that time, this was so close to the speed of light that Maxwell himself assumed that light and any other radiation is an electromagnetic wave. Experiments by Heinrich Hertz later confirmed this assumption.

Maxwell, however, believed that light waves moved through a carrier medium—the aether, which uniformly fills the entire universe. This aether should affect the motion of light. The US physicists Albert Michelson and Edward Morley tried to prove this in 1887 with the experiment named after them. If the earth moves relative to the aether, the speed of light should change depending on the direction of movement ("against" or "with" the aether), which Morley and Michelson wanted to prove by means of an interferometer. In fact, they got no result, and neither did later experimenters. A plausible reason for this was to be found only by Albert Einstein with the special theory of relativity.

Classical physics summarized

Before I release you again into your familiar world, here is a very brief summary of what physicists at the end of the 19th century considered to be confirmed once and for all and to be absolutely true—and what was soon to prove to be a small part of a more comprehensive reality.

- The three dimensions and time are absolute, thus independent of the choice of reference system. Velocities therefore depend on the state of motion of the observer.

- All physical processes take place in a three-dimensional Cartesian space in which the laws of Euclidean geometry apply. Time and space are independent of each other.
- The gravitational force is described by the law of gravitation as a remote effect. It has nothing to do with the inertial force of a mass.
- Mass and energy are constants.
- Electromagnetic waves can exist at any energy level.
- The location and momentum of a physical object can be determined simultaneously at any time with arbitrarily high accuracy.
- With exact knowledge of all laws of nature and parameters, the behavior of a given physical system can be predicted exactly.

Tip: As always, you can get an illustrated version of my little tutorial by requesting it at hard-sf.com/subscribe. Would you like a topic that I haven't covered at all yet? Then feel free to write me!

Printed in Great Britain
by Amazon